Thank you for pu
support is hugely ap]
my gratitude at   ......,
I'd like to offer you a free story.

Yep, free.

Just visit my website to get your very own
copy of *Building*, an award-winning short
story observing the lives of the dysfunctional
residents living in a block of flats. *Building*
is part of short story collection, *Echoes*.

Get *Building* here: www.author-
karinaevans.com/building

VOLCANO

KARINA EVANS

KARINA EVANS

© 2020 by Karina Evans.

All characters in this publication are fictitious, and any resemblance to real persons, living or dead, is purely coincidental.

For my babies: you taught me how exciting words can taste, and how the monologue of a four-year-old is one of the most beautiful things a parent can hear. Never stop reading. Never stop listening.

For Tony: HELP ME. THE COVER IS TOO BIG. THE COVER IS TOO SMALL. THE COVER IS TOO CRAP. Every time, you sorted it. Thank you, from the bottom of my heart.

For my family and friends: your patience and constant feedback upon being forced to read and reread every edited, re-edited and re-re-edited sentence has not gone unnoticed. This book will sell at least ten copies, so at least ten people will know how grateful I am.

Natural diamonds are formed inside some dying volcanoes. The beauty thrives, long after the volcano's death.

PROLOGUE

Paul Bennett
July 22nd 2001
0930

*Falling...falling...falling
Screaming...screaming...screaming...
I love my family*

I open my eyes and grunt. I am waiting for the inevitable. The sunlight forcing its way through the window is sharp and painful.

I rise slowly to my feet, surveying the mess surrounding me. Bottles, cans, toys, clothes; strewn haphazardly on the cream carpet. Debris. Debris from the hours before.

My life before.

The shrill ringing of the doorbell is not unexpected. I remember. I remember.

She fell

She is dead
Falling...falling...falling
Screaming...screaming...screaming...

I remember. I remember that although I love her with every piece of my being, it is my fault.

It is over. I have killed her.

'POLICE. OPEN THE DOOR.'

'I am arresting you on suspicion of murder.'

Falling...falling...falling...
Screaming, screaming, screaming...

'You do not have to say anything.'

'What have I done? What have I done? I did it, didn't I? I fucking killed her.'

'You are charged with the manslaughter of Eloise Katherine Bennett.'

'I am refusing bail.'

'PAUL BENNETT. I SENTENCE YOU TO TWELVE YEARS' IMPRISONMENT FOR THE MANSLAUGHTER OF ELOISE KATHERINE BENNETT.'

'TAKE. HIM. DOWN...'

ONE

Jessica Louise Bennett aged 5 years and 2 months
April 2001

I am five years old. It has been my birthday
ages ago and I got most things that I want which
makes me happy. On my birthday my Mummy
whispered to me in my ear that next year I will
be old enough to have shiny gold earrings in my
ears like my Mummy has sometimes. They have
pointy bits that go right through your ears and I
think that might hurt a bit but they look pretty. I
love my Mummy. We live in a house together and
also with my brother called Baby Joe and Daddy
too. The house isn't a proper house and it isn't a
flat like where my best friend lives but it is a bit
like a square. It has stairs and it has my favourite
stair, and it has a neighbour who lives downstairs
so it doesn't belong all to us. I like the carpets
most. My Mummy says that the carpets are old
and horrible and that one day the landlord man

might buy some new ones because he owns the square house but I hope he doesn't because they have patterns on them that I can walk on and they have string bits in the corners by the walls that I can pull and make longer and wrap around my fingers and around my Buggly Bear's paw. Buggly Bear is my favourite bear.

My Mummy is like a volcano. She doesn't look like a volcano she looks like my Mummy all pretty and soft with a round tummy a bit smaller than my space hopper and a pretty face and lots of hair. A teacher at my school who has a name I can't remember said a volcano has lots of hot stuff coming out of the top but not all the time because sometimes it is dormant. My Mummy is sometimes dormant then she gets all cross and her crossness comes out of her mouth like a lava. Then sometimes she doesn't have any crossness and she just has kisses and sweets and cuddles. I love that Mummy most so I told her that I don't love her when she has crossness and she got more cross and more cross and sent me to my room where I got bored and drew on my wall.

My Daddy has a different crossness. He has a smelly crossness that he gets from the pub and sometimes from a big bottle at home and it makes my Mummy scared. When it's light and he comes in and he doesn't smell of funny drinks he isn't cross, but when it's dark and he comes in and he smells of funny drinks and sometimes when it's light too, he shouts at my Mummy and she looks at me with her eyebrows all funny and I know I have to go to my room and tell my baby brother Joe that we are safe and that Daddy won't hurt us because he loves us and Mummy loves us and she will PROTECT us because she's our Mummy. When he did hurt me that day the month in February it was because I was in the way on my favourite stair. My favourite stair is where I can see down the stairs and if I turn round I can see up the stairs too. Daddy had hit my Mummy that day because I saw him do it because my Mummy had told Daddy that I wanted him to give me a bath. So I think it's my fault that Daddy hit my Mummy. Daddy was very sorry and my Mummy said it's okay because it will mend quickly. It was only a little bone. The lady at the hospital was quite fat and tried to make me remember how I broke my little bone in my arm but I couldn't remember because Daddy said that remembering is dangerous and I'd have to live with strangers. I had to tell a lie and it makes me sad because Santa might have heard and not bring me a real doll that walks and talks at Christmas time. I told the nice lady that I fell over on the stairs and that was only half a lie because I did fall over on the stairs but it was because Daddy pushed me hard when my arm was holding Buggly Bear through the gap. Buggly Bear is my best toy friend. My Mummy gave me lots of sweets and kisses and cuddles and gave Daddy lots of sad looks with her sad crying eyes and one of her eyes was red and her nose had blood on it.

The next day my Mummy had a funny eye, it was the eye that was red the day before but then it was green and black and purple and I would have laughed but I remembered that was how my arm looked a bit before they put the plaster on, which is what they call it, but it is bigger than a plaster and it is like a big funny hard bandage and it's not funny at all. I still have the plaster on now because it has to be on my arm for six weeks to stop it moving and breaking into pieces and sometimes it gets really scratchy and I can't scratch it because my arm is trapped but I will be able to scratch it soon because the hospital will take the big plaster off on April which is this month so it will be very very soon.

I go to school a lot, even the day after we stayed up really really late because the policeman came to our house after Daddy said that stuff about killing people and getting a thing called a divorce which I don't know what it means and then the policeman went away because Daddy and my Mummy told him that everything was ok and he put his hat back on and I cried with my Mummy. And sometimes at school I talk to my friends and they are happy but I'm not happy all the time and I don't want to ask them the stuff that their Daddies do because then they might have to lie and then Santa won't give them presents either. But I know it was an accident and also I know that it was only a little bone.

My Mummy walks me to school because we have a car but it's cheaper to walk. We go up the hill and over the hill and cross the road and past the shop and round the corner. Sometimes which is usually on Tuesday, my Mummy takes us into the shop and sometimes buys some milk and sometimes I get sweeties and Baby Joe gets white chocolate because it's not messy like brown chocolate. The shop smells really nice because they have sweeties in pots in the shop and I can smell them when I walk past them. They have white mice and they have chewy snakes and they have lollipops that look really nice but the time I chose one it made my tongue a bit too fizzy and then when I looked in the mirror, my tongue was all blue! I like walking with my Mummy, she smiles a lot and kisses my hair and laughs and looks like an angel. When I grow up I am going to buy a big house with a big lock on the door and my Mummy and Baby Joe can come round for chicken and gravy at night-time but Daddy can't get in because the lock is sooooooooooo big that not even Superman can open it.

I have to think about Daddy quietly because I think some nasty things but I can't help it. I want Daddy in the daytime but only when he doesn't have that big bottle with him; I don't want him here at night-time. I wish a monster would take him away and put him in a cave and take away the bottle and put it in a box and let Daddy out in the morning but never let the bottle out. But I am only five and a bit so I can't make that happen. At the weekend sometimes Daddy takes me to the rides like the big caterpillar one that is green and goes through a giant apple and we spend loads of gold coins and he puts me on his shoulders and I am his princess and he loves me. I try to be really good so he'll want to stay at home and not open that big bottle and not go to that pub place. I want us to be happy all the time I want us to love each other all the time I don't want to have a punishment when I have been asleep and not naughty.

When Baby Joe cries at night-times my Mummy runs really fast into our bedroom and picks up Baby Joe so that he doesn't wake Daddy up and sometimes my Mummy doesn't do that and I have to pick up Baby Joe or sing him songs. Maybe crying makes Daddy cross. I hear Daddy say cross things that are funny and naughty and I'm not allowed to say them or my Mummy will shout. My Mummy says them too when she thinks I can't hear. She said a funny naughty word to Daddy once and I think she meant she wanted him to go away but he didn't go away he broke three plates instead. I know he broke three plates and not two or four because we used to have four white plates and now we only have one but we have blue ones instead because Daddy bought some more so that we would be able to eat our dinner. Sometimes dinner smells funny but only when dinner isn't my favourite and it has those vegetables with it that my Mummy makes me eat because they will make me strong.

My poorly arm with the big hard bandage on is so hard that you can write words on it with a pen. My Mummy wrote words and told me that it says 'To my Jess. We love you, be brave, from Mummy and Daddy and Baby Joe,' and lots of kisses and Baby Joe can't write which is why my Mummy wrote for him and Daddy can write but maybe he was tired and so my Mummy wrote it for him. And when I went to school and everyone wrote their names on it and one teacher who is called Miss Scott but we just call her 'Miss,' she asked me how it happened and I told her all the things I was allowed to remember and she looked at me all funny and said 'Jess, I am your friend and you can tell me if there is anything wrong at home.' And people call me Jess because it is short for Jessica I told Miss all the things that were wrong at home, like there never being any peanut butter or chocolate mousse and that Baby Joe wakes me up before the sun is awake, but there are secrets and I can't tell her Daddy shouts. Tomorrow I might tell her that I had to tell a lie but not tell her the lie and ask her if she knows Santa. Because if she knows Santa she can tell him how sorry I am and that I had to lie and I still want all my presents and I promise so much that I'll be good and I'll try not to lie again.

Paul Bennett

Can I be honest?
I lie
I love my life
My life is shit
I love my wife
I beat my wife
I love my children
I scare my children
I'd die for them
I'd die without them

Eloise Katherine Bennett

I fell over. That is what I shall say.
I FELL OVER.
How hard can it be?
Is it possible to fall into something and blacken your eye so perfectly? It is almost a work of art. 'Perfection.'
I cannot pinpoint where it changed; I cannot recall the moment my life turned into an advert for charity. However, I can tell you which part of the slippery slide I am on now. It is the part where all I can see are the hungry mouths waiting to eat me. The salivating mouths that have been waiting for

me to lose my grip.

Waiting
Anticipating

Do I change the names to protect the innocent? Or do I stand on the badly-tiled rooftop and shout 'It's HIM, it's Paul: it's not the table, it's not the door, it's not the drawer, it's not the cooker, IT'S NOT A FUCKING ACCIDENT; it's the man who loves me'?

My daughter has amazing insight. Jess knows that the white chocolate buttons are there as a distraction whenever Daddy's head is going to explode. The chocolate buttons sit there within the haphazardly arranged contents of the kitchen cupboard; in their perfectly packaged, structured, innocent, white glory; until my babies' Daddy decides that my skirt is too short, the sink is too dirty, or his wife is a slut. Then my eldest child, with her five-year-old wisdom, climbs on the worn wooden kitchen stool; the stool she has lovingly covered with stickers of ladybirds and flowers. She opens the cupboard door and reaches with her beautiful, chubby hands to clutch what have become her earplugs, her blindfold, and her comfort.

My heart breaks as I filter the shouting and accusations to watch Jessica concentrating on her distraction; a tiny face creased into a frown; a frown that shouldn't exist for many, many years.

She pretends, you see—my Jess. She lives in her imagination, and after the event she tells me that the frown is pushing happy thoughts from the back of her mind to behind her eyes. Each and every time, the tiny pieces of my shattered heart melt and I wish, oh how I wish, that the melting would somehow bond it back together, like the sticky chocolate reshaping itself in my beautiful baby's hands. Each time, I feel I should tell her not to allow the chocolate to melt in her hands; to insist she eats it before she makes a mess, but the words will not form. The words I need to say will never form. Instead, I stand in my ignorant silence, Paul in the background, running like a muted film, and I watch my daughter. I watch her examine the slightly melted chocolate in her hands; squashing it and poking it until it becomes the shape she requires. I watch her close her hands and reopen them, observing with wonderment as the chocolate stretches into a matt white puddle within her palm.

The frown disappears and Jess looks at me with a tentative smile, just as Paul is making his way towards me. Then I am brought back to reality with a bump, or a thump, or a slap, or worse; an angry face inches from my own, demanding, asking, terrifying me. Jessica is unimportant, once again.

I love that man, you know. I love that man who cheats on me. Please do not think that I am too stupid to realise, because I am not. However, I know it has gone too far for me to allow myself to do anything about it. I love the man who ridicules me, who loves me, who hits me, who hugs me.

I do not love him enough not to be scared.

My life was a mistake. From the moment I knew I existed, I knew I should not. My parents looked after me; they dressed me, they fed me, they read stories to me, but I felt so strongly that I did not belong. I felt like a cheat. I longed to hear the words 'I love you.'; to see their eyes melt and pool when they looked at me, but emotion surfaced so rarely in my childhood home, that I can recount every single time I felt loved.

It is an evening at the end of summer: too hot to sleep, but I am sensible enough to realise I have to at least try.

Through the open bedroom window, I can hear the crackling of next door's bonfire and I inhale as the sharp smell of smoke wafts through my bedroom window. I hear my mother run up the stairs; I can feel the urgency in her footsteps. I watch the door, through half-closed eyes; the brass handle turns quickly before the door swings wide open, hitting a bookcase behind it. How I love the smell of that bookcase, it was purchased from a furniture store two weeks ago. The smell of fresh pine awakens me every morning, whereupon I ball my hands into fists, rub gritty sleep from my eyes and slide to the end of my bed to absorb the aroma, before carefully choosing which of my many books I am going to bury my head in that very evening. The bookcase shakes a little as the door hits it, then my mother makes her entrance, she steps quickly inside my bedroom, deftly avoiding the creaking floorboard that I was not aware she knew existed. I struggle to keep my eyes closed, anticipating a telling-off when my mother realises I am awake so late, my eyelids flickering as I fight the urge to ask her what is wrong. She gently lays her hand on my chest, leaving it resting there for what feels like an eternity, and as if she is now satisfied that I am alive, turns her back. I open my eyes and watch her walk slowly to the bedroom window, pulling the curtains slightly apart to watch the bonfire. She quickly turns back to look at me, but I am unable to close my eyes in time. My mother forces a smile, rubs her eyes, then silently pads over to my bed to brush my hair from my face, before turning on her heel and marching out to the hall to become herself again.

Through the years, my mother has displayed a wavering support; one minute telling me to leave Paul to live with her and Dad, the next telling me to hold my family together at all costs. I choose to follow the latter advice.

I feel I need to explain why I love my man. I love him because I remember I loved him when we met; I remember I loved the excitement of our first kiss, I loved the nights we sat together;

drinking together; talking about music, love, life, sex, our plans, our future: *our life*. The silences between conversations were comfortable, beautiful. Our glasses would sit on the table, close in companionship, identical inside and out, save for the lipstick kissed on the rim of the glass I had been drinking from.

A lipstick kiss
next to emptiness
The darkness;
startling silence.

We would sit awake, on a worn bench outside the front door of Paul's tiny shared flat, smoking crackling cigarettes in the darkness of night; anticipating our future, anticipating *us.*

Night-time hangs;
a banner of love
crackling, and
softly vibrant.

I would hold Paul's hand and stare at the sky, absorbing images like photographs inside my mind.

A snapshot, reflecting
the vivid moon
dancing inside
a silver plume
contain a feeling
we silently hold

Two empty vessels,
never alone
Of course, this could never last.

'It's a honeymoon period, Eloise. It won't last for-
ever. Just wait until you're darning his socks...'

But, those moments were mine: ours. Ours to absorb, to retain, to call upon when things changed.

I looked forward to the phone calls when we would arrange to see each other, then I would spend hours trying to look effortlessly gorgeous for when he took me out. In those first few months, Paul taught me that I was beautiful, that I was worthy of being loved. We quickly whirled into a life of love, hope and mutual attraction; together we attended parties, clubs, bars, and restaurants. We had a circle of friends—real friends. He was an accountant and my poor education had afforded me a position as an administrative assistant at a computer parts factory. Together, we had a reasonable income, so we pooled it.

I remember.
I remember how it was.
I remember how it could be.

We rented a tiny two-bedroom maisonette in the town centre. It was beautiful. I painted it, dusted it, cleaned it, vacuumed it, and hung pictures of our families.

The paint is now cracking, the carpets are threadbare, the bathroom walls exhibiting an abstract installation of cracked plaster decorated with black mould.

We lived in our maisonette, our haven, our little bubble. We lived, we loved, we laughed, we were happy; so happy that we scraped together some money and got married at the local registry office. I was so proud to take his name: Mrs Bennett; Mrs Eloise Katherine Bennett; the happiest bride in the world. Little did I know that I was steadily climbing the ladder to the top of the slide. Little did I know that within eighteen months, my partner would have no job, and I would be gripping on to the top of the slide with so much force that my fingernails would be bending and ripping and shredding with every painful second.

After our beautiful Jess was born, the bubble burst; Paul was made redundant. It was a huge blow, one that pushed Paul to cope by drinking. Day and night, night and day. The smell of superstrength lager soon cancelled out the smell of the polish and air fresheners, the sound of Paul tripping over chairs and swearing under his breath soon cancelled out the gurgles of our baby; our much-wanted baby, who spent her days lying contentedly in the basket that we had bought when she was still our entire world.

Paul had every opportunity to find a new job;

friends offered positions, adverts circled by families and not-so-subtle hints dropped by everyone we happened upon. All in vain. Paul was intent on self-destruction; his masculinity had been compromised. I wonder now whether this was actually him. The man who I thought I knew was a façade; this drunken 'thing' was my life partner. I now know that this is when I should have left, before he hit me, before I was absorbed by the whirlwind which has become my life. I should have left because he was not the man that I knew and fell in love with; he was a man I loved yet resented in equal measure.

Do you ever wonder why you let everything go so wrong? Why you think that if you just change those imperfect parts of you, you'll be more wonderful, more accepted, totally perfect? I wonder why I let him tell me what make-up to wear the first time.

'I'M WEARING EYESHADOW BECAUSE IT MATCHES MY DRESS, YOU BASTARD.'

Why I let him tell me what clothes to wear, what underwear to wear, who I could speak to. I wonder why I let him follow me everywhere: down the stairs, out the door, to the shop, to the kitchen, to the toilet, to the bedroom. My life was no longer mine, my life was him: he was me. Then I wonder how I became a frizzy haired frump, wearing grey underwear and no make-up, staring at the floor when I walked.

'Because there's no need to look up, unless you want to fuck the guy walking towards you.'

So now, here we are. I am that person. I am the person in front of the cracked mirror trying to fix her cracked face. My lank, unwashed hair is hanging in greasy strands around my bruised, lined face. The hair that he used to bury his face in and inhale at every opportunity.

'You are so beautiful, Eloise.'

My once youthful face, broken by lines, frowns, and unhappiness. The make-up that should enhance my blue eyes and flawless complexion now applied thickly to disguise the bruises. There could be anyone underneath. Anonymity. The anonymous woman, shuffling down the street, laden with shopping bags, looking at the pavement, tears rolling silently down her face as she realises that she could do anything, say anything, and nobody would notice her. She is nobody. She is not colourful, or vibrant, or even distinguishable. She does not have a great personality. She is grey, and, quite frankly, may as well be dead. She pastes a smile upon her face each morning, but the truth is still apparent: her soul has died.

Wanting, with space

to guard the night
that, by chance
we stepped inside
There they thrive
and will remain
holding droplets of our
lives.

I close my eyes, remembering. Wanting to forget. Wanting to forget the day my husband broke my daughter. Wanting to forget February the twenty-third.

'You promised Jess that you'd bathe her today.'

Pleading, begging a drunken father to spend time with his daughter.

'How dare you accuse me of being a bad father?'

Jessica standing on the stairs, four stairs up, holding on to the banister, her favourite teddy bear under one arm, her bubble bath clutched in her tiny hand. Looking at us, willing us not to have this argument.

'I didn't, Paul. Jess wants you, she needs you, she's been looking forward to you bathing her all day.'

Jessica's face falling slightly, her little body tense.

'She's waiting for you, Paul.'

She was. Jess was waiting for her Daddy to lovingly scoop her in his arms and lower her in the bath as he does when he is sober.

'Like a crane, Daddy. Like a crane.'

I felt Paul looking at me, his eyes boring into me, then glancing briefly at Jessica, before swinging around on the ball of his foot. Somehow, I knew it was coming, but I was powerless to stop it. I tried to duck, or move, or say something, but I couldn't. I felt his fist slamming into my face with a force stronger than I could ever have imagined.

'For fuck's sake, Eloise. I'll run her fucking bath if it means that fucking much to you.'

Stunned, I watched as Paul marched towards the stairs.
Marching to martyrdom. To be a crane.
I could feel the warm trickle of blood running slowly from my nose to my mouth.

It all happened so fast…

Jessica, trying to block out the hate around her by distractedly playing with her Buggly Bear, pushing him through the railings on the banister.

Paul pushing past Jessica. My eyes widening in horror, realising Jessica's left arm was stuck between the railings.

'Paul. Be CAREFUL!'

The heartbreaking, terrifying, soul destroying scream, the sound of my beloved daughter's tiny bone snapping.

'MY BABY!'
What to do, what to do, what to do?
They mustn't know what happened; they'll take her away from us. What will I do without her?

Paul running past me, Jessica screaming in his arms.
'Drive us to the hospital.'
The baby.
Joseph

Running up the stairs to the children's room, sniffing back the blood that was threatening to pour out of my nose. Lifting Joseph out of his basket, holding him close, hearing his contented murmurs as he nestled right where he belonged. In his mother's arms.

If only you knew, Baby Joe.

Blanket, dummy, keys, blanket, dummy, keys, blanket, dummy, keys.

Joseph's tiny fingers tightly clutching the thin material of my vest top. Looking for Paul and Jessica. Running towards the car, feeling the sensation of the gravel ripping apart my bare feet, but not feeling the pain. Gravel, concrete, tarmac, life. Tearing me apart.

'ELOISE. Hurry up.'

Shaking hands, unlocking the car door. Sitting, unable to comprehend.

What's happening, what's happening, what's happening?
'Drive, Eloise. Please. She's hurting.'
Driving. Screeching. Screaming. Crying. With the man who broke his daughter.

Bastard
Cunt
Call yourself a father?

Red traffic lights staring angrily at me. Accusingly.

'Come on come on come on come on.'

Speeding into the hospital car park, screeching into the parking bay. Opening the car door, needing to hold my baby.

'You're a fucking mess, stay here.'

I did as I was told, you know; I waited right there, in the car, staring at Joseph sleeping. Aching to hold my daughter, aching to tell her that everything would be ok, aching to be with her. Hours passed, and the sky gradually turned from black to an ominous blanket of reddish-grey.

Darkness and blood.

The longest five hours of my life passed without event. I didn't have my phone with me, I couldn't go inside to check what was happening. I was helpless. I had been told to stay where I was. I was pointless. I was a fucking mess.

I HAD BEEN TOLD.

Then, it clicked. Temporarily, my addled mind pieced itself together. My baby was hurt, and I was doing as I was told.

Why?

I was entitled to be there: to hold her, love her, and comfort her. I reached for the door handle, looking in the wing mirror as I did so. Two figures caught my eye. I blinked to clear my eyes, and then looked again. My daughter, skipping towards the car, her arm in plaster and a sling, Paul holding her good hand. Father and daughter. Together, loving each other. Then there I was, sitting in the car, doing as I was told. It's all my fault. I'll take the blame.

So, who am I?

I'll tell you that:

I am the woman who broke her daughter.

<u>Paul Bennett</u>

I love my family. My Eloise, my Jessica, my Joseph. I have made many mistakes in my life, but I am so proud of my family. I admit that I have a temper, that I am not constantly the epitome of the perfect man. But, I am not a bad man. However egotistical it sounds, I know that I am not rotten through and through; I am strong enough to change. I have a heart, I have a soul. I love my family. I love the hubbub in my house when we are all there together. I thrive upon the moments when Jessica throws herself into my arms, demanding a squeeze. I love the smell of our clothes hanging on the radiators to dry, when we have been for a walk in the rain. I love Joseph; his impatient squeals if we don't get out of bed when he wants us to, the smell of his hair when I have just bathed him. And, Eloise: I adore her. I adore her grumpiness in the morning, as she sighs and throws on her dressing-gown, her hair messed-up and her eyes bleary. I love them all. So, please don't misunderstand me. My primary function is love. I am not a bad man.

I realise there are many people out there who cannot, who will not, understand me. I am unsure whether I understand myself. However, I do know that the person I sometimes become is not who I aspire to be.

Blame it on the alcohol

Oh, the alcohol

Blame it on provocation

She winds me up, your honour

Blame it on depression

Who wouldn't be depressed, when life is so fucking shit?

Just don't blame me.

I read about it all the time: another wife battered because her husband saw fit to punish her for something she may have done. Another family torn apart because of domestic violence. Another family wiped out because 'he snapped.' Another heart broken. Another life ruined. Another murder. Another bruise. Another secret. Another death. Another suicide. That's not me: I can change.

I can't vocalise what goes through my head when I lose it. You know how people say that they 'see red' when they get angry? I see black. My entire head shakes and thumps with anger and then I black out. Time and time again I've been dragged back to reality by Eloise begging me to stop, or Jessica sobbing quietly in the doorway. I know I have to change, and I will: I am determined that this is not the man I should be. Am I the man who I despise when I read about the dead wife in the newspaper? The man I despise who beats his wife and scares his children, who has affairs and blames them on his wife? Am I that man? I hope not.

I am the man who can change.

TWO

Eloise Katherine Bennett

I am a puppet, tied tightly on the strings that Paul holds. Yet, although I cannot escape, the strings can be cut at any time, and my legs will crumple beneath me, dumping me in an uncere-monious heap on the floor.

Useless and broken.
Used and broken-hearted.

You can't understand the way life is
Why there's somebody there, but there's no-one around
Why you're holding his hand
But there's no one to care
Sitting around a crowded table
Surrounded by faces of people you know
But you're feeling alone

As a child, I prayed to be loved. I dreamed of

white dresses and bouquets, and someone loving me so deeply that it bore a hole into their soul. As a teenager, I broke my own heart over and over and over again; nobody loved me enough. Nobody could love me enough to make it stop hurting. I cried into my pillow, I transferred the pain; I watched the razor cutting through the fragile skin of my arms, I watched the emptiness filling with red, raw emotion. I felt the frustration melting from my chest and congealing in tiny beads on my forearm. I felt the pain disappear, and then I wiped the tears of terminal frustration from my cheeks. I did not want anyone to heal me; I simply wanted someone to love me.

My only guess
Is if you had that wish
He'd take away the pain
And give you the chance
To live life again

So simple, so defined, yet so impossible.

'There are plenty more fish in the sea.'

I waited for the phone to ring. I waited for them to love me. I cried. I hurt. I loved them all.

Give yourself to them. Give them everything you are, everything you have, everything you can be. They will devour it, they will grow, they will need you.

You give someone your soul, completely, wholly and totally, because you TRUST them, because you connect with them. But, after weeks, months, or perhaps years, you realise they are sucking out the life and colour inside you, until your soul is a carcass: blackened and lifeless. They suck out your faith, your trust, your life, until finally you are writhing with the pain of emptiness, and left with nothing. Crying, weeping, begging for love, for life, for HIM.

Tears on a pillow.

Every poignant song wipes the clown mask from your face, and briefly but intensely you show the world your pain. A once vibrant being disintegrating into a faithless, loveless cynic.

I learnt that if love is not allowed to grow, to evolve, in its natural environment, it turns into a dependency: an addiction. I learnt that love can be beautiful, but it is not pure, nor simple, because love is defined within the complexities of your soul.

It begins as a tiny pupa destined to transform into a beautiful butterfly, destined to flutter inside the soul, lightly, carefully, and eternally. But, if your soul has a dark corner, the butterfly can become trapped, like unsaid words stuck in your throat. A fluttering butterfly caught in a net of desolation, its beautiful wings mangled as it tries to free itself from the memories. The love has not grown, it has not been nurtured, and so it is invented; relying on needs and desires to build it, to make it the biggest and the best.

Magnificent.

So, you climb to the top of the tower you have built; it's so high that you can see the world. You made this: it's fucking amazing. From this height, you can feel the beautiful warmth of the sun, you can see people scurrying like ants miles away, and you realise they are the people that hurt you. Fuck them. The little people. They do not matter. Then, you wonder whether you are better off on your own. So you test it. You jump up and down on the unstable foundations, which you have recklessly but passionately built upon; you ask and you demand. You need more. You need an entire heart, you need an eternal promise.

Then, you fall. You fall from the euphoric height so fucking quickly and hard that it literally knocks the breath out of you. The smile fades, and the darkness descends, because you have identified love; you have named it, you have accepted it, but then you changed it. Because, to enable self-destruction, it has to be unattainable. It has to be an impossible challenge. The more you get, the more you need. The more you need, the less you can scrape together. Remnants. You pick yourself up and you run through the tunnel, chasing that image that you want to hold in your soul. You chase the passion and the definition, reaching with desperation, grasping with panic. You have changed your mind; you are now willing to accept the old love, the love that you owned, but threw away.

It has gone; it has let you down. It will always, always let you down.

It will always let you down, because you did not allow it to exist.

Jessica Louise Bennett

It's my birthday in two hundred and thirteen days. I know this because I asked my Mummy and my Mummy sighed and took the calendar off the wall and the pin on the wall fell out and my Mummy says that all the walls are going to fall down because they are old, and it was the calendar that I made her with the rippy off pages and the picture of our house and me and my Mummy and Daddy and my Baby Joe. Then my Mummy got a big gold pen that I use to draw pictures for my best friend Charlotte and circled every week and then did some sums with her calculator and then said 'two hundred and thirteen,' really loudly. Me and Charlotte love each other more than chocolate and ice cream and cheese and we have Best Friend days where we hug more than we do on days that aren't Best Friend days. I hope that my poorly arm is better by the time we have our next Best Friend day because I can't hug people properly at the moment.

Daddy walked into the kitchen and hugged my Mummy, my Mummy looked so tired. My Mummy hugged Daddy back a bit, but not very tightly and then she looked over his shoulder at me and then she kissed him like you see in the films. Then Daddy picked me up upside down and my good arm hung downwards and Daddy said he had better start counting gold coins because my birthday was VERY soon. I told Daddy that what I want the best is a doll that walks and talks and some music and a player to play my music on and a milkshake maker so that I can have milkshake EVERY day. I want to have a vacuum cleaner that sucks up real fluff then I can help my Mummy when she gets cross and stressed because I don't like it when she gets cross and stressed. My Mummy goes outside the front door when she is cross and stressed and smokes a cigarette which smells bad and my Mummy says it is bad for you but it is okay for her to do it because she is an adult and makes decisions.

I love my Mummy. I love Daddy too and I love my Mummy but I'm not always happy. Baby Joe cries more when I am sad I think it's because he can feel that I am sad and so I put a bottle in his mouth and he sucks it and makes cute noises.

Sometimes when I am sad at night-times and I

hear the shouting and I feel the crossness I look at my Baby Joe and my cheeks get all wet and I know that there's a number I can call and a nice lady will give me money to make me happy, but in those adverts the children hide behind the sofa and I haven't hidden behind the sofa because I don't think it's a very good place to hide. I'm scared with the door closed because the light doesn't come in but if the light comes in the shouting comes in and the footsteps are on the stairs and I can't hear giggling and I think something bad is going to happen like that time with no footsteps and no light when my Mummy was hurt really bad last year and left and left us and went to the house on her own.

THREE

Eloise Katherine Bennett
April 2000

Something is different this time.

Please don't wake Jessica

Weight on top of me. A mouth. A tongue. It gags me. It silences me.

Help me, Jessica
The stench. Stale beer is forced deep into my mouth. It becomes part of me.

Stare at the ceiling, count the cracks.
I force my head backwards against the wall behind the sofa; backwards until it hurts; trying to escape the claustrophobia.

Why?

A sweaty hand snakes around my wrist. It hates me. It wants me. It haunts me. It needs me. A knee pushes between my thighs.

Wake up, Jessica. Save me

The rain on the roof tiles. The wind howls. The stench of unwanted passion.

'No. I love you.'

A hand pulls. Trembling, dirty, powerful fingers rip material. Searing. Cutting. Silently.

'You're hurting me.'

A shift in weight. A zip. The fear. The pain. The tears. The noise. The hate. The love. The silence.

Why? Lying beside me, pretending I wanted it. Pretending I consented. Now, just like a satisfied beast you sleep, unaware of the darkness falling around me, your love, stifling my thoughts and feelings, drowning my soul. Am I living? Can I love? Do I leave? Living. Loving. Leaving.

I watched him sleeping, afterwards. I watched him lying there, so innocent and at peace. I could not wonder why, I could not ask 'why me?' I had to go. I wish that I had gone into my baby girl's bedroom, lifted her warm, sleepy body out of bed, and taken her with me. But, I was destroyed, my life had shattered and I needed to escape from the pain.

Now I am sitting in a room in a friend's cold flat, without the laughter of my baby girl, without anything. I have a purse, I have my mobile, and I have some cigarettes. I also have the stark realisation that I abandoned my saviour, I abandoned my Jessica.

Paul Bennett

Can you ever force someone to be with you entirely, wholly and completely? Maybe you can, maybe I did, and maybe I will pay for it forever. I am not a good man, by any stretch of the imagination, but I never thought I could turn into someone, something, so monstrous and disgusting. Would you believe me if I said it was not me, if I said that for those twenty minutes I was outside my own body, watching a sick, evil monster rape my wife? Is there a justification for what I did?

Please can I make excuses and blame my childhood, blame the alcohol, blame the pressure, blame Eloise? Will I ever forget my wife's face, contorted with confusion and fear? Will I ever forget the anger I felt as we argued about nothing? The rage I felt as she sat there, denying me, telling me that I have broken her, that I have made it impossible for her to want me?

Will I ever forget the split second it all clicked

into place, the second I knew that if I wanted it I had to take it? With or without her permission.

I am not going to say she asked for it, I am not going to pretend that she consented; I refuse to fall into the cliché of a typical, cowardly, perpetrator of domestic violence. Yet, I do blame her for leaving me. What sort of mother abandons her daughter and runs away from her life, from the people who love her most? There she is, my wife, in the big wide world, free to meet other men. Free to fuck other men.

My wife.

She's probably sitting in a pub right now, free from the constraints of a relationship that she cannot be bothered to fix, while I sit here missing her and needing her home, having bathed and fed her daughter. Not a care in the world, my wife. What can I do to get her back? Do I sit and wait and hope that she will see sense and return? Do I text her and beg her to return to me? Or, do I play on her biggest weakness, Jessica? I could tell her Jessica is ill.

Could I?

I could hurt myself. She would have to come home if I hurt myself. I could throw myself down the stairs. I could take an overdose. Yes, an overdose, that is what I will do. Just enough to scare her, just enough to make her realise that she loves me and needs me and cannot survive without me.

Here I am. Her husband. Sitting on the sofa on

which I raped her. My wife. Trouble and strife. On the table in front of me, there are two blister packs of paracetamol. Twenty-four.

Count them. Twenty-four.
One, two, three
Love, hate, fear.

Swallowing them with whisky, I am laughing. Who will find me? Jessica?

Four, five, six
Wife, husband, child.

I do not want to die, I just need her to be home. My wife.

Seven, eight, nine
Together. Forever. Always.

My wife. Fucking other men. My wife. Come home.

Ten, eleven, twelve
Want. Need. Control.

They could never want her the way I want her.

Thirteen, fourteen, fifteen
Live. Life. Death.

Shall I take them all? Twenty-four hours in a day. One for each hour she's been gone. My wife.

Sixteen, seventeen, eighteen
Tick. Tock. Tick.

The whisky is warm, burning the back of my throat. This is good. This will work.

Nineteen, twenty, twenty-one
Asking. Questions. Silence.

Did she ever love me? She said she loved me. Where's my phone?

Twenty-two, twenty-three, twenty-four
Weakness. Bully. Bastard.

CAN'T COPE ANYMORE. TAKEN TABLETS. SO SORRY. BY THE TIME U GET HERE I WILL B DEAD. PAUL X

Jessica Louise Bennett

Today I feel very very sad. My Mummy didn't wake me up and I was in bed and I thought that if I get up it might be too much earlier than I usually get up because sometimes the clocks go backwards and forwards and the sun wakes up at a different time. I waited in bed and I spoke to Buggly Bear and I pretended that my pink dressing gown was Buggly Bear's dressing gown but it was too big for Buggly Bear and it has a picture of a princess on it and Buggly Bear is a boy. Silly me.

I couldn't hear the noises in the kitchen when my Mummy makes the kettle boil so she can have her coffee drink. Then I thought that I might be hungry because we have those things that you put in the toaster that are hot and have chocolate in the middle. My Mummy says that they are unhealthy and they are just like eating a big sweet for breakfast so I'm only allowed them at weekends. Sometimes I have two. So I got out of bed and I sucked my thumb, and my Mummy says that if I keep sucking my thumb my teeth will stick out and my thumb will grow really big but I do it anyway because it feels nice and a little bit tickly at the top bit of the inside bit of my mouth and I have been doing it for years without my Mummy knowing and it hasn't made my teeth stick out and all that has happened is that my thumb goes a bit wrinkly sometimes like when I stay in the bath for ages. And I put Buggly Bear under my arm and I went down the stairs to the kitchen. Then I walked past the lounge and Daddy was asleep on the sofa and I don't know where my Mummy is. I asked Daddy where my Mummy is and he didn't wake up, he made a snoring noise instead.

I went to the kitchen and I put my Buggly Bear

on the table so he could go back to sleep in case it was really early and he was still tired, then I opened the cupboard door but I couldn't see inside so I got my stool and I climbed on it and I saw the chocolate things so I put two chocolate things in the toaster. I'm allowed to use the toaster but I'm not allowed to use the kettle and not the cooker because they are very hot and might burn my fingers. I watched the toaster turn hot and I thought about where my Mummy is, and I thought my Mummy might still be asleep. My Mummy's special coffee plunging thing was next to the toaster and I thought that if I make her a coffee she would be really happy and might be so happy that she would forget that I'm not allowed to use the kettle. I can reach the kettle but not the tap. I took my stool to the sink. Have you ever had a favourite stool? My stool is my favourite stool and so I have put my best stickers all over it to cover up the scratched bits. And so Buggly Bear was still asleep. Where's my Mummy? I put a small bit of water in the kettle and I put the kettle on the stand and I switched it on and I put some coffee in the plunging thing and I spilled a bit but I think that's okay because it went on the floor and maybe nobody will see it. But it is brown and the floor is white so I kicked it a bit and got it stuck between my toes and it felt a bit scratchy. Then the kettle made a swishing whooshing sound and stopped boiling so I tried to pick it up to pour it on but it was too heavy to pour it.

Where's my Mummy?

My Mummy loves coffee so I took the plunging thing to the sink and climbed on my favourite stool and put some water from the hot tap in it. Then I sat down to let it get cold a bit and my chocolate breakfasts had popped so I ate one even though it was hot. Then I picked up my Buggly Bear and I put him under my arm and I put a chocolate breakfast on a plate and I picked up the plunging thing and I walked up the stairs to give my Mummy breakfast in bed. I like to get in bed with my Mummy because she is warm and cuddly and she might let me eat a bit of her chocolate breakfast. But when I went into my Mummy and Daddy's room there was nobody there.

Where's my Mummy?

I thought that maybe my Mummy was having a shower so I listened at the bathroom door and I put my hand on the door to see if it was warm from the very hot showers that my Mummy has that make her look all red all over. I couldn't hear the shower squirting water and so then I opened the door. There was nobody in the bathroom. I walked back down the stairs and there was nobody anywhere on the stairs.

Where. Is. My. Mummy?

I walked into the lounge and the lounge has wallpaper that I like that has flowers on it and they are blue and green and yellow and it used to have a picture on the wall but Daddy broke it and where it used to be there is a square, and I always look to see it because the wallpaper is clean on that bit. There was just Daddy on the sofa. So I asked Daddy again: where is my Mummy? Daddy made a noise and lifted his head and said my Mummy has gone and I knew that he wasn't lying and that she has really gone because her keys have gone because they are not in the black box next to the coffee thing in the kitchen.

Where's my Mummy?

That is why I feel very very sad today.

FOUR

Eloise Katherine Bennett

Sometimes, I want to give up. I try so hard to keep it all together, whilst wondering what would happen if I stopped trying, just for a while. What is the worst that could happen if I lay down and allowed the world to turn around me, without my input or permission? Just for a while. Could it be worse than this prison cell I am trapped within? I can see the light through the window, sometimes it even seeps inside and makes me smile, makes me laugh, makes me remember. But, it's still a prison; there is no escape. Here's the killer: I chose to be here. Laugh with me.

I hate him.

When the bad times are more painful than the good times are happy, that is when I will leave.

The grass is never greener on the other side. Sitting next to him, I want to be alone. Sitting alone, I want him next to me. How do I decide whether I have done the right thing?

There was intensity to our relationship, which was demonstrated in equal measures by passion and violence. The relationship was constantly the opposite of itself; it was unstable, yet stable; it was aggressive, yet gentle; it was love, yet it was hate.

When it was good, I could look into Paul's eyes and see deep inside his soul. I could feel the love that he had for us, and I knew that he was hurting because he couldn't be the man we wanted him to be. I know he loves me, I know that I love him, I know that we can be better together than apart. I can fix him, I will help him.

I love him.

How do I know which is the 'genuine' Paul? I know the person he can be, yet I know the person he has become. When does the divide become permanent? When is it safe to assume that the person he once appeared to be was a facade?

When I ran away to Emma's last night, it seemed like the right thing to do. I ran. I ran from physical pain, only to take it with me, plus the inevitable price of my daughter's happiness. That is what I'm selling right now. Tendering my child's sanity to the highest bidder, all the while running, running, running, with the truth hot on my heels.

Eventually, I will fall to my knees with exhaustion, the truth will catch up and I will be dragged back to reality against my will.

I hate him.

I need to believe in my own capabilities. I could return on new terms. No more hitting, no more shouting, no more pain. Just happiness, laughter and us.
Me plus Paul. Paul plus me. Plus Jessica. My family. Us.

I love him.

Emma and I stayed up all night, talking in circles. What to do, what to do, what to do...? Round and round we went, but each time we ended with the same question: do I return? Like teenagers, we formulated a list of pros and cons. This time round, instead of discussing the virtues of a nice arse, versus the drawbacks of body odour, we discussed the virtues of a family unit, versus the penalty of rape.

I hate him.

Like any good friend, Emma doesn't want me to

return, I suppose I can understand why. From an outside perspective, it must appear I am living a nightmare: beaten, shouted at and degraded. Nobody truly understands.

I love him.

Does love truly exist; or it is just a tool one can use to control another being?

I hate him.

There are two sides of me fighting to win the argument. The side that desperately wants there to be a reason, a point, behind this pain, versus a side that doesn't believe, or want to believe, that love exists.

I love him.
I need him.

Lust is a chemical reaction, devised by Mother Nature for the purpose of procreation.

Love is a chemical reaction, devised by Mother Nature to hold a pack together, to protect and nurture the young, to ensure the species continue.

I suppose that having borne a child, Mother Nature couldn't really give a fuck whether I live or die.

I hate him.

There's the old joke, isn't there? The one the married men tell in the pub, about watching their wedding video backwards, so that they can see their beloved walk back down the aisle, get in the car, and be gone for good.

I love him.

They joke about it, but deep down they know that if they opened the door to an empty house, they couldn't cope. They would close the door and slide down it in utter devastation. Yet, they can't admit this. Testosterone. Bravado. Women should be chained to the kitchen sink. Women should cook, women should clean, and women should ensure that the children are bathed and fed and then put to bed, all shiny and clean, by the time he returns from telling his sexist jokes at the pub.

I hate him.

And pain. They say that suffering pain makes you stronger. Does it? Does it, really? Alternatively, does it eat away inside and crumble your soul, like disintegrating vertebrae? Pain upon pain upon pain. Just as a body would eventually give up; a mind, a heart and a soul surely cannot be strengthened by constant trauma.

But, I love him.
Go on, now go.

I should leave him. He doesn't deserve me. I see what he does to me, I listen to the words he says to me, and I observe how he looks at me.

I hate him.

I absorb how it feels when he holds me. I smell the warm crease between his shoulder and his neck. I hold him, I feel him.

I love him.

He needs me, he loves me, he does not mean to. He is all I will ever get. Stand back. Step forward. Watch the drama unfold. Enter the turmoil. See the fireworks explode, but do not go in. Open the door. Be a victim. Stay. Stay. Stay, so I can tell the story of survival. Go. Go. Go, and sell my story to the magazines. Hate him. Be the victim. Be the survivor. She could not leave. That's what they will say. She left him. Loved him. She did, you know.

My phone bleeps, temporarily distracting me from my own, tragic, self-indulgence.

PAUL

Part of me wants to throw the phone at the

wall in rage. How fucking dare he take the control from me? After that? After he did that to me? Doesn't he have enough remorse to leave me to think for a few days? How fucking dare he try to take the decision away from me? If Emma hadn't had to go out this evening, undoubtedly she would have implored me to leave the text unread and unanswered. Wonderful, supportive, beautiful Emma. Emma, who I haven't seen for four years, because I haven't been allowed to. Emma whose doorstep I turned up on; crying, broken and bruised.

My mobile glows ominously in front of me, a wave of hatred burning through me. I hate Paul for putting me in this position, he has Jess, what if something has happened to her? I have to read the text.

CAN'T COPE ANYMORE. TAKEN TABLETS. SO SORRY. BY THE TIME U GET HERE I WILL B DEAD. PAUL X

'Fuck...'

I hate him.
I love him.
I hate him.

Instantly, I fantasise that I can leave him to his own idiotic devices, allowing the poison to travel through his body, hijacking and stifling his organs, until finally they give in and he collapses into an agonising unconsciousness. Then, he'd be gone, and I could grieve. I could grieve for the man I once knew, for the hope and the love that I once possessed, the hope and love that he slowly, yet cruelly ripped away.

Jessica

I visualise Jessica, my wonderful Jessica, with her beautiful, pleading brown eyes. If I don't go home, Jessica will find Paul. What sort of childhood memory is that?

What sort of childhood memory is recalling the day your mother abandoned you?

For the second time in twenty four hours, I pick up my cigarettes, my phone and my keys.

HOW MANY, BABY? I'M COMING HOME X

I'm going home…

I'm going home…because I love him.

Paul Bennett

She came back.

HOW MANY, BABY? I'M COMING HOME X

Oh, how my pounding, broken heart leapt when I read those six words.

She has forgiven me.

Home to her husband, to the man who loves her more than life.

Home to her violent, rapist husband. Home to the man that she should hate, the man who has made her life hell.

This is the beginning.

The beginning of the end?

This is a brand new start.

Today is the first day of the rest of my life. Today I will be that man: I will be that man who changed.

I will stop drinking, I will become the man that I should be; the man who everyone wants me to be. But, is it akin to putting a square peg in a round hole? I have tried it sideways, but it doesn't fit. I have tried it diagonally, but it still doesn't fit. Can I do it? Is it where I belong?

Outside the box, I am surrounded by my heaven: beer, *power,* vodka, *control,* cider, *manipulation.* Inside the box are my beautiful wife and my amazing daughter. My heaven: their hell. Therefore, I will get the hammer, and I will bang and I will push and I will force myself into that fucking hole, because that is where the important things are; that is where I am needed. I will change; I can love them, I can be husband and I can be father.

It all starts from somewhere, doesn't it? Every wrong, every right, every mistake, every choice. They all originate, they were all planted, and they all grow.

It all stems from his childhood, you know.

In the great scheme of things, I had a wonderful childhood; I led a charmed existence. I was my parents' little blue-eyed boy and could do no wrong. My elder brother and sister resented me from a very early age because of this, not that I cared. I got the best toys, the best room, the most hugs and the biggest praise.

'He's the angel of the family.'

As I grew up, I realised that I could do pretty much whatever I wanted, and get away with it. If I was good, I was rewarded. If I was bad, I was bribed. Bloody fantastic. Or, so I thought.

At the tender age of ten, I was suddenly thrust into the big, wide world of adulthood. My parents decided that they no longer loved each other enough to stay together, and that it was acceptable for their three children to grow up in a broken home.

Bitter, me?

That is when it all fell apart. My fifteen-year-old brother, William, decided that he wanted to live with Dad. Jane, my seventeen-year-old sister, decided that she hated everyone, and thus should be self-sufficient and live in a bedsit in the town centre. Not such a great plan, as by the end of the year she was hooked on heroin and an embarrassingly crap shoplifter.

I stayed with Mum—she was in her fifties and absolutely adored every bone in my body. Dad: not so much, I visited him every Sunday and we would indulge in two hours of stilted, shallow conversation. I know he blamed me for the breakdown of his marriage. It transpired that my Mum had had an affair a few months before I was conceived, and the band-aid merits of my arrival had slowly dissipated and eaten away at the delicate flesh of their matrimony, rendering it in a worse state than it was before. Dad resented Mum for looking elsewhere, and Mum was forever indebted to the man who overlooked her extra-marital faux pas. Mum and Dad did not speak again after the split. They had spent eighteen years sharing the same bed, drinking out of the same cups, walking on the same carpet, and raising the same children, yet now they could no longer bring themselves to exchange a few pleasantries, they used William and I as messengers.

'Tell her that Dad says you can come round Sunday, if it's ok with her.'
'Tell him that Mum says I always visit on Sundays, so why is he asking her?'

Over the months, these exchanges became more and more elaborate and colourful, without Mum and Dad's knowledge.

'Tell her that Dad says she's a disgusting, horrible, lazy slut.'
'Tell him that she wouldn't be a slut if he'd managed to get it up once in a while.'

In hindsight, it was the only way that William and I could vocalise our frustrations. My frustration was that he treated Mum with amazing disrespect. This wonderful lady had given him life, yet he despised her, and he spoke to her like shit. He would phone solely to verbally abuse her, to demand money that she didn't have. He terrified her. His frustration was that his Mum had never loved him as much as she loved me. He was my polar opposite, whatever he did, whether good or bad, he was told off.

'Go and wash your face.'
'I am.'
'Don't use that tone with me, young man.'

However hard he tried, however much love he gave, it was never returned. He was older, and should know better. Jane was incidental. Jane caused the marriage in the first place, and as it disintegrated, this became her fault. The words were never said, but hung in the air, like damp washing. Heavy, dripping with unsaid resentment. So, she left. Sometimes I see her, walking down the road, with her shit of a boyfriend, and I cross the road to avoid her. Am I any better than she is? Am I actually worthy of snobbery? I, after all, am a wife beater. The worst she did is ingest chemicals and take things that did not belong to her. Nobody got hurt. Nobody died.

Eloise Katherine Bennett

Cope: Noun. To cope. Coping. Coped. To face and deal with problems, responsibilities, or difficulties, successfully, or in a calm manner.

Self-harmers, they do it for attention; it is just a cry for help. Bollocks. I spent my teenage years wearing a variety of long-sleeved tops to hide my shredded arms. I did it for me, nobody else. It started the week after I lost my virginity. I was sixteen, he was twenty-nine, and I met him during a vodka-fuelled binge in the town centre. He excited me, far more than my first love, my untouched love, my Sam. Sam was my friend, who became my boyfriend, the boy I sat on benches with, held hands with and kissed with no tongues. The boy who did not love me. The boy. A boy.

The man who took my virginity showed me that there was more to life; there was flirting, there was expectation, there was excitement. Romance. Lust. Expectation. Paedophile. Afterwards, he was never to be seen again. No phone calls, no flowers, no marriage proposals, no nothing.

It creeps up on you when you're happy
It's always around when you're having fun
It hits you when you're already down
Always there on your shoulders
Weighing a ton

I fantasised that perhaps he had died—a hideous car crash, or maybe even abducted by aliens. How else could it be explained? That I was so disgusting that nobody would want to touch me for a second time?

It makes daytime feel like night
And a night feel like eternity
It makes a bed feel so big and bare
And being part of a crowd feels so lonely

I had friends around me, all saying he wasn't worth it, I'll find someone else, he is clearly emotionally inept. But, it was me, all about me. My fault, my life, my mistake.

It makes sure the phone never rings
And the doorbell seems to have died
It makes the mirror appear so ugly,
There's no one there to see the beauty inside.

I curled myself into a ball to protect my heart, I spent my days pretending to be sick to avoid school, and my evenings staring at the stars through the window of my bedroom, periodically changing my focus so that I could wallow in the misery of my tear-stained reflection.

Misery loves company...?

Misery doesn't love company; misery loves to be left to its own, self-indulgent ways. It loves to be alone; it doesn't wish to spread itself. Misery doesn't demand that someone knocks on the door every two minutes to check its welfare; it thrives on the feeling of emptiness and loneliness. Misery loves to hear the heart-breaking warbling of love songs; it listens to them repeatedly, it learns the words, it absorbs them, then it expels them in a stream of salty water. Emotional bulimia. I am misery. Misery is me.

I stood in the shower and sobbed as the warm spray stung my cold body. If only it could have cleansed the dirt inside me. I scrubbed my skin until it turned an ominous shade of red. Staring at my red arms, I reached for the razor and tentatively pushed it against my skin. Nothing. I pushed harder until the pressure turned the skin beneath it white. Taking a deep breath, I pulled the blade quickly across my arm, watching as the skin pulled slightly apart, and then fill with bright red blood. I watched the droplets and I waited until the pressure inside me had dissipated, then I collapsed on the floor of the shower with relief. Curling myself into a ball, I watched with satisfaction as the warm water washed away the blood containing my dirty secret. Washed away HIM. Washed away the pervert who touched me, who fucked me, who dumped me. I stepped out of the shower and soaked up the remaining blood on my forearm with a tissue. Nobody must know. Nobody must see. Eloise must keep smiling. I pulled on my dressing gown, grinning with a macabre satisfaction as I studied the cuts on my arm. Marked and branded. History, right there, etched on my arm.

Time to go to bed.

Time to dream away the pain.

I used this coping strategy for years, until I met Paul. For the first time, I was truly content. Paul

LOVED me. Nobody had ever truly LOVED me before.

'Mum. I love you.'
'Do you?'
'Dad, I love you.'
'Ok, dear.'
JUST SAY IT.

The scars on my arm healed, but were always a constant reminder of how to survive. Scars, waiting to be ripped open.

Now, I sit at Emma's kitchen table, staring at the scissors for what feels like an eternity. I feel the familiar bubbling of anxiety in the pit of my stomach, travelling towards my chest, constricting me, stifling my breaths. I take the scissors and purposefully drag them over the old scars, transporting myself back to 1992.

Flounder: Verb. Floundered. Floundering. To struggle clumsily or helplessly. She tries to get her life on track, but flounders helplessly.

FIVE

Jessica Louise Bennett
May 2000

Daddy was poorly five weeks ago. I know it was five weeks ago because I have been writing lines on the calendar so that I know how many days it is until I get to go to the cinema to watch that film with the cartoon animals in it that talk with big voices. It's seven days. On the day that Daddy was poorly, my Mummy came home and I was so pleased that my Mummy had come home that I smiled a lot and I forgave her for going away. I go to playschool because I am four years old and two months old too and I go to big school in September. At playschool we learn to smile and forgive people if they make a mistake because everybody makes mistakes. One time when we went to a farm I made a mistake and I put my arm through the fence to stroke a donkey and my teacher shouted at me and told me 'I told you not to put your arm through the fence,' and I was really sad and cried because I don't like to be naughty, but now I know that she only told me off because the donkey gets angry at people's arms and sometimes bites them. She told me for my own good so I think that when my Mummy made a mistake it was for her own good so I can forgive her. I think my Mummy was poorly that day too because when she came back from Auntie Emma's she had a bandage on her arm. Auntie Emma is my Auntie because she has been my Mummy's best friend for a long long time, and I think they've been friends for a longer time than me and Charlotte. My Mummy hasn't seen Auntie Emma since I was a baby but my Mummy told me she is called an Auntie because they are really good friends.

Daddy was so poorly that he had to go to the hospital and I don't think I know what was wrong with him except I heard my Mummy talking on the phone to Auntie Emma and saying that at the hospital they were going to pump something. I think the hospital fixed Daddy because he is happy and smiling and not hurt now. I was sad about my Mummy's arm because there was blood on the bandage and we had run out of plasters so I couldn't make it better so I told my Mummy to let the air get to it. My Mummy wouldn't tell me what hurt she had on her arm but I think she hurt it when she went away because she went away in the middle of the night and it was dark so she might have banged into something. It is better now though.

We live in a house that has another house underneath it and the other house used to be empty but now there is a neighbour there. The neighbour has got a cat and brown hair and I really want to go and see her cat because when I am older I want to be a vet. When I think about what I want most I decide that I want a pet and I want that doll and I want no poorlies and I want my Mummy and Daddy to smile and hug forever like they have been smiling and hugging since my Mummy came back from Auntie Emma's.

Today when we went to the park my Mummy looked a little bit poorly and she said she felt a little bit poorly and I want her to not be poorly but when I heard her being sick I knew it was bad. Then later on I heard my Mummy telling Daddy she had been sick and then my Mummy was laughing and crying and Daddy was laughing and crying and then I was confused, because if you are sick it is horrible and it comes out of your nose and makes it sting and you need to drink water which makes your throat taste funny. Then my Mummy came into the lounge and I was trying to watch the television and my Mummy stood in front of the television and I tried to look around the side of her to see the picture but she pressed the button to turn it off. Then Daddy came into the lounge and stood next to my Mummy in front of the television and my Mummy told me I am going to have a baby brother or sister to look after and to love. I am very happy about that because I like babies but I am not very happy that I missed all of my favourite programme.

Eloise Katherine Bennett

I am pregnant.

Celebrate or commiserate?

How can something so amazing be born from something so hideous?

The rape.

It is a brand new start, a new beginning. The house has been filled with the joyous sound of laughter for the last few weeks: exactly what I prayed for.

Happy or sad?

Paul is ecstatic.

Another person to control.

He has stopped drinking.

Ignore the bottles hidden under the sofa.

There have been no arguments.

Avoiding confrontation.

My mother called me yesterday; Emma had contacted her to express her disgust at the life I am living. Now my mother knows everything. Apparently, Jessica and I are more than welcome to move in with her and Dad. Ha. Move in with that controlling, emotionally inept pensioner?
Not much different from the life I am living now?

I politely declined, which was 'ungrateful and bordering on insanity.' When will she realise I am no longer the little girl that she can mould and control?

For a brief, a very brief, period of time, I considered an abortion. Would it be right to bring another life into this hideous, fucked up world? Into *my* hideous, fucked up world? But, then I realised how much happiness this baby has brought us already—Paul hasn't as much as raised his voice since I returned from Emma's, and Jessica seems happy that she will finally have somebody who is completely on her side.

Band-aid baby. It will never work.

Perhaps we can now return to the happiness we had before it all went wrong? Paul has been looking for a job, he spends hours each day at the job centre trying to find something that will bring in enough money to support us, maybe even enough to move to a house.

Is that where he is? Really? What about the perfume and the lipstick? Tell them about the perfume and the lipstick.

In conclusion: life couldn't get much better. Really, it couldn't.

To summarise: patch it up because, Eloise, that's the best you're going to get...

Paul Bennett

It is three AM. I am alone with my can of beer and my thoughts. The can I grasp in my hand is slightly crushed; the force of my self-loathing denting it between my fingers. The blood rushing to my fingertips pounds with every heartbeat: a rhythmic tattoo of hatred. There is a mirror on the wall to the side of me and I stare at the loathsome man trapped within it, his pale, ageing face, tangle of greying hair and charcoal smudges beneath his eyes. I slowly close my eyes, blocking him. I hate that man, that man must change.

Eloise and Jessica are in bed, and I am in the process of deconstructing my life once again. Everything was perfect.

Everything is perfect.

Everything could be perfect?

No sooner has Eloise come home, and I'm playing away. Pregnant wife, four-year-old child, and a mistress.

Time for another beer.

Eloise thinks I spend my days looking for a job to support my ever-expanding family, when in reality I spend my days fucking her best friend, Emma.

I laugh.

It was inevitable, like mixing two unstable components and wondering when they are going to explode. Emma came round to see Eloise the day she returned home, but she was out taking Jess to playschool. That day, we exploded.

I truly hadn't set out to hurt Eloise, I don't know how this started, and I certainly don't know how to end it.

Don't want to end it.

I have told Eloise I've stopped drinking completely. In reality, I'm having a few cans a day. It causes no harm, as long as I can control my temper.

Just one more beer.

Oh, who the fuck am I kidding? I hold my hands up: I am a bastard. I will call her, I will tell her I can't do it anymore.

Maybe another beer.

What if Eloise checks my phone and sees that I have called Emma late at night? She might realise what's been going on. What if Jessica comes down the stairs and hears my conversation?

I'll call her tomorrow.

Two beers left, I will have another.

Definitely tomorrow.
Maybe tomorrow.

I am certain that, given the chance, Eloise would do the same, I've treated her like shit, so why wouldn't she? How do I know that this baby is even mine? She could have been out fucking all the men in town for all I know.

Because that would make my behaviour acceptable.

I need to ask her, it's time to know the truth. I'm

not a mug, I'm not a fool, and I won't take this behaviour from a slut like her.

Another beer?

I need to know now.
I'm going to ask her.
I rise from the sofa, and, stumbling slightly, make my way to the living room door. The door creaks as I drunkenly ease it open.

Shhh. Don't wake Jessica.

Holding on to the wall for support, I edge my way along the dark hallway, stepping on one of Jessica's plastic building blocks as I do.

Shit
Fuck
Why is this place such a mess?
Bloody woman, what the fuck does she do all day?
Biting my lip to stop the string of expletives threatening to escape, I begin to make my way up the stairs to our bedroom.

Bitch
Slut
Whore

I can feel the anger welling inside me, as I struggle to understand why somebody who says they love me would fall pregnant with another man's baby.

I creep into our bedroom; I watch Eloise sleeping, watch her chest rise and fall with every deceitful breath. How can someone so deceitful look so beautiful? She is lying on her side, facing away from where I would be sleeping. Her head is resting upon her hands, which she has clasped beneath her cheek. There's a strand of hair falling across her face, resting on her upper lip. I want to gently brush it away; I want to be that man. But, I'm not.

I know that if I speak, I will wake Jessica, so I slowly climb on top of Eloise, and gently ease my face forward so she will be able to hear me. Eloise wakes with a start, a horrified look in her eyes.

She knows that I know. She is scared now.

'I know what you've been up to, Eloise,' I whisper, inches from her face.

'You've been drinking?'

'Yes, and I know what you've done, I know it's not my baby.'

'Paul, get off. Please. What are you talking about?'

'You've been fucking other men. FUCKING. OTHER. MEN.'

'Paul, please be quiet, you'll wake Jess. When have I had time to fuck other men?'

I hadn't thought of that.

Now she's trying to make me feel stupid.

Eloise starts to struggle beneath me, so I put my hands either side of her neck to stop her moving.

'DON'T TRY TO MAKE ME LOOK STUPID,

ELOISE.'

I tighten my grip on her neck, feeling the anger coursing through my veins, furiously pumping blood to my throbbing temples.

Red and black and red and black and red and black.

Eloise's eyes have moved to the open bedroom door, because bathed in the light from the hallway is Jessica. She looks like an angel.

'Daddy? Why are you shouting at my Mummy? Please don't shout at my Mummy, please, please, you're scaring her.'

I stare at Jessica, and then shift my body weight so Eloise can take my princess back to bed.

That's my kid, that's my daughter, that's my life.

I lay face-down on Eloise's pillow, smelling her scent, remembering our baby, knowing that one day I could push Eloise too far and she could take everything away. I think I have fucked up again.

I'm so sorry.

Truly, honestly, God's honest truth: I fucking love my family.

Jessica Louise Bennett

Last night I was tired and went to sleep but I

can't have been as tired as I thought I was because then I woke up. I thought I heard a noise and a bang from downstairs but maybe I was hearing things because sometimes that happens. I picked up my Buggly Bear to cuddle and then I remembered I was excited because I was wearing my new pyjamas that had a picture of a princess on them. I tried to look at the picture but I couldn't see it because it was night-time. My Mummy always leaves the landing light on because I get scared of the dark and I'm glad she left it on last night because I realised that meant I could quickly go into the hall and have a look at the picture on my pyjamas and then go back to bed to go to sleep and not get into trouble. My door is only four big steps away from my bed so I got out of my bed and walked four big steps to my door but my legs must have been tired because it was four and a half really big steps.

My door is normally closed at night-time just in case there is some shouting which really scares me but my Mummy says there won't be any shouting anymore so I let her leave my door open so I can see in case I need to get up to go to the toilet when it is dark. I can see a little bit out of the door and I saw Daddy walking really slowly like a snail across the landing bit and I think he was doing that so that he didn't wake me and my Mummy up because it was so dark. I thought that I should wait until Daddy had got into bed before I looked at the picture on my pyjamas so I quietly spoke to Buggly Bear and we decided that I should count to twenty buttons before I went to the landing. The landing is like the hallway but it is upstairs and it's not downstairs like the hallway. It's the most boring bit of the house because it hasn't even got a carpet and it has only a floor and even the floor has bits of paint on it. And I get a bit worried because there are gaps in between the bits of wood on the floor and the gaps are big enough for great big spiders to crawl through and I don't like great big spiders because to adults they look tiny which is why adults aren't scared of them, but to little children like me and like Charlotte they are really really big and we think they will climb into our bedrooms and sit on our eyes when we are sleeping. I only got to five buttons before I heard Daddy say something and he sounded a bit cross but I know that when people get tired they get grumpy so I thought that Daddy might go straight to sleep because he must be very tired as he sounded very grumpy. Then I counted to eighteen buttons and I got a bit bored so I decided that I would stop counting buttons and so I walked out onto the landing. My Mummy and Daddy's door was open and it is only next to mine so I could hear that my Mummy's voice was very quiet and shaky like when I see a spider so I know that she was scared and Daddy was shouting and I wished so badly that I had closed my door and not woken up and not wanted to look at the picture on my pyjamas.

I thought that my Mummy might need me to give her a cuddle because I know it's not nice to be scared and it is nice to have cuddles. Then when I went in to my Mummy and Daddy's bedroom and saw that Daddy was kneeling on top of my Mummy and I thought that must be a nice cuddle but Daddy was still being grumpy and he had his hands round my Mummy's neck and it looked like he was squeezing her. My Mummy saw me, and her eyes looked scared and so I asked Daddy to get off my Mummy because she was looking scared and he did, so maybe they were just playing a grumpy game. But when my Mummy put me to bed she kissed me and her face was wet and she hugged me and put her wet face in my hair and when she went I thought my hair must be wet because the wet on my Mummy's face was tears. And then I thought I don't want my Mummy and Daddy to play grumpy games if it makes my Mummy sad.

Then I counted more buttons and hugged Buggly Bear under my arm and cried and went to sleeps and wished that my Buggly Bear had told me to count to a hundred buttons.

Emma Woodgate

I have no excuse.

I have nothing I can say to redeem myself.

I cannot justify why I betrayed my oldest friend in such an abhorrent way.

I care what people think of me, I care what they say about me, I care whether they laugh or frown when they hear my name. I care for Eloise, I care for Jessica, I fucking hate Paul.

I had a good childhood.

I have never been beaten, I have never taken drugs, I have never been arrested, I have never been dumped.

I have a car, I have a flat, I have food in the cupboard, I have an ashtray somewhere, although I have never smoked.

I drink ten to fourteen units of red wine a week, usually spread evenly over the seven-day period.

I have a job, a reasonably well paid one at that, I wear a suit and heels to work.

I have a car, a little one, but a car nonetheless.

I eat organic, I drink smoothies.

I buy fair-trade and I donate to charity.

I turn the television over if warned that a programme may contain violent images.

I help old people cross the road.

I tip the taxi driver, I tip the waiter, I tip the hairdresser.

I refuse to purchase throwaway fashion. Someone, somewhere has dripped sweat to make that.

I have perfectly manicured nails. Nails that scratched Paul's back.

The man of my dreams exists and he is looking for me. He has styled hair and uses moisturiser. When he runs out, he borrows mine. He runs me a bath and lights a candle or two, before sitting on the chair next to me and telling me about his day. We eat dinner together every night, except when he is away on business. In between mouthfuls, we laugh, because our relationship is based on fun. We have two children, they are named Millie and Max; we like the rolling rhythm of alliteration. We live in a house; the flat was not large enough to house our expanding family, so we rent it out. It is our investment, our pension, our future. We have a future, you see, because we are perfect. In this life, I drive a 4X4 and I have joined the parent-teacher association. Twice a year, I bake cakes for the school fair; they are moist and delicious. They are perfect.

Even when pregnant, I was still beautiful: untouched by swollen ankles, stretch marks or heartburn. This is because I am perfect.

My parents are still married, I visit them twice a week. They sit on the sofa next to each other, and sometimes doze off holding hands.

I cried for three hours last March, because I saw a cat die under the wheels of a car.

I do not need to diet. I am a perfect size ten.

Yes, I am perfect, pretty much perfect. Yet, I still fucked my best friend's husband.

<u>Eloise Katherine Bennett</u>

If it isn't written down, it didn't happen. Life could be convenient and tolerable if it existed solely in black and white. The painful, horrible things not even worthy of putting pen to paper for, dissolving before they have even begun. I try to control my life according to this fantasy, I remember everything, yet waste no time pitying the dross. I spent my teenage years writing in a diary, conveniently leaving out the bits that I wouldn't have wanted anyone to read if it had been discovered. Most of my thoughts, feelings and emotions were there, scrawled ominously in black and shades of grey, tainting the white purity of the paper. Yet, the things that happened to me that I couldn't accept, or that embarrassed me, were locked inside a box in my brain, to be aired once in a while when myself and my razor shared some quality time. The razor that was not permitted a debut in my tattered, exhausted diary.

If I wrote a diary now, I would scribble about last night. I would tell how Paul and I had an argument, which woke up Jess. I would omit that I woke up to Paul sitting on my chest, suffocating me, with the menacing look of a maniac upon his face. I would omit the fact that I lost control of my bladder because I was fucking petrified. I might mention that when I put Jessica back to bed, I cried. I wouldn't tell that I suspect Jess saved my life, and that left to his own devices, Paul would have continued throttling me until I died.

Escaped.

Nor would I tell that I am such an appalling mother that I let her go to sleep sobbing her heart out into her pillow, yet I couldn't bring myself to comfort her, because that would mean admitting that I need to change the life I am forcing her to live.

I would perhaps write that Paul and I aren't getting on so well at the moment, we are snapping at each other over the smallest of things. Who ate the last of the crisps? Whose turn is it to put the washing on? Where are my fucking keys?

Perhaps I would say that we are bickering, and that I am considering marriage counselling of some description. I certainly would not write that our arguments are so loud and nasty that Jessica has nightmares and wakes up crying. I would write that on the nights I feel brave enough, I hold her to my chest, with my face buried deep into her hair as I rock her back to sleep. I would admit that at times, Paul can be nasty, but I would not let anybody know that he pushes me, or throws things at me. That would be admitting I am too weak to stand up to him. I would say that he is trying to give up drinking, but omit the discovery of the empty cans underneath the sofa.

Perhaps I would lighten the mood by mentioning that Paul is looking for a new job, but not state that he returns home smelling of perfume, with the clichéd lipstick on his collar.

I think I would write about the time I stepped backwards suddenly, then tripped and cut my face on the corner of an open kitchen drawer. I definitely wouldn't mention that the reason I stepped backwards suddenly was because Paul was threatening me, or that the drawer was open because that is where Paul had got the knife he was holding inches from my face, whilst Jessica watched television in the room next door.

Maybe, I would even say that he scares me, but I would never write that I think that if this continues, one day he may really hurt me.

Because, if all these things are written in black and white, then I would have to admit they are real.

Sandra Alice Harrington

Externally, I am a cold creature of habit. You will know where to find me at any given moment; I will be where I always am on that particular day of the week, at that time. I am fundamentally the same structure as every other human being, yet I am devoid of emotion.

I clean my oven on a Monday—it always needs it after Sunday's roast, and I cook a casserole on a Thursday—using the meat I purchased from my local butcher on the Wednesday morning. Every other day, I wash my hair, and I have it hot-brushed once a week at the salon I have been visiting for the past thirty years. It concerns me when my regular hairdresser leaves, and palms me off to a new, anonymous young slip of a girl who is fresh out of training. I always close my eyes as she wraps my hair around the hot barrel brush, because I do not wish to see the panic in her eyes as it becomes stuck; the fresh, sticky scent of hair-mousse quickly replaced with the biting catch of smoke. I realise that I do not cope well with change. But, before long, I find myself singing the praise of the new hairstylist, and the whole cycle starts over again.

Life was not always so organised, in contrast, as a young child my life was hectic and out of control. I was adopted at the age of five, after my mother and younger sister died in a house fire. My father could not cope with the loss, and struggled to deal with the thought of the emotional trauma it had caused to his two remaining small children, so we were palmed off on grandparents for a year, until their frailty gave them no other option than to pass us to an adoption society to deal with. We were relatively lucky, I suppose, inasmuch as we all remained living together, in my grandparents' house, until a 'suitable' family was allocated to us, like lost luggage at an auction. The highest bidders were the Clarks, who lived on the South Coast. They were stable and solvent, and to all intents and purposes, the epitome of the 'perfect couple'.

As each day went by, the treasured images I held in my mind of my natural parents faded like an old Polaroid. I desperately tried to grasp them back, but their faces were fading, and their vibrant personalities paling. This saddened me, because my mother was beautiful and artistic; she spent her days painting stunning landscape pictures, and her evenings making clothes for my siblings and me. My father was a little more stoical, everyone could see he loved his family, but in a manner typical of his time, he maintained a constant business-like air.

Together they were perfect; my mother's constant whims were grounded slightly by my father's sensible nature. However, her wings were not clipped, they were merely held gently and loosely to stop her floating away from us.

I remember the day of the fire, albeit in a manner not unlike an old, crackly cinema reel. I remember being scared.

'The children, Jack, save the children!'

I remember struggling to breathe, but I couldn't

understand why. In my five-year-old mind, a fire was hot, and I would burn to death. This was thick, acrid smoke, snaking around my head and burning the back of my throat. I tried to scream, but no noise came out. I tried to call out for my Mummy, or my Daddy, or anyone, *someone*, to help me, but my voice was strangled by the smoke around me. I could hear the screams of my sisters and brother, but I could not see them. I didn't know what panic was at the time, but I now know that the tightening in the pit of my stomach, and the feeling that my heart was going to beat out of my chest was just that.

'I want my Mummy. MY MUMMY. I WANT MY MUMMY.'

I tried to comfort the others, I reached out my arms to grab them, but felt nothing but air.

'Sandra, William, Diane, Linda. Where are you?'

I felt relief wash over me as I heard the comforting sound of my father's voice outside the house. With every ounce of my energy, I managed to lift an arm to the window to show him which room we were trapped inside. Seconds later, I heard a smashing as my father threw a metal bucket through the windowpane, smashing it and showering me in tiny, painful shards of glass. I now know that it was this act that saved me, but killed Linda. My eight-month-old sister, lying in her cot, her mouth open as she gasped for air, was pierced in the throat by a flying shard of glass, killing her instantly.

William, Diane and I were carried to safety by our father's strong arms, but when he returned to save his beloved wife; my mother; she had perished. I will never forget standing huddled on the front lawn with William and Diane, neighbours milling around with blankets and cups of tea, watching as my soot-covered father carried out first the lifeless body of my baby sister, her tiny form splattered with blood, then the limp body of my mother. Linda was clearly dead, but my mother: she looked asleep. My father sank to his knees, pumping my mother's chest and I watched, mesmerised. I prayed: oh, how I prayed. I prayed my mother would cough and splutter and sit up on the lawn, exclaiming profanities at my father for having bruised her. This was not to be so, there she lay, and in my mind there she remains. That day was the last day I cried. That day was the day we all died inside.

The day we buried my mother and Linda was the last time I saw my biological father. I awoke on the morning of the funeral, expecting the weather to match my mood, but there were no tornadoes, there was no torrential rain, just warm sunshine and a few scattered white clouds. I was washed and preened by my maternal grandmother, with whom we were staying whilst my father 'sorted out the funeral arrangements.' My cheeks were scrubbed so clean that they stung when I went outside, and my Sunday-best dress had been given a new lease of life with a brand-new, heavily starched petticoat. I felt guilty that I was excited about wearing a hat, guilt that I had not cried for my mother, yet I had smiled when my grandmother placed the black headpiece on my neatly combed hair. I knew my mother would have been so proud of me, her eldest daughter, beautifully groomed like a proper young lady, standing stock still, shoulders back, chin raised slightly in a defiant manner.

Being a reasonably well-off family, we were able to give my mother and Linda a heartbreakingly beautiful send-off, in the form of a procession of horse-drawn hearses. My father read an eloquent, unemotional speech; he always was a man of few words, and by detaching himself, he was able to save face in front of the hoards of people who packed out the church. Unfortunately, the body never lies, and shortly after the speech, as my father made the short walk back to his seat, I watched in horror as his legs crumpled beneath him, people leaping from their seats to catch the proud man as he fell. My father never truly recovered, and fifteen years later, I was dutifully informed that he had died in his sleep of a heart attack, having never seen us again.

A broken man, killed by a broken heart.

A year later found us on the South Coast, living in a four-bedroom detached house with an herbaceous border and net curtains. On paper, it was perfect—the bedrooms were beautifully decorated, the cupboards tidy and neatly organised, but there was something lacking. I cannot recall laughing with Walter and Alice Clark; Alice was brusque and rarely smiled, definitely didn't hug, and would rather have died than tell us she loved us. This lack of affection withered the bond between William, Diane and me. Like a plant starved of water, the roots of love shrunk and died in that house. If my mother were alive, she would have been devastated that her much-loved children had grown so cynical and uncaring. I do not doubt that Walter and Alice loved us deeply, they certainly looked after us, and they rarely chastised us. I suspect that somewhere in the past, something killed their ability to demonstrate that they loved, just like the fire burned away the receptors that carried my love from my heart to my hands, my lips, my arms, my mouth, my soul. It stays right where it is, wrapped in walls, so I cannot feel it. Broken cynics store love internally and indefinitely, until eventually we explode with the pressure.

I have not been in touch with William or Diane since my wedding to George in 1975, they spoke about the fire that day, they tried to make me remember, tried to make my eyes sting with forgotten tears.

Walter was not dissimilar to my real father, in that he marched to work at six o'clock in the morning, returned at five pm, solemnly ate dinner with us, and then had a brandy before going to bed. Yet, there was no fire in his eyes, no emotion when he kissed Alice goodbye in the mornings. I could not imagine this man dissolving in grief as he buried two-fifths of his family.

This, my friends, this is why I am the way I am. And for that I do not apologise.

SIX

Jessica Louise Bennett
July 2000

I think that maybe Daddy is going to go on a holiday. I asked my Mummy if we were going on holiday this year and my Mummy said no but then I heard Daddy on the phone to somebody and he said he will meet them there and he can get away for a whole night and he has made sure that nobody knows about it. I have drawn a sun on a piece of paper with my best crayons that I keep for my best pictures and also I have drawn some sea and some grass but I don't know if there is grass in hot places because I know that in the summer if there is no rain, the grass goes all brown and I think that in another place in the world where it is summer all the time, I think that the grass would always be brown so I think that they just wouldn't plant grass.

I know we can't go on a proper holiday because

I know that we have no money because my little baby brother or sister is growing in my Mummy's tummy and will cost lots of money when it comes out. Maybe that is why Daddy is going on a holiday on his own.

When my baby brother or sister comes out I want my Mummy to call it either Baby Joseph or Baby Mary like in the nativity play at nursery school. If my baby brother or sister is called Mary or Joseph then they will get to be Mary or Joseph in the nativity play and be happy. Because I am called yucky Jessica I only get to be a star or an angel and there are lots of them so it's not as special. Last year I practised my singing extra specially in front of the mirror in the hall but they still didn't choose me. That made me a bit sad so when I did the singing in the play I tried to do it with a sulky face so that the teachers would see that I didn't want to be an angel and then they might let me be the Mary on the next year. What makes me sad too is Daddy going on holiday without my Mummy and me and my baby brother or sister bump. Maybe if I ask Daddy nicely he will take us with him?

Daddy and my Mummy are sitting in the kitchen with Auntie Emma at the moment talking and drinking coffee so I am going to ask Daddy now whether we can all go on holiday with him.

Uh oh.

I've had to run away to my bedroom now because I asked Daddy where is he going and why is he going without us and why it is a secret and he looked all surprised and so did Auntie Emma, and my Mummy looked at Auntie Emma and looked at Daddy and looked at Auntie Emma again and then Daddy again and then looked really angry but she didn't say anything and then stood up and then threw the big glass coffee plunging thing and it went on the wall and on the floor and on Daddy's hand and I think he got a bit hurt. I am so so sad now and I wish someone would come to give me a cuddle and I can't wait for Mary or Joseph to be born so that Mary or Joseph can cuddle me when I make everyone cross and make everyone hate me.

Eloise Katherine Bennett

Desolation.
Unhappily.
Ever.
After.

Sandra Alice Harrington

I have my daughter home, at long last. Finally, she has seen sense, left that volatile pig of a husband, and moved herself and Jessica back home with her father and me. George was reluctant to have her home, reluctant to shoulder responsibility for a small child in the house, but I asked him: what else are we to do? I didn't tell him that the idea of having both my girls under my roof made me so happy that I wanted to dance on the rooftops.

Made me feel useful again.

Made me feel in control again.

During Eloise's birth, I suffered catastrophic trauma, which left me physically incapable of falling pregnant again. This is why Eloise is so precious to me, to us. She is, and always has been, the single most important person in our lives.

I just wish I could tell her so.

I find it difficult to express emotion, my adoptive mother was Victorian-esque and looked disdainfully upon emotion; it was a sign of weakness. I find it almost impossible to say those dreaded three words that seem to bandy about so freely in everyday life.

I love you.

Eloise and Paul have been in a relationship since Eloise was seventeen. I approved, at first. Paul was solvent, appeared quite sensible, and Eloise was smiling for the first time in years. How could I not be happy for her?

You have to understand that Eloise was not the easiest of children to raise, she got in with a 'bad crowd' and developed a taste for alcohol, cigarettes and boys at a very young age. Eloise was so rebellious that I gave up grounding her; it was just punishing me and George, having Eloise mope around her bedroom for days on end. By the age of thirteen, she was smoking, drinking by fourteen, and I have no doubt that she was sexually active by the age of fifteen. Eloise was difficult, you see. She was headstrong and argumentative, nobody could tell her right from wrong, and she only ever listened to her own self-centred opinions.

Loved the sound of her own voice, that child.

Eloise had a series of unsuccessful 'relationships', as she called them. I tried to explain to her that they were just puppy love, she had her whole life ahead of her, and there were plenty more fish in the sea. Yet, she continued to mope around, and at some point started cutting herself. I did not tell her I knew about the cutting; I threw away the blood-soaked tissues in the bathroom bin, I ignored the neatly lined scars on her arms, and I worried when she spent more than ten minutes in the shower, because I knew what she was doing. Yet, still I could not bring myself to hold her, to tell her that I loved her and that I would try to make everything better for her.

Self-harmers do it for attention, you know. They want people to notice the cuts and the scars, so they can tell them just how terrible life is.

How Mum and Dad don't love them.

I ignored it, hoping that without the attention she would stop.

Suddenly, it stopped. My little girl was smiling again. She would bound in from work, fling her work-bag on the table, smile at me and talk to me again. No more long showers, no more sad songs, no more pain. Because she had Paul.

She didn't need me anymore.

When she brought Paul home for dinner the first time, there was a glow about her. I knew that, despite everything, she wanted us to love him as much as she did. How could we not? He was smartly dressed in a charcoal-grey suit, and arrived armed with a bunch of my favourite flowers. Lilies. Oh, he was a charmer. Within weeks they had set up home together; a poky little maisonette on an estate in the town centre. Paul is still living there now. Eloise was happy, so I kept my mouth shut. I still did not intervene even when Paul proposed, although he didn't ask George for his permission. George was furious; his little girl was going to walk up the aisle with a man we barely knew. Oh, if only there was an aisle! They wed in our local registry office, Eloise wearing a monstrosity of a dress, barely covering herself. Yet, still she was smiling.

When they had been married for a few months, Paul was made redundant. I started to worry about their rent being paid, and how on earth were they to feed themselves on the paltry income Eloise brought home? Then the silly girl got pregnant. As if there could be worse timing, so I told her so. Eloise started to confide in me after Paul lost his job; she told me that he was drinking a lot, that he shouted a lot, that sometimes he scared her, that she was concerned he was sleeping with somebody else. Yet, she always had a slight smile on her face, almost as if she was fond of this newly-exhibited behaviour, and a large part of me believed her to be exaggerating, for attention. I told her repeatedly that if it ever got too much, she could return home, but in my opinion he was a charmer and she should fight for her marriage. 'Don't give up, Eloise,' I would say. 'Fight for him.' I wish I could take back those words. However, Eloise's room would always be waiting for her, and her father and I would be more than happy to have her home.

Throughout her pregnancy, Eloise appeared to become 'depressed', a diagnosis I honestly don't believe in. Why can't people just pull themselves together? The vibrancy I had seen when she first met Paul seemed to lessen as her tummy grew. I had no idea what to say to her, George and I had never experienced the problems that face youngsters today. George and I met, married, had Eloise and settled into a routine as easy as pie. Every Monday, George goes for a round of golf. Every Thursday we eat a casserole. Every Sunday we have a roast. There is nothing wrong with a routine.

Boredom.

How was I meant to help Eloise, when I didn't understand how it felt?

I will never forget the day Jessica was born; it was the happiest day of my life. I saw her when she was just a few hours' old, and I swear the little mite smiled at me. From that moment on, I knew that whatever happened, I would be there for her.

'Hello, you,' I whispered in her tiny, perfectly formed ear.

Whilst Eloise and Paul's relationship was falling apart, I desperately hoped that she would call me and ask whether she and Jessica could move back in with us. I regretted advising her to stay for the sake of her marriage. Divorce is so easy, these days. I desperately wanted her to ask me if I would look after Jessica for her, while she got her life back on track. That call never came. I confronted Paul about his behaviour; I told him he is not good enough for my little girl. He cannot call himself a man; he is a pathetic little boy, masquerading as a grown-up.

'If it's not her nagging me, it's you.'

Now another poor baby will suffer at the hands of this abhorrent man, a man who turned a beautiful smile into a river of tears. A man who made my daughter bear a baby from violence; a baby who will need love and attention to thrive. I can give that. It is too late for Jessica, she has witnessed and experienced so many terrible things, and unfortunately, her life is irreparably broken. Not so for the new baby. I can save the new baby. Eloise and Jessica live in my house now. My house, my rules.

Faultless.
Perfection.

George Edgar Harrington

Thumbs are very useful. Sometimes I peer from beneath the thumb under which I have lain trapped for the last one hundred and fifty thousand years, just to breathe in the beautiful, fresh air. But, alas, for Sandra sees that I am making my escape and pops me right back where I belong. It sounds like a dire existence, yet I quite like it; the regime is a comfort and the orders and the punishments a reason to get up in the morning. With a matriarch comes a routine: one o'clock, two o'clock, three o'clock, four o'clock, they all exist because of their tasks. If I forget to make the three o'clock tea, I hear the tongue clicking against the roof of the mouth, whereupon I rise from my seat and boil the kettle. When I pass her the freshly brewed cup of tea: brewed, not stewed, dear, I expect her face to crinkle in disapproval; I expect the next hour to pass in tedious silence, broken only by the silence of my thirsty wife, occasionally slurping the tea from her favourite porcelain mug. It sounds miserable, yet inside I am smiling, filling up with an overwhelming fondness for this slightly crazy, yet completely grounded wife of mine. I honestly would not accept life any other way.

Eloise is always going to be a cause of disagreement; if either Sandra or I believed in divorce, our darling Eloise would certainly have caused it by now. I enjoy a quiet life, I like to sit and observe until events are whirling around my head, forcing me to untangle them. Conversely, Sandra likes to poke her nose into everyone's business. If the neighbours forget to put their bin out, there she is, hauling it up their steps, muttering under her breath. If the council fail to fill a pothole in the road, there she is, on the end of the phone telling them exactly why she paid her taxes and what to spend them on. 'National Health Service? What a pile of rubbish. They left poor old Doreen in a pile of her own excrement, you know.'

Now, Eloise Katherine (not a name I chose— a little Austenian for my liking—I much preferred something more traditional: Kate or Louise), Eloise is an adult, a reasonably intelligent, slightly whimsical adult, who has made some horrendous decisions with disastrous conse-quences. There is no need for me to intervene, un-less told to do so by Sandra, because our Eloise is headstrong and interference riles her. As a father, I have a duty to protect my child, my only child, my first and last born. I have a duty to protect my grandchildren, and I will. If I have to stand in front of a bullet for them, I will. If I have to lie, cheat, beg, steal, to get her away from Paul, I will. But not until she admits that she needs my help.

Until that day, I am very much just her mother's husband.

Under the thumb.

SEVEN

Paul Bennett

My name's Paul and I am an alcoholic.
My name's Paul and I am a love addict.
My name's Paul and I am a wife-beater.
My name's Paul and I am an absent father.
My name's Paul and I am a rapist.

If I could do it all differently, I would have driven straight home from work the day I was made redundant. I would have driven the three and a half miles, without stopping at the supermarket. I would have opened my slightly creaky front door, smiled at my beautiful wife, and then I would have calmly informed her that I had lost my job.

I would have held her whilst she cried, then reassured her that we would be ok; we will always be ok, and the very next day I would have gone to the job centre and taken any job offered, no matter how menial.

Instead, I stopped at the supermarket to get our final supper, a pizza. A broken, potentially bankrupt husband, sadly looking for the cheapest pizza he could find for his last supper.

Then I saw them. They still had a hold on me.

Bathed in golden light.

I used to joke about it, but who is laughing now? Cans of beer, bathed in the golden light of the fridge: angels sent from above to cleanse my soul.

I sloped down the alcohol aisle, like a naughty child, knowing that I did not belong; I was not allowed to belong. That day, I succumbed. I knew I should not drink. I could not drink. I had never told Eloise, there was no need. I was teetotal when I met her, and I will be teetotal when she comes home. I used to be an alcoholic, you see. Apparently, this is my mistake; I need to accept what the therapist tells me. My homework for the week is to accept that I will ALWAYS be an alcoholic.

My name's Paul, and I'll always be an alcoholic.

I have what is commonly referred to as an 'addictive personality', or perhaps I am merely a man of excess? Not only will I always be addicted to alcohol, I will always be a 'love addict'. I teeter on the precipice of infidelity every sad day of my lonely life—waiting to be a victim, waiting for the rush of endorphins when somebody decides they need me, even if it is only promised for a short time.

All my life I have been lonely, holes of despair

littering what should have been, what could have been, a wholesome and desired existence. I temporarily plugged these holes with sex, with alcohol, or with 'love'. I stopped plugging the holes when I met Eloise, because she gently covered them for me, and I did not need anything or anyone else. I married my remedy.

Very soon after I was made redundant, whilst I was caught up in my whirlwind of drinking, I met Amelia. Amelia was stunning; forty-five years old, with a youthful and boundless energy about her. I watched her float effortlessly around the shop, her curls bouncing with an energy of their own. The first time I looked into her eyes I lost myself. I am still there, you know. I am still there: alive in Amelia's eyes.

Amelia deserved much more than being stuck working in the off-licence down the road. I fell in love with her: hook, line and sinker. It began with witty banter in the shop when I went to purchase my daily beer, then we swapped numbers. Whilst my wife was gently sleeping in the evenings, I would stay up to text the beautiful Amelia, text her all the things that I wanted to do to her. I thrived on the excitement of somebody wanting me. Somebody other than my poor, long suffering Eloise.

My name's Paul, and I am an addict.

Amelia declared we were like two peas in a pod:

we had a connection. We met up a few times, despite my initial protests that I would never cheat on my wife, never risk shattering my family. I drove to her home—a flat on the outskirts of town. Every room had her personality stamped on it. I could see her in the broken teapot in the kitchen, in the artwork on the living room walls, and in the floral bed-sheets arranged haphazardly on her queen-sized bed. Amelia. My queen. We used to drink together, she didn't know, you see: she didn't know of my 'problem'. The glasses sat next to each other, just like Eloise's and mine once had, before she ruined it.

We spent wonderful hours watching films, listening to music, and having mind-blowing sex. We had a connection. We would sit in a beautiful silence, emotions whizzing around like fireworks, exploding occasionally, making me jump with a surprise that made my heart flutter with excitement. I fucking loved her. If Eloise found out, surely she would understand?

I cannot help it. I am an addict.

The fireworks became less frequent, but I still hung on. I hung on to the memory of the last time I saw her, those snatched hours together. How we had laughed, how we had listened to the songs that told the story of how I felt, how I wanted her to guess that those songs, those words, were for her, but I was too scared to declare.

Then the texts became sporadic, the sex incidental. I could feel the connection breaking, yet I could not understand why. I struggled to hold us together, to force the connection to fit again, but I could not.

My name's Paul, and I am addicted to you.
Karma.

I spent days wondering, beating myself up. What had I said? What had I done? What had changed? So, I asked her. I text her, I asked where our connection had gone, told her that I felt it had suddenly and inexplicably been broken. For five long minutes I waited for a reply, praying for her to answer that she had backed off because she loved me, but could not have me.

The answer?

'To be honest, I hadn't really thought about it, but I suppose you're right.'

My heart shattered. Tiny pieces of my life, streaming from my eyes. It could have been so special, if only she had let it.

My name's Paul and you have broken me.
My name's Paul and I am hurting.

Two painfully lonely days later, I decided to text her. I text a witty, meaningless random observation—she would have to respond, because it proved that I could be who she wanted me to be,

I could be fun. I could be who we agreed I'd be, adhering to the rules that *I* initially laid down, I could be the man with no strings.

The man with no strings, emotionally tied to someone who wants to be free.

My name's Paul, and, oh, how I fucking love you.

That text remains on my phone, that secret, meaningless text, cruelly symbolising a secret, meaningless relationship.

I vented my anger and feeling of worthlessness on Eloise and Jessica. I was not worthy of being loved by anyone.

'I hadn't really thought about it.'

Cutting, like a knife.

I needed to share my pain with somebody, but nobody would understand. Everyone would judge. The clichéd drunken husband, fucking everything in sight. Perhaps I was, but I LOVED her.

I fucking loved her.

The bitter irony throughout was that I knew there was only one person who could make me feel better, only one person could utter the words of wisdom that could comfort me. The one person I could not confide in. My best friend. My Eloise.

My wife.
My best friend.
My life.

I stumbled into a chasm of depression, a depression that made me believe there was nothing wrong with drinking from dawn until night fell, when darkness enveloped my unwanted heart once again. I now accept that this is my default coping mechanism, this is how I am programmed to deal with life. This is my strategy. Everyone copes in a different way, we all have a means of expelling pain. Eloise self-harms. I am an alcoholic. Is drinking that far removed from self-harm? Is ingesting the poisons that could eventually rot me from the inside out, any better than aesthetically marking pain upon skin?

A diary written in blood.

Jessica does not need to learn to cope. Jessica lives in a bubble of innocence and four-year-old naivety. Jessica asks me to stop hitting, she begs me to stop drinking, and she pleads with me to stop scaring her. Then, Jessica goes to her bedroom to play with her toys, as if this fucked-up life is normal, the arguments a blip, and the violence an advert break.

I am desperate to learn lessons from Jess—how I wish I had stepped outside of myself all those years ago, before I dragged other people down with me. I cannot redeem myself, I cannot expect forgiveness, and all I can truthfully tell you is that I love them.

I love my family.

I need my family.

Please forgive me.

My name is Paul and I am a fucking mess.

I am so sorry.

EIGHT

<u>Jessica Louise Bennett</u>

We're living at my Grandma's house at the moment with Grandma and Pops. My Mummy is living here with me and her tummy is getting bigger because there is a real Mary or Joseph in there and my Mummy said that when she next goes to have a photo taken of my baby Mary or Joseph that I can go with her so that I can see Mary or Joseph too and that will be a lot of fun and also my Mummy's tummy button has gone all funny and flat and my Mummy said that soon it will pop right out I will be able to see it through her t-shirt that she wears that used to be Daddy's t-shirt! Maybe my Mummy will give it back to Daddy when baby Mary or baby Joseph has been born. Daddy isn't living here with my Mummy and my Grandma and my Pops and me. I think Daddy stayed in our house that has my bedroom in it or maybe Daddy is staying with Auntie Emma because my Mummy is very angry that they were planning to go on holiday together. I am a little bit angry about that too because I am more important than a holiday and so Daddy should have known that and should have come to stay with us. Staying at my Grandma's is very boring and it makes me yawn because she has no fun things.

My Grandma and my Pops watch the television in the evening and they watch all the boring things like when they tell you about the Queen and about the man that lots of people don't like who owns the country and about boring things that are happening in places that we don't live. I like to watch television things with animals in and with the man that sings funny songs and flies on a wooden spoon. The only fun thing about staying with my Grandma and my Pops is that when my Mummy says I can't have a biscuit because I haven't eaten all my dinner, my Grandma gives me a biscuit anyway and tells me to keep it a secret. I don't like keeping secrets because secrets are bad and they normally make shouting happen, so I did tell my Mummy really quietly and my Mummy said she would keep it a secret that I told her, so it is her secret and not my secret. I can nearly tell the time and I know that it is nearly three o'clock in the afternoon because the little hand is at the three and the big hand is nearly at the twelve. I know that at four o'clock Grandma will make potatoes and yesterday when she made potatoes she told me that she wants me to stay in her house forever and that baby Mary or baby Joseph can stay here too. But really more than anything I want to go to my bedroom in my house with all my things in it and with Daddy.

I saw Daddy standing outside Grandma's house yesterday and I heard my Grandma shouting at him to go away and my Mummy was at the shop and didn't hear it, and then I heard Daddy say that he loves my Mummy and me and I wonder if that means he doesn't love Grandma and Pops and baby Mary or baby Joseph. And then Daddy said that he is trying hard to change himself and Daddy looked very sad. Daddy was looking at the window and I pulled back the curtain and I looked at him and he saw me and I think for the first time ever I think I saw Daddy cry. And guess what? Then my Mummy came back from the shop and my Grandma didn't tell my Mummy that Daddy had been there and had been crying and then I thought that I should tell my Mummy and so I did and Grandma did that face that old people do when they are cross and it goes a bit droopy and shaky. And my Mummy was cross with my Grandma and they shouted at each other and I wish they hadn't because when my Mummy and Daddy were shouting all the time, that's when we had to move into Grandma's and I don't want to have to hear more arguments and have nowhere to live.

Today my Mummy was reading the boring newspaper and I was sitting next to my Mummy and I was yawning because it was so boring. Then I saw a picture of a man who looked all lonely and he had a sleeping bag and he was sitting on the floor and I asked my Mummy why he was sitting on the floor and she said he was homeless, which means he has no house to live in. He looked really cold and I decided that if I have nowhere to live I will make sure it's in the summer or I will take lots of clothes with me, and probably my dressing-gown too. It's the summer time at the moment because it is in July but it keeps being a bit cold and rainy and the other day I had to wear my winter jumper and my Mummy said it's because we live in England and it can rain at any time and I think it's that man's fault who owns the country. Of course Buggly Bear will come with me because he is my favourite. Then I thought that because I keep telling the truth I keep getting people into trouble, like when I told my Mummy that Daddy was going on holiday and then when I told my Mummy that Grandma made Daddy cry. Then I thought that if I wasn't here then I couldn't make people sad and then I thought that maybe I could run away. I have a bag and I have put my Buggly Bear in it and my dressing gown and my favourite blanky and a packet of biscuits from Grandma's cupboard and I suppose that is stealing but I don't like to be hungry. I can reach the handle on the door but Grandma puts a funny chain thing on it that is high up so I am going to try to reach it when I stand on the little stool that I sit on sometimes when there are too many people. It is in the lounge which is next to the front door and it is brown and I know that I can move it to the front door and nobody will notice if they are asleep. I want to write my Mummy a letter to tell her where I have gone but I only know how to write my name and I know how to write kisses because I'm only nearly five years' old. If I could write my Mummy a letter I would write a letter telling my Mummy that I have gone and tell her that I will come home but only if they all promise to stop shouting and to stop stopping me telling them the truth. Tonight I will move the little stool to the door and tonight I will run away like on the news and then my Grandma and my Mummy and Daddy will all stop shouting and look for me and be happy again.

Eloise Katherine Bennett

'Jess!'
'Jess, where are you?'
Shit...
'JESSICA.'
'Jessica, wherever you are, you stop hiding right away.'

The front door is slightly ajar; the footstool from the lounge next to it and the chain is swinging freely and ominously in the light of the hallway lamp. For a second, I stand silently in the hallway, trying desperately to gather my thoughts. What was the last thing I said to her? Had she said anything about running away? Had a stranger come in and taken her? I run upstairs in a final desperate attempt to find her; I can't see her. I look under her bed, behind the dressing table, even in the wardrobe.

'JESSICA. IT'S NOT FUNNY.'

Realisation dawns on me: my first instinct was right. The door is open, because she has gone.

'Mummy? Where do those people with no houses go when they are tired?'

'I don't know, darling. A bench or something, probably. Eat your dinner up.'

Why didn't I entertain that conversation? Why didn't I ask her why she wanted to know? Why didn't I wake up when she opened the door?

I pull open the front door, praying that by some miracle my Jessica will be sitting on the doorstep, clutching her Buggly Bear in her tiny hands, while she chews on his soggy ear. The door swings open, slightly assisted by a gentle, whispering breeze; a direct contrast to the tornado of emotion whirling inside me. A flash of black and white catches my eye. A newspaper cutting. I pull the creased, jagged-edged piece of paper from the letterbox and study it, tears filling my eyes. It is the newspaper article I was reading yesterday, whilst cuddling Jessica on the sofa. At the bottom, scrawled in crayon, is an almost illegible 'Jess XXXX'.

I stare at the cutting, wishing that I were imagining it. I run back into the kitchen, thrust the note into my shocked mother's hand, before running out of the front door, hot tears blurring my vision. I blink furiously, hollering Jessica's name. Where the fuck is she? I briefly turn around, and catch sight of my mother standing on the front door step, her mobile in one hand and the newspaper cutting in the other. Curtains are twitching as the neighbours look out of their windows, wondering why this barefoot, pyjama clad woman is screaming, crying and running, running, running at six o'clock in the morning.

Running where?

Just ahead of me is a shopping plaza, surrounded with benches and trees. Straining my eyes, I scan the area, praying to God that Jessica will be curled up on the bench, sleeping soundly. I can see something.

'JESSICA!'

I run as fast as I can towards the bundle on the bench, the chilled air stinging my tender eyes, my heart painfully pounding with adrenalin and fear.

'JESSICA!' I scream, as I reach my destination. I pull back the blue bundle of material, to be greeted by a sharp, acrid stench. I fall to the floor with utter devastation.

'JESSICA...'

The homeless man stares at me, a mixture of shock and confusion upon his heavily lined face.

'What you doing, Miss?' he asks, raising his gruff voice slightly to make it heard between my screams.

'Jess...Jess...Jessica.'

He looks at me with disdain, gathers his belongings and makes his way to another, less dramatic location. I am just a mad woman, cruelly judged by a man who does not know me; a man with nothing, a man with nobody. Holding my head in my hands, I silently cry, tears falling for my baby, my baby who has run away because she does not want to make me sad.

'ELOISE!'

I turn around at the sound of my name, to see my mother running towards me, her hands full with the items only my mother could find time to grab in an emergency of this magnitude: a pen, a phone, keys, a packet of cigarettes.

'Have you found her?'

Genuine concern is etched upon her softly lined face, and for the first time in years, I feel affection towards her.

'No, Mum. Please just call the police.'

'A bench where, Mummy? Are there any comfy benches?'

'I don't know, Jessica. I don't know. The park? Eat your carrots.'

The park.
THE PARK.
'The park.'

I am running again, faster and faster, until my legs feel like they are going to collapse with the exertion. My throat is burning and my mouth is watering, but still I run. I run through alleyways and over speed bumps, I dodge people and cars, I keep running, running, running. I know she is there. I know she is. I run down the hill into the park, building up so much momentum that I think I might never be able to stop. I have stopped crying, because I know she is here. I trip over a branch on the floor, almost stumbling, but still I do not miss a stride. I run past the toilets, past the bridge, past the stream, past the trees. The ten-minute run feels like a marathon, because I need to reach the finish line so desperately. Then I see it, the bandstand.

'It's cosy in here, isn't it Mummy?'

Pushing myself harder and harder, I finally reach it. I run up the two steps onto the wooden platform, knowing that I am right.

'Jess,' I whisper tentatively, into the sleeping girl's ear.

'Jess. I love you baby, please come home.'

Jessica yawns and, still holding onto Buggly Bear, reaches her arms towards me. I pick her up, wiping the biscuit crumbs from her face as I do, and begin the journey home. The beautiful journey that makes me realise that today is, in fact, the best day of my life.

NINE

Jessica Louise Bennett
November 2000

I go to big school now. I have a new uniform which is a skirt and tights and a T-shirt and a cardigan and some shiny shoes with toys in the bottom that my Mummy said were too expensive. I got to choose if I wanted a skirt or if I wanted trousers and this time I wanted a skirt but next year I might have trousers so that it's fair. Today and yesterday and all the times I have been to school I only go to school for a little bit of a day because I am not that old. But after Christmas I will go for a whole day and I am really happy because I get to have a lunchbox with a cat on it or a dog, and a flask with a lid. But guess what? I don't see Daddy anymore. That makes me a bit sad because I know that Daddy can be naughty sometimes and sometimes he scares me, but I can be naughty sometimes and I'm sure that sometimes I will scare my baby brother Joseph but I still will want to see him. I know that the baby in my Mummy's tummy is a Joseph and not a Mary because my Mummy took me with her when she had a special photo taken and it showed that the baby had a little winkie that means that it is a boy. Boys can be disgusting sometimes and they smell a bit but I will make sure that my baby brother Joseph doesn't smell because I will make him have a bath every day.

I really want to see Daddy because it is the first of November today and guess what that means? That means that it is my birthday in two days or is it three days? My birthday is on November the third and I am very excited and we are still living at Grandma's house with Grandma and Pops and we have lived there for years or months or a long time anyway. Grandma and Pops have said that I can have a little party. It was my Mummy's birthday two months ago and my Mummy didn't have a party, my Mummy just hugged me a lot and told me she loves me and helped me make her a big cake that tasted of lemons and even let me put chocolate buttons on it even though it was my Mummy's cake and she didn't think that lemons and chocolate would taste very nice together but they did. My birthday is on a Friday this year and it is the day before the weekend which means that I am lucky because I can have a party on Saturday which is only one day after my birthday. I hope I can have some biscuits and little sausages. On my birthday I like to wake my Mummy and Daddy up. This year I won't be able to wake Daddy up because he won't be here. I will be able to wake my Mummy up but not too early because she has Joseph in her tummy and it makes her tired and grumpy. Grandma said that my Mummy is grumpy too because she's not allowed to smoke with Joseph in her tummy as it would be like making Joseph smoke and I heard my Pops tell my Mummy once that she should stop smoking as it isn't very nice and she must stop right now because it is making me and Joseph smoke too and my Pops is always normally right, except when Grandma sighs at him and then that means that my Pops is wrong again. When I ran away from home on that day that I didn't go very far my Mummy said she ran all the way to get me with Joseph in her tummy and she carried me all the way back because she loves me and she was so pleased to see me. I haven't had to tell the truth or any lies since then and I am happy because truths and lies make crossness. I'm a little bit happy that Daddy isn't living in Grandma's house with me and Mummy and Grandma and Pops, because I know that Daddy sometimes argues with Grandma and that makes me sad. But I don't know why Daddy doesn't want to see me and my Mummy any more. And I do know that Daddy has sent my Mummy some letters and that is the only secret I have because I know that Grandma put them in the bin in the front garden so that the dustbin man would take them right away. When I get up early on my birthday I am going to have a look to see if Daddy has sent me any letters and cards and presents and then I can get them before Grandma puts them in the bin.

Paul Bennett

When I was a kid, I used to lie in the bath, deliberately and slowly slipping down until the water began to gently pull my sodden hair. Then I would close my eyes, raise my feet to rest against the cold tiles behind the taps and slowly dip my head, until the water trickled into my ears. It wasn't ever an unpleasant feeling at first, until my heart began to race, as fear kicked in. The fear that my elevated feet would slip, the water would rush into every orifice: blinding, deafening, muting me. My screams would be translated into a stream of bubbles that nobody would hear, my feet and hands—slippery with bath oil—unable to grip the bottom of the bath, unable to push myself back into the air. There I would stay, there I would silently drown. Hours later, my mother would find me, my face bloated and distorted, a look of fear in my staring eyes.

As an adult, I have struggled against a fear that induces a similar panic. A fear that has recently become a reality. My life— my troubles, my fears, my anger, my weaknesses: rushing towards me as if a dam has broken. Each time I battle to my feet, another torrent hurtles through, washing over me and knocking me back down. I am getting stronger, and I am learning to stand my ground, but nonetheless, it is a frightening journey. I am drowning in my own mistakes. The latest torrent of destruction is so fierce that I am tempted to give up. Tempted to lie down and let the water take me, let it gently take my hand and lead me to peace. To death.

Deal with it. I deserve no better.

I love my family.

Behind my eyes, there's emptiness, an aching chasm.   Aching to look into Eloise's eyes, to see the love, to be loved again.

The adoration.
The fear
The beauty within.
The blackened heart.
The wonder.
The confusion.

I cannot view the world in its amazing technicolor without Eloise, I cannot appreciate the beauty of the trees, the colours of the flowers, the enchanting call of birdsong on a summer's morning. Corny, I know, but devastatingly true. The sound of other children's laughter serves only to remind me of what I have pushed away – thrown away. I love her, I miss her, I need her, I cannot live without her. Eloise need not be afraid of me any longer; there is nothing left to fear. I am not drinking anymore, not properly, not devastatingly. Just a pick-me-up every so often, when I feel life is getting on top of me. Perhaps once a week, maybe twice, at a push.

Wake
Eat
Sleep
Wake
Drink
Sleep.

Every single day, I call Eloise. Every painful day, her mobile goes straight to answerphone and every day I punch the redial button repeatedly, desperate to hear her soft voice once again.

Perhaps she just doesn't want to speak to me?

I have text her every morning and every night. I have called her mother's phone on numerous occasions, yet Sandra promptly hangs up the second she hears my voice.

Controlling bitch.
Stop it.
Mantra.
Forgive and forget. Forgive and forget. Forgive and forget.

Breathe.

Every week, I send a letter to Eloise and a letter to Jessica. Every week, I sit, I wait, I hope, and I pray that I will get one in return.

Deserving?

I have explained to Eloise and Jess how desperately sorry I am, how I am getting help for all the issues that have torn our family apart.

My family.

I explain how I am looking forward to seeing my new baby in two months. How I wish Jessica could wake me on the morning of her birthday, oh, how I long for her to jump on me and insist that five o'clock is the perfect time for presents. How I will miss her countdown to Christmas, the countdown that starts immediately after she has opened her birthday presents.

And, Eloise. What can I say? How I miss the smell of her hair, the inane chatter, the smoke wafting through the front door as she has a sneaky cigarette when things became a little too stressful. How I miss her looking at me with those stunning eyes.

The eyes you beat black and red.
Those beautiful eyes you broke, time and time again.

Upon waking from my fitful sleep each morning, I check my phone, hoping for a text from Eloise. Each morning, I am disappointed.

Like I waited for a text from Amelia. Like I waited for a text from Emma. Like I will always wait for a text from someone, from someone I need to love me. But, I don't need that any more. I am in control. Paul is in control. My name is Paul, and I am in control.

Each morning, I turn over to bury my face in the pillow that Eloise should be resting her head on, my tears saturating the unwashed mustiness of the pillowcase.

Wash her away. She doesn't want you anymore. She doesn't need you anymore.

Each morning, I walk around the house, trying to feel her presence. I walk into the kitchen, and I reflect upon the image I have absorbed of Eloise waiting impatiently for her morning coffee to infuse. I see Jessica climbing on to the stool to reach the sugar for her Mummy's coffee, knowing as well as I do that Eloise will be in a more amiable mood once she has drunk it. I recall Jessica's eyes lighting up when she sees the hungover mess that is her father; running towards me, before I brusquely brush her off.

Give me my time again and I will change that. I have changed. I can love you all properly now. Real love, the love only a man who has hated is able to give.

Each morning, I walk past the fridge that occasionally houses my beer, and I grab a drink of water from the tap Eloise touched so many times. I walk into the lounge, where Eloise should be sitting, her cold legs covered with the soft white throw-over. The throw-over I mocked her for buying.

'You're not an old lady yet, Eloise.'
'Oh, I am, Paul. For Christmas I want a cookery book.'

Then I wonder how so many things could remind me of her, so many things could *be* her, yet she is gone. She has left me.
Oh, Eloise. However am I to survive without you? Without your strength, without your weakness, without your forgiveness?

I put her through so much during our time together; my flawed personality tortured her. It hit her, it shouted at her, it scared her, it punished her. Yet my unforgivable meetings with Emma were to be the final straw. I deserve punishment: hit me, call me names, have me sent to prison, but please, please, please do not rip my family away.

I love my family.

I am so sorry.

Eloise Katherine Bennett

Clearly, Paul couldn't give a fuck whether he sees his family again. Clearly, Paul has too much on his plate, what with Emma, and whoever else he has decided to fuck in my absence. Clearly, Paul does not think that his wife, his beautiful daughter, and his unborn son are worthy of any time and attention.

Yes, I made the decision to leave him.

No, he pushed me to leave him.

Yes, I have made the decision not to contact him.

He should contact me first. He should be begging for my forgiveness.

What's to stop him sending a letter? What's to stop him calling me at my mother's? He has her number.

Maybe he's tried? Maybe your mother won't allow him to speak to you.

Excuses, excuses, excuses in my head. He is not worthy of excuses. My mother agrees. Paul does not deserve me, Paul does not deserve Jessica, Paul does not deserve his unborn son. Paul does not deserve a family.

Is it time to start divorce proceedings?

Divorce. So final. Like the final bell on your last day at school. You feel a sense of relief that the hard work is over, but now you are out there in the big, wide world, on your own. This is why, as an adult, when you are struggling to pay the bills, and struggling to hold your family together, the cotton-wool wrapped days of your schooldays hold certain affection.

School days are the best days of your life.

When the pennies will not amount to the cost of a loaf of bread, you yearn for the packed-lunch days of your youth. You think back to how you thought you would do everything differently to your parents when you grew up, how your house would be so much tidier, your children would have better clothes, your wallpaper would not be floral. Now you realise that whatever their faults, your parents tried their best. You were clean and clothed, educated and unbeaten. Today, I am living with my mother, and in my marital home is a broken boiler, along with my husband who beat me black and blue. Before we left, my daughter had eaten pasta for three days in a row, because we could not afford to feed her anything else. This is not how I imagined it to be.

Is this hell?

Is divorce the answer?

First thing tomorrow, I will go into town to speak to a divorce solicitor, because if Paul cannot be bothered to think about us, then I do not wish to spend another wasted minute being his wife.

I can feel my baby son rolling around in my stomach, almost in a protest. Is it the right thing for the children? Then again, what choice do I have? I know in my heart that if Paul says the right words, I would take him back in an instant, despite everything. Because, when all is said and done, whether whole or broken, my heart belongs to him.

TEN

Jessica Louise Bennett

It's my birthday today, my birthday today, my birthday today. I am so happy. This morning I didn't have Daddy here because he is still living in my old house with my old bedroom and my other toys. I thought I would be allowed to visit my other toys and I think they probably miss me too because I have only taken Buggly Bear but Grandma and Pops have bought me things that I think they got from one of those boot sales because they have scratches on the plastic with dirt in them. My Mummy has a new telephone and my Grandma has thrown my Mummy's other telephone in the bin. My Grandma bought my Mummy's new telephone as a present even though it wasn't her birthday. I learned that people have telephone numbers and I think everyone has one so I thought then I would be able to speak to Daddy and wake him up on my birthday and that it would make me happy. I'm not sure my Mummy and Grandma and Pops would be happy when I speak to Daddy because I have heard them speaking about Daddy and I have heard them say that it is probably for the best that he doesn't speak to me or my Mummy or my Joseph, who is still in my Mummy's tummy. This morning I thought I would speak to Daddy and I am very lucky that I wake up when the sun isn't even awake and before my Mummy or Grandma or Pops wake up, so this morning I walked downstairs on tippytoes and went to the kitchen and looked for my Mummy's telephone but it wasn't there. Then I went into the lounge where the sofa is to look for my Grandma's telephone and it was there in a silver thing on the little table that my Grandma says is a coffee table. My Grandma's telephone didn't have a wire and I thought it might not work if it didn't have a wire but it might, so I picked it up anyway. My Grandma's telephone had a button that looked like a book and I thought Daddy's number might be in the book because it looked like my address book that Santa put in my stocking one year before I could even write numbers. I know that Daddy's name is Paul because when Daddy got cross with my Mummy sometimes my Mummy would get cross right back at him and shout 'Paul!' really loud which scared me. On the screen on the telephone there were only four words and I thought it was because Grandma didn't know how to put words into the telephone because I remember my Mummy telling Grandma that she would put the most important ones in there for her last Christmas, when she bought it for her. I hoped my Mummy put Daddy's number in Grandma's telephone because I know that Daddy is important but I don't think Grandma thinks he is. I pressed a button but it didn't do anything at all and then and I saw two telephone buttons and one telephone button was green and the other telephone button was red. I thought it looked like traffic lights and I know that a red traffic light means stop and a green traffic light means go and I wanted the word to go to the telephone people so I pressed the green one and it started making a beep beep beep beep beep noise. And then it started making a ringing noise in my ear and then a voice answered and it was a man who didn't sound like Daddy and I started to ask the man if Daddy was there but then the man said it was a doctor's surgery and the surgery was closed and to ring another telephone number if it is important. And I know it's important but I don't think a doctor can help. So I thought then that I should press the green telephone for the next word on the screen and then I wished I could read properly. The second word on the list didn't make a ringing noise it made a talking noise and it was a lady this time, the lady said that she couldn't connect my call. And then I sighed because it was a bit difficult. So then I pressed the green telephone for the next word on the list and that one didn't have a voice and it just rang and rang for a long time and nobody heard it or picked it up. So then I knew that the screen only had one more word left so I pressed the green button for that word and it made a ringing noise and it did the ringing noise eight times, and I know because I counted. And then Daddy's voice spoke on the telephone and said he couldn't take my call at the moment but I should tell him who I am and why I'm calling and then he will call me back. So I did. I said 'Daddy. It's my birthday and I wanted to wake you up. I love you Daddy,' and then I pressed the red button and then I waited for Daddy to call me back and then I cried.

Paul Bennett

I am awake. The sun is streaming through the tiny gap in the bedroom curtains, and I can feel the November chill in the air. I am filled with a feeling of despair and excitement, as today is Jessica's birthday, a bittersweet occasion. I am hoping that Eloise will soften and bring my daughter round to see me, or at the very least let me speak to her. I yawn and debate aloud whether I will treat myself to a drink today. I reach towards my phone lying on the bedside cabinet. I don't know why I bother, as it never reveals anything. The only people ever to call me are my various coun-sellors, arranging appointments for me to sort out my fucked up head. I'm certain they have a variety of graphs and bar charts to chart my pro-gress.

On the fifteenth of August, Paul Bennett was ninety-five percent fucked up.

On the third of November, Paul Bennett woke up in a happy mood. He is now only three percent fucked up.

I start laughing at my own stupidity.

Laughing? Paul, you aren't allowed to laugh. Your life is a mess.

The laughter peters to a halt as I look at the phone screen. I frown as I try to comprehend what it says through my sleepy eyes.
One missed call.
One voicemail.
Who would be calling me before eight o'clock?

Eloise?

I tentatively unlock my phone and press the missed call button.
Sandra

What's happened?

Sandra cannot even bring herself to pass the time of day with me, let alone call me. I curse my insistence on turning the volume down at bedtime and lift my phone to my ear, preparing for a tirade of abuse via voicemail, or a nonchalant message revealing a disaster.

'Daddy. It's my birthday and I wanted to wake you up. I love you Daddy.'

I am filled with a mixture of relief and sadness.

My baby.

I call Sandra's number, my stomach churning with the anticipation of speaking to the daughter I haven't seen for months. It rings three times, and then a voice I recognise picks up the phone.

'Hello?'

'Eloise?'

'Paul?'

'Jess phoned me and left a message. Can I please speak to her?'

I hear Jessica talking in the background, but then I hear Sandra's voice.

'Is that Paul?'

The line goes dead.

The dam reopens, pushing me back against my pillow.

On the third of November at ten past eight, Paul Bennett was one hundred percent fucked up.

Eloise Katherine Bennett

I have a song on a loop in my head, like a twelve-inch vinyl, which refuses to stop. Like the smell of warm bread in the supermarket, or the flashing neon advertising signs that you are never quite sure whether you imagined or not, I suspect it is attempting to subliminally control my next actions. Therein lies the problem, like most things in life, this message is ambiguous, mouldable to my own requirements. Lyrics can be deliberately misinterpreted, words reshaped, and sayings adapted, to suit one's own needs and desires. It is much like asking for advice, then disregarding it when it does not suit you to follow it. My mother advises me to divorce Paul, her advice is so strong and constant that I cannot hear myself think. The ridiculously chirpy song in my head advises me to move on, be strong, be happy and be right. The solicitor, a man whose very presence makes me feel like I have done something very wrong, advises me to be certain in the steps I take, for fear the emotional damage will be irreparable if I change my mind. That makes me feel guilty, before I have even begun. Despite my mother's protestations that I should forgo the shiny leaflets, and start the divorce ball rolling immediately, I managed to make myself heard over her shrieks and squeals of indignation. I took the leaflet, I folded it in half, and I placed it in my handbag, should I decide in a day, a week, a month, a year, or indeed a century, that divorce is the answer. Or, as the leaflet so eloquently asks:

Is Divorce The Answer?

Divorce is the question.

A few days ago, when I thought Paul did not care/would not care/could not care/would never care, I had almost found in favour of Divorce being the Answer. Then Paul mixed it up again: he phoned Jess. My mother pulled the telephone wire out of the wall and guarded it like a rabid dog, until I assured her that neither of us would return his call.

Temptation washed over me, my fingers itched to dial his number. He needs us, I could hear it in his voice. Without us, he is lost and he is broken. Each time I felt the temptation, I would take a step back to try to remember how he actually made me feel for all those years we shared together. If I go home now, I have nobody but myself to blame for anything that happens in the future. He didn't ask, did he? He didn't ask us to go home. He didn't say the words.

I shake my head, furiously. I have made a clean break, I am on the road to freedom, and walking backwards would be the biggest mistake I have ever made. It is perpetually unhelpful that time dilutes everything; experiences, pain, pleasure, happiness, sadness, love, hate. Everything is covered with a misty film that you can't quite see through, can't quite reach through to get hold of that feeling to relive it, to make an informed decision about your next move.

I will keep the leaflet until after my baby is born, a decision waiting in my handbag, for summarisation and conclusion. A life changing moment cunningly disguised as a glossy A5 leaflet.

Is Divorce The Answer?

Move on, be strong, be happy and be right.

Don't give up the love you need
Not without a fight

ELEVEN

<u>Jessica Louise Bennett</u>
<u>December 2000</u>

That baby who is my new brother Joseph, that baby makes a LOT of noise. I haven't changed my mind about wanting a new baby brother called Joseph because I love him lots already but I really want Joseph to sleep some more and not make funny noises all night when I am trying to go to sleeps. My Grandma has run out of bedrooms so my baby brother called Joseph sleeps in my Mummy's room but I can still hear him because I think everyone can hear him because he is so noisy. If Daddy was here I think he would give my baby brother called Joseph a big cuddle because baby Joseph is his son and he is my Mummy's son too but he is my brother.

When my Mummy went into hospital I was really really excited about seeing my baby brother for the first time and I made him a card and I put my new toy that I got for my birthday in a box and I gave it to Grandma to give to him because he was in hospital because he was born four whole weeks early. He had a yellow face and my Grandma said he had a pointy head too because his heed got squashed when he was being delivered. I think that whoever delivered him to the hospital should be a bit more careful because he is my baby brother called Joseph and he is very delicate and he is very special. Then guess what? This is sad news. Grandma told me my baby brother was too young for stencil toys and I was sad about that because then he won't be able to have fun with me. I don't think babies do a lot of playing but my baby brother called Joseph has got a toy that is just a boring mat but it has fun things on it like fishes and mirrors. I will lie down next to my baby brother and play with him so that he knows that even though I get very very cross that he cries so much I still love him more than I love chocolate, and if Daddy doesn't ever let us live in our house again, I will do things that Daddy would do so my baby Joseph doesn't miss him. I will take my baby brother to the swings and to the Caterpillar and I will save up my pocket money and buy my baby brother white chocolate so that his face doesn't get in a mess. And I will stop people shouting when he is sleeping because even though my baby brother makes lots of noise I think that other people making a big noise might scare him. And I will tell him about that time that I phoned Daddy on my birthday on a Friday and tell him that one day Daddy will phone me back because he said he would on his telephone. And I will cuddle him and I will tell him not to cry and I will be his best-est big sister that he could ever ever have. Now I think that I wish I had a big brother or sister to cuddle me and tell me not to cry because a cuddle might stop me crying real tears every time when I go to bed with my Buggly Bear.

Paul Bennett

I am a Daddy again.

You have no right to call yourself a Daddy.

I desperately want to see Joseph, I want to hold him, feel him, bond with him, and be his father.

Break him.

I have had no contact with Eloise, or Jessica. On the day of Joseph's birth, I received a curt telephone call from Sandra.

'Paul, Eloise has given birth to your son. I'm only telling you because she begged me to. STAY AWAY.'

Do I have a choice?

My heart was so full of daggers, so numb with the pain of constant battles that this dagger did not hurt. I was incapable of feeling pain; my brain was numb, my heart was numb, my life was numb. For two days, I walked round in a semi-daze, expecting more bad news. It would not have surprised me if my house blew up, or my heart stopped beating. It would not have surprised me at all.

Resigned.
Empty.
Stop feeling so fucking sorry for yourself. Get out there and fight, fight for what you believe in, fight for those you love, for those who should love you. Make them realise that you may have got carried away, but your baby, your son, was still born from love, not hate.

At some point, something had to give. I would never have guessed that something as innocuous as a questionable joke on a comedy programme would be the thing that cracked me. It was funny, granted. I started laughing, I laughed so much that I cried. I cannot recall when the tears of mirth turned to tears of insanity; they shifted without my knowledge or permission. I curled up on the sofa, head in hands, sobbing like a baby, tears wetting my cheeks, soaking my T-shirt. When it was over, I furiously wiped them away, feeling stronger than I had felt in years. The last of my emotions purged from my battered soul and I knew I would have to step up my fight. Let the battle commence.

Fight for them, Paul. Fight for your family. Be a hero, show them what you are made of. Cowards always come last. Nice guys come last. Bad guys come first. Be nice. Be strong. Be bad. Be good. Be you. Do not show them who you really are; show them who you can be.

I picked up the phone and made an appointment to speak to a solicitor, I wanted to spend the rest of my life being a father to my children. I needed to see my children.

The solicitor's waiting room was sleek and uncluttered, a direct contrast to the mess and baggage that must arrive at their doors each day. On the table were various leaflets, to advise me on every aspect of my home life.

Is Divorce The Answer?

No.

Are You Attempting Reconciliation?

Yes.

Are You a Fucked up, Wife Beating, Abusive, Scumbag Rapist?

Yes.

Do You Deserve Another Chance?

Do I?

Probably not...

TWELVE

Eloise Katherine Bennett
January 2001

I walk, clutching the handles of Joseph's push-chair, anticipation in the pit of my stomach. I shuffle past complete strangers, I feel them staring, I feel them judging me.

What the fuck are you doing, you crazy woman?

'What the fuck am I doing?'
I wish that I had parked the car a little closer, to avoid the pejorative journey of the eternally unstable.

The last march.

My heart is pounding, as I head towards my destination.
Neutral territory.

Perfect place for a battle.

Then I see him, sitting casually on a wall. He looks a little more tanned than when I last saw him. He looks a little like the Paul I met years ago; clean-shaven, confident, and almost serene. I stop walking, knowing that I am not yet in his line of sight. Reaching into my handbag, I touch the leaflet, hoping it will guide me in the right direction.

Is Divorce The Answer?

Onwards, or homewards?
Last chance, Eloise. Last chance.
My fingers brush my key-ring, which is nestling between the leaflet and my mobile phone. I clutch the familiar rectangular piece of plastic, knowing that on one side is a photograph of Jessica, and on the other a photograph of Joseph. I am doing this for them. Taking a deep breath, I march onwards.

Marching towards my destiny.

Paul catches sight of me and jumps from the wall. I had forgotten how handsome he is. He starts to walk towards me, glancing rapidly from my face to the pram. I stop walking, and wait for him to reach where I am standing. Without saying a word, a tear rolling down his face, he puts his head in the pram and silently kisses Joseph's nose. I look intently at the back of his head, wanting to hold him, wanting to smell him, wanting to love him again.

'Eloise,' Paul says softly, his lips and tongue forming my name so beautifully.

'Eloise, I am so sorry.'

I bite my trembling lower lip and reach out towards Paul. He tenderly clasps my shaking hand between both of his, rubbing it gently like he used to when I was cold. My emptied heart refills with love for this man. This man, my husband, my protector.

'Eloise, please come home. Bring my family home, baby. I love you.'

No, no, no.
Is Divorce The Answer?
Yes, yes, yes.
Is Divorce Still The Question?
No.
Divorce Is Escape.
Yes.
Fighters March Onwards.

I need my family together, in one house, a unity.
I need the laughter.
I need the love.
I need my life back.

I need the sadness.
I need the violence.
I need the hate.

I remove my hand from Paul's clasp to lift my

sleeping baby from the pram.

Do not hand him over, Eloise. Keep Joseph safe. Do not allow him to be hurt.

I will give him to Paul. I will show him that I trust him again. I will show him that love is not the only factor. I will show him that I choose to be with him, that I choose to start again. I will give him to Paul. I will hand him over.

Sacrifice.

For a second, I stand still, waiting and listening, and wondering.

Listen to me, Eloise.

Listen to the loudest.

Listen to common sense.

Listen to your heart.

Sacrifice.

I tentatively hold out my arms, offering Joseph to Paul. A peace offering.

Sacrifice.

Paul takes Joseph and, nestling him in the crook of his elbow, looks at his watch then reaches for my hand once again.
Our minds click together, an indefinable bond.

Unbreakable. Hand in hand, we stroll slowly and silently to collect our daughter from school. To unite our family once again.

Jessica Louise Bennett

Today I am very very happy. Today I am more happy than I was when I got my birthday presents and more happy than I was when it was Christmas at my Grandma's house. But Christmas made me a little bit sad because Daddy wasn't there but Baby Joseph was and I am going to call him Joe so that he will be happy and surprised when his teachers tell him he can be Joseph in the nativity play and wear Joseph's clothes and wear a dress like Joseph. Guess what? Grandma and Mummy kept locking the front door before we moved out of Grandma's house and my Mummy said that it was because I ran away and they need to lock me in so I don't run away again. That is really silly because I won't run away again because everyone promised they won't be sad when I tell them the truth anymore. My Mummy and Grandma are a bit silly sometimes. Pops isn't silly. Pops is very clever because he pretends he is asleep a lot of the time and then my Mummy does the washing-up for him because she thinks he is tired, but one time I watched him and he opened his eyes and looked at me with both eyes open and then he closed one eye and then opened both eyes and then my Grandma came in the room so he closed both eyes again. I am going to do that a lot now. I am going to pretend I am asleep and then I won't have to tidy my room and I might even not have to go to school on the days when I am feeling very tired.

I feel like singing because I am back in my house with my Mummy and my Baby Joe. And guess what? WITH DADDY! Daddy is here and I know he has been here all the time, but we are here too, so we are all here. Yesterday I was coming out of my class with all my friends and I made sure I had all my things with me, or then I would have had to go back inside and walk up all the stairs again. And I was looking down at the ground because I was watching my feet walk and I always see my Mummy's feet in the same place, which is five footsteps forwards and three footsteps towards the wall and then there's the bench. And if my Mummy doesn't get there early enough to sit on the bench then she stands next to the bench which is only one extra footstep if I make it a big step. So I was watching my feet and watching other people's feet to make sure I didn't bump into them and I saw my Mummy's shoes which are her trainers and they are a bit old and a bit grey but my Mummy likes them. Then I saw Baby Joe's wheels which are big and black then I saw some other shoes which were trainers and they were white. The trainers were standing right next to my Mummy's grey shoes and one of the trainers was touching the side of my Mummy's shoe. So I thought I should look up to see who was with the trainer and then I heard Daddy's voice say 'Jess!' and I was so happy that I jumped up and down and up and down and made a squealing noise and my Mummy was laughing and I was so happy because then I knew that Daddy was still my Daddy and he hadn't forgotten me.

That is why I am very very happy today.

Paul Bennett

Cloud nine. Wherever cloud nine is, I'm there. It is a long way from square one, but it is floating in the stratosphere far away from reality, surrounded by chirping birds and angels. Eloise, Jess, Joseph and me, holding hands and laughing. If I had known that something as simple as a note left under a car windscreen wiper would be sufficient to piece together my shattered family, I would have done it months ago.

I feel almost bereft of emotion as I set off towards our agreed meeting place, having wept all the tears I could possibly weep before writing the letter.

Do you remember, Eloise? Do you remember when you loved me? When we laughed at those stupid curtains your mother gave us? When we cried together as we looked at our perfect baby Jessica for the first time? How we held each other and danced so close

at our wedding? I hold those times deep in my heart, and there is some room left for more. For better, for worse, Eloise. I have done the worst I can possibly ever do, I have lost everything, and I have suffered the worst punishment I could have been given. Our house is empty without you; the laughter that once filled the rooms has been sucked into the hollow, which has formed since you left me. I did wrong, Eloise, I know I did wrong. From the bottom of my heart, I beg your forgiveness. I promise you Eloise, I have changed. Please meet me at 14.30 tomorrow under the tree, where I proposed. I love you. Paul
XXXXXXXXX

I stride purposefully to the tree where we sat all those years ago, legs dangling off the wall, holding hands, laughing at something innocuous and pointless. I remember being filled with such an overwhelming emotion for Eloise that I could not ever imagine my life without her. I am praying that today is the last day I will wake alone.

I can see Eloise walking towards me, pushing the pram with one hand, the other fiddling about in her bag. I try to look casual, although my heart is beating so loudly I would not be surprised if everyone could hear it. My stomach is churning, making me nauseous.

Make or break time.

I jump from the wall and smile, genuinely.

Eloise has stopped walking, so I make my way towards her, adrenalin pumping through my veins. I look at Eloise's face, seeing a mixture of apprehension and fondness in her eyes.

It's looking good, Paul...

The five seconds it takes to reach where Eloise is standing feels like a lifetime. My arms are itching to hold my baby, my lips yearning to kiss his soft, baby skin. I finally arrive at my destination, and tenderly drop a kiss on my baby boy's beautiful face.

I cry one last tear, but this time it is a tear of joy, for the battle has ended.

Onwards, marching soldier. Take your family with you, for there are no more battles to fight.

THIRTEEN

Jessica Louise Bennett
February 15th 2001

When I was at school today we had to write a poem about what we did at the weekend and so I remembered all the things we had to do at the weekend and I wrote a poem about it. I'm not very good at writing and nobody in my class is very good at writing so we had to tell the teacher what we wanted to write and so she wrote it down and we had to copy it underneath to practice our letters. I'm not very good at rhyming-sounds either but I know that cat rhymes with hat but we haven't got a cat so I couldn't write about one. I wrote that we went to the park and that it got dark but it didn't really get dark it was light all the time until after I went to bed. Here is my poem:

I went to the park
And it got dark
And I was with my Mummy

And Baby Joe isn't in her tummy
And I was with Daddy too
And he lives with us too.

My teacher said that I shouldn't use the same word two times to rhyme but I couldn't think of another word except glue, and I didn't have anything to say about glue. But I like my poem and when I can write properly I'm going to write it for my Mummy and Daddy and draw a picture of the day we went to the park together and we had fun and even Baby Joe giggled a bit. Baby Joe has learned how to do a lot of things now and I am allowed to give him his bottle if he is hungry because he can't eat biscuits. My Mummy and Daddy laughed a bit last week at the weekend and I remember when they didn't laugh and now I think that I like it more when they laugh, except they are not laughing this week. And I know that my Grandma is sad that me and my Mummy and my Baby Joe don't live with her anymore because she came round and rang the doorbell and shouted things and my Mummy got upset and cried a bit, but I think Grandma was being quite nice because she said that when it all goes wrong we can live with her again but I don't want it to all go wrong, I want it to stay right because I don't like to be sad. I think my Mummy and Daddy might be getting angry with each other again because yesterday Daddy smelt a bit like those funny drinks that he smelt like before he got angry before.

My Mummy wants Daddy to get a new job because if he gets a new job we can move to a big house and even though I like that my Mummy has let Baby Joe move in my room I'm worried that when he is older he will want blue things and I want pink things so maybe we will have one wall blue and one wall pink or maybe purple, I can't decide properly yet. Baby Joe still makes noises at night-time but my Mummy says I am an expert because I hear the noises and I put his dummy in his mouth and he makes some sucking and goes back to sleep. When he doesn't go back to sleep it's because he is hungry which is weird because if I wake up hungry I wait until the sun is awake and I eat my breakfast, and I think my Mummy would be cross if I ate my cereal before the sun is awake. If Baby Joe gets scared when my Mummy and Daddy start shouting again I will put his dummy in his mouth. Because that's what expert big sisters do.

Paul Bennett

One. Just one? Surely, one won't hurt? I'm in a good place right now, I'm not trying to block anything out, I won't be using it to cope. I'll be drinking to celebrate the reunification of my family. A celebration. That's all it is. Just one.

Just one.

It will never be just one, Paul. Never. Your name's

Paul, and you are an alcoholic.

Just one...
Just one beer...
Just one argument...
Just one...

Eloise Katherine Bennett

Like an ostrich, I am burying my head in the sand. Why rock the boat, when the boat is just about handling the choppy waters without intervention?

Paul is drinking again, I can smell it, I can feel it hanging thickly in the air, the stench of a relationship rotting from the inside out.

I thought it would be perfect.

He promised it would be perfect...

FOURTEEN

Paul Bennett

Just one?
Bollocks.
I'm drunk.
Do you want to know why I'm drunk?
She wants a fucking divorce.

She's probably fucking someone else.

Denial.
Denial.

Denial is bad for you, you know, Eloise. It is bad for the soul, it drowns the spirit.

Denial is oppression.

'STOP IT DADDY. STOP IT.'
'Paul, I don't want a divorce. Stop it. I picked the leaflet up when I left you. Remember? You're hurting me.'

Stupid slut.

*'If you hadn't gone in my handbag, Paul. Why did
you go in my handbag? LET GO OF ME.'*
'DADDY, you'll make Baby Joe be scared. DADDY.'
'Make that baby shut up.'

Divorce?
DIVORCE?

'I'll kill you first.'
'DADDY.'
'SHUT THAT FUCKING BABY UP.'
'Who the fuck is that at the door? Oh. Hello officer.'
'We're fine, aren't we Eloise?'
'Everything is just fine, isn't it Eloise?'
'She's upstairs, officer. Yes, you may.'
*'No, officer, it's fine. I understand. There are some
nasty people out there. Thank you for your time.'*
'WHO CALLED THE FUCKING POLICE?'...

Jessica Louise Bennett

Yesterday I was so scared because Daddy had
some of those drinks again and I woke up because
he was being noisy and shouting at my Mummy.
I listened to the shouting and then I put my head
under my pillow and tried not to hear it any more
but that didn't work. Then I got out of my bed
and tippy toed over to look at Baby Joe because
sometimes when I look at his face it makes me
feel happy because he is very very cute. Baby Joe

was asleep and my Mummy and Daddy were still shouting and I knew that if Baby Joe heard them he would be scared like me. And I thought that it's ok for me to be scared because I am a big girl but I really didn't want Baby Joe to be scared because he is only a baby and he wouldn't understand.

So I listened for another minute which I counted in my head, but I can only count to ten and twenty and thirty, so I did it slowly so it would be sixty. Then they were still shouting and I heard Daddy say that my Mummy had something in her handbag that he didn't like and that is probably why he was angry. And my Mummy was saying that it had been there for ages and I heard Daddy say lots and lots of rude words and then I thought I should go and stop them shouting. I went down the stairs and went to the kitchen and Daddy was standing very closely to my Mummy and he looked like he was going to hit my Mummy so I got all my voice in my mouth and I shouted at Daddy to stop. And then my Mummy had her hand on Daddy's arm and Daddy had his hand on my Mummy's wrist and I think he was holding it a bit too tightly because my Mummy was telling Daddy that he was hurting her and so I told Daddy to stop again but Daddy didn't listen to me. So I told Daddy that he might wake Baby Joe up and make Baby Joe be scared, because I know that Daddy loves Baby Joe and he wouldn't want him to be scared, but Daddy still didn't listen to me. And then I wondered if Daddy could hear me and then I heard Baby Joe start crying and then I was worried because I knew Baby Joe would wonder where his best big sister was. Then Daddy said he wanted that baby to shut up and that was a horrible thing to say. And then Daddy said he wanted to kill my Mummy and that really scared me and I tried not to cry and I was so scared and I wanted to stop Daddy hurting my Mummy and then I shouted again. Then the doorbell rang and I wondered who was at the doorbell because I knew it was dark and it wasn't the morning. And then I heard Daddy talk to some people and he didn't shout at them and my Mummy ran upstairs to cuddle Baby Joe and so I went upstairs too because I needed a cuddle so badly. And my Mummy was sitting on the end of my bed holding Baby Joe and Baby Joe stopped crying and my Mummy held one arm out because she was holding Baby Joe with the other one, and so I sat next to my Mummy on my bed, in the dark, and we had the biggest cuddle ever.

And then two policemen came into my bedroom which made me a bit scared again because I hadn't done anything wrong. And one of the policemen who was holding his hat, he asked my Mummy if everything was alright and my Mummy said yes and then they asked my Mummy if she was sure and my Mummy said yes and I didn't say anything and then they said that the neighbour had called them and my Mummy had to be quiet and children should be in bed and then they went away without helping us.

<u>Eloise Katherine Bennett</u>

...it was meant to be perfect.

Why do we strive to reach perfection, when perfection itself is unattainable? We strive for the impossible, and then feel like failures when we cannot reach the pinnacle of the elusive mountain peak, to place our flag. If we could somehow reach the summit, where would we go from there? When you're at the top of anything, there are only two choices. Stand perfectly still, like a statue, hoping that by not moving you will stay exactly where you are.

Don't rock the boat.

Or, you could steadily make your way back down the mountain to face the reality at the bottom. The perfection is a fiction; it is a place invented by your imagination to keep you going in life. Perfection exists in your mind to give you a purpose, to give you something to strive for. Perfection is a long, hard trek to nowhere, invariably ending exactly where you began.

Paul has given up on ever reaching perfection. When he is sober, he respects me; he takes my advice, he takes the leaflets I pick up for him at the doctors, but three hours later, when he is steaming drunk, he throws them back at me, telling me I am judging him. I don't even have to walk on tiptoes around him anymore, because my seemingly unpredictable life has suddenly become painfully predictable. As soon as I hear the fridge door open, or the front door close, I know that within a matter of hours he will be the man I despise. The drunken man, slurring insults, spittle congealed in the corners of his angry mouth.

Not so perfect.

I see other people: strangers in the street, neighbours I nod to as I walk past, and I wonder how they remain so perfect. Holding hands, talking to each other, communicating, not a shred of fear or hate between them. Are they displaying the same façade, which has become so tiring to me? Or, are they truly, madly, deeply perfect?

A mask
A play
A performance

Paul has been a little more considerate of late. Instead of constantly using our home as a base for his alcoholism, he has been taking it to the pub. If he is going to do it, he may as well do it elsewhere. My quality time with my unemployed, alcoholic, husband amounts to a cuddle in bed in the morning, and occasionally a cup of coffee at nine o'clock, when I get back from the school run.

For five minutes, I spend time with my real husband; with the man I adore. We talk, we laugh and we gather the strength from each other that we need to get through the day ahead. This is when I see guilt etched upon his tired face, guilt for everything he has put me through, guilt for forcing me to be a victim. I assure him that I am here because I choose to be, I will never leave him again, because we belong together. Perfection. Then my husband, my Paul, gets out of bed, like a real person, like we all do. He walks to the bathroom, and I listen to his bare feet padding on the tiles, sometimes sticking slightly as sweat mingles with floor cleaner and the hand-soap that Jess has spilled. I hear the toilet flush, then the sound of him vigorously brushing his teeth. The water runs. It is right now that I know he is splashing his tired, grey face. Then, he will look up and he will study his face in the mirror, as I have watched him do so many times. He will pull tight the wrinkles around his eyes, and examine his receding hairline. He always looks so sad, so broken. He will then shake himself back to reality, this is when I close my eyes and concentrate. There are fourteen stairs from the landing to the hallway. Five strides from the hallway to the kitchen door. Two strides from the kitchen door to the fridge. I count:

One.

Two.

Three.
Four.
Five. Six.
Seven. Eight. Nine. Ten.
Eleven. Twelve. Thirteen. Fourteen.
One two three four five one two.

Reality.

Perfection.
Perhaps one day I will own it, and then I can describe it to you in finer detail.

FIFTEEN

Paul Bennett
March 2001

'Good luck, baby,' Eloise whispers, kissing me tenderly on the cheek.

Such a contrast to the life I made last month. The life I
invented. The life in which I hit my wife, blackened her eye. The life in which I broke my daughter's arm. That life.

I get out of the car, and look up at the looming building, catching a splatter of spring drizzle on my upturned face. For five years, I have claimed that I am too sick to work; too sick to contemplate looking for a job. It is a lucrative, yet soul-destroying situation, one that feels slightly fraudulent, because I know that if I just put down the cans of lager, I would be as capable of working as anybody.

The money that kindly taxpayers give me every week is enough to get by: we have a rented maisonette, we can run a car, and we can just about afford to feed a family of four. Yet, encouraging me to do nothing is certainly not helping me, or my family.

Today is the first day of the rest of my life.

Again.

Today, I will find myself a job.

Taking a deep breath, I push open the glass doors to the job centre and step confidently inside, although my stomach is churning—almost painfully. I look around at the other unfortunates who have found themselves in the same position as me. Standing to the left of me is a desperate looking man, he looks approximately thirty-five years old, but the years have been unkind. His hair is unkempt and greying at the temples, strands sticking to his perspiring forehead. That man needs a drink, I think to myself, bitterly.

Judgement.
Judge yourself, before you judge others.

The man is looking straight into my eyes, and all I can see are fear and despair. His clothes are cheap, but smart: a black suit, complete with tie, and a well-ironed, crisp, white shirt. His hands are shaking slightly, so he clenches his fists to stop the tremor being obvious to those around him. The man puts one hand in his suit jacket pocket, and, at a guess, I would say that he is clutching a photograph of his family, because he is here, in this hideous place, for them. A younger man, wearing a hooded top and jeans, pushes past him, almost knocking him over, whilst talking loudly on his mobile telephone.

'I'm just signing on, mate, I'll meet you outside the pub.'

The older man steadies himself, then shakes his head sadly, as he knows that he cannot judge, for he is in the same sinking boat. He visibly takes a deep breath and pulls a sheath of paperwork out of his briefcase: certificates, a CV, references, and a battered Record of Achievement from his school days. I know that this man is not here to save just himself; he is here to save his family.

'SIR. Sir, can I help you, Sir? There's a queue here, you know.'

I stammer an apology and tear my eyes from my reflection in the window.

'Yes, Sir?' the young woman questions, a little more impatiently this time.

I sit in the worn, blue office chair, feeling sweat beading on my brow. My heart thumps loudly. Thump. Thump. Thump. Thump. They are all looking at me, they are all judging me. I am me. I can feel myself. My body is coming back to life. Tingling and thumping and hurting. I am the unemployed. I am the alcoholic. I am the wife-beater. I am the scumbag, bullying, drinking, selfish, loathsome, intolerant bully. That's me. Me. Me. Me. They stare. They hate me. They are staring at me, they are hating me.

I pass my documents to the impatient, judgemental lady. She takes them with a puzzled look on her face.

'And these are...?'

Thump.
Thump.

'My references, my C...'

'Sir, sorry to interrupt, but this is a job CENTRE, not a job INTERVIEW. There's a machine over there, go and enter your requirements and it will show you the current vacancies. NEXT...'

Thump.
Thump.

Every beat of my heart, I can feel. Every bead of sweat forcing its path from my pores, I can feel. Every drop of saliva evaporating from my mouth, I can feel disappear. My tongue sticks to the roof of my dry mouth, just behind my front teeth. A heat ascends from my toes, up my body. Up, up, up.

I trundle dejectedly to the indicated machine, and stare at the flashing screen, which is requesting I input my current location. I dutifully type in my postcode and speed through the next three pages of boring questions.

Thump.
Watch me.
Thump.
Watch me fail.

Job type? Any.
Salary? Any.
Location? Any.
The machine informs me that there are too many jobs fulfilling my less-than-exact criteria, therefore I must refine my search.

Thump.
Fail.
Thump.

Job type? Retail assistant.
Five jobs appear in front of me, each within a reasonable distance from home, and each with similar salaries. I print the details, pick up my briefcase, and stand back in the queue in front of the bored woman. There are three people ahead of me, each clutching a telltale piece of paper.

'Bugger,' I mutter, as I realise that I left the contact details for the jobs on top of the machine. I make my apologies, and slide out of the ever-growing queue. I need a fucking drink, that's what I need.

There is a woman standing at the machine I had been using, and unsure of job centre etiquette, I politely tap her on the shoulder, so that I won't have to reach over her shoulder to get the piece of paper. The woman swings round defensively, almost as if she expects the phantom shoulder-tapper to attack her.

For a moment, her face is blank, but then a familiar smile appears.

'Paul!' she exclaims.

I run my fingers through my sweaty hair.

'Hello, Amelia,' I answer sharply, trying to hide the pain in my voice.

'Long time, no see, how on earth are you?'

How can she ask such a casual question, after everything? After everything she didn't do, didn't say, didn't want, all those years ago. Every part of me wants to scream at her, wants to grab her and shake her and ask why the fuck she so callously broke my heart.

'I'm...I'm...good, thank you. What brings you back down here?'

'I got bored, I came back hoping to catch up with some old friends. Paul, I'm sorry I left like that. I'm sorry I didn't get in touch. Truly, I am.'

I had always sworn to myself that if I ever saw Amelia again, I would casually say hello then walk away, like she walked away from me. Yet, I cannot do it, my feet are rooted to the spot. I love this woman. I love how she used to make me feel, and I love the thought that she could make me feel like that again. I hand her my mobile number, and walk outside before I say what I really want to say.

I love you.

I gulp in the damp, spring air, hoping it will clear the fuzzy confusion inside my head. I send Eloise a text to let her know that I am walking home, as I need the fresh air. A tiny lie, but still I feel a slight pang of guilt as I start walking, smiling wryly at the image of Amelia's stunning smile that has imbedded in my mind. I walk past a pub, gratefully inhaling the familiar fragrance of hops.

Thump.
Thump.
Thump.
Thump.
One won't hurt.
I've had one a day for months, and it hasn't hurt.
One a day. Two a day. Three a day. Who's counting?

I take a seat at the bar, and wait for the barman to take my order. I don't care how long I have to wait, today is a beautiful day, and I need to savour every last second.

'So, did you get an interview then?'

She looks pointedly at my pint and sighs, plonking herself down beside me. I motion to the barman to pour another pint, and now realise I have it all figured out. This woman wants me, ergo, this is the woman I need.

This is my Amelia.

<u>Eloise Katherine Bennett</u>

I stare intently at the photograph on the computer screen. The faces blur in and out of focus, and I squint in an effort to squeeze them out. I looked so young and vibrant, as if I didn't have a care in the world.

The camera never lies

I beg to differ; the smile is hiding secrets, lies, pain and love. I return my gaze to the computer screen and the blurb swimming in front of me, to the left of the photograph. Should I? It's innocent, just communication with an old school friend.

An old boyfriend.

Why did he choose that photo for his profile? The photo where my arm is swung casually over his broad shoulders, and I am looking at him with the expression of a teenager in love.

I look around the lounge, which we have filled with cheap, cheerful furnishings. The threadbare patches on the sofa are expertly covered with a throw-over. A rug is placed over a stain on the carpet, patching up the things we cannot afford to replace.

Patching up our marriage.

Last month, Paul paid for a computer out of his 'disability' benefit, supposedly so that he could use the internet to look for jobs. However, the history tab on the web browser tells another story, as it appears that he has only ever logged onto a porn site. No point quizzing him about it, I think. He will only get defensive. I read the blurb again.

Hi, I've been in love, out of love, employed, unemployed, educated and re-educated since I last saw any of you lot. Would love to contact any of my old school buddies. Sam.

It's innocent.

Say it enough times and I may convince myself.

I have no ulterior motive.

It's innocent.
Innocence. Guilt. Innocence. Guilt. Hand in hand they go.

I have no desire for anything other than a chat with an old friend.

A secret friend?
Is this why I joined this website? To find Sam?

Suddenly, I feel fifteen again. I close my eyes and I can almost hear the sound of motorbikes roaring past Sam and I, as we stroll along the seafront. If I concentrate a little more, I can hear myself weeping as I dump him, a red herring I chucked at him in the hope he would then tell me he loved me. I wanted him to follow me; I wanted him to fight for me. Instead, he frowned a little, bit his lip and waved me a fond farewell. We had such fun together: Sam and I. We met in the canteen at school, two innocent eight-year-olds, our eyes met over a chocolate sponge cake. At break-times, we would sit on the bench in the playground reserved solely for those who wanted to hold hands and kiss on the lips. 'The snogging bench', it was fondly named. No tongues.

So, Sam and I grew together: from primary school to secondary school, where I finally decided that we should 'be together.' We were best friends, we were inseparable, we were destined to be married, destined to have babies, destined to add to the series of photographs that had been taken of us together. Primary school kids, with scrubbed clean cheeks, holding hands in the playground; secondary school teenagers, with spots and braces, arms swung fondly over each other's shoulders; wedding day photographs, the glowing bride looking adoringly at her groom, knowing that this is the beginning of the happiest years of her life; friend, girlfriend, lover, wife, mother. This is how it could have been. This is how it should have been. This is how it would have been.

If only he had said that he loved me.

Instead, I made what could have been the biggest mistake of my life, I pushed him away, I made him hate me, and then I lost my hold on him.

I type frantically on the keyboard, as if the faster I type, the more accidental my betrayal becomes.

Hi, Sam. So good to see that you are still alive, and that my dumping you didn't finish you off. Ha-ha. I would love to keep in contact, email me. Elly XXXXXXXX

My finger hovers over the 'send' button; several times I almost clicked it. I look around, almost expecting Paul to appear behind me, his face contorted with rage as he realises that his wife is entertaining communicating with another man. My mobile phone bleeps, making me jump with guilt.

I'LL WALK HOME, DARLING. I NEED SOME FRESH AIR AFTER THAT HIDEOUS PLACE. SEE YOU SOON XX

Fresh air? Bitter air freshened with the sweet smell of a few double whiskies, no doubt.

I take a deep breath, and then slowly lower my finger again…

MESSAGE SENT.

Jessica Louise Bennett

I don't think Daddy likes to spend time with me and my Mummy and Baby Joe anymore. Sometimes I get bored of things too like when my Mummy bought me all those cards with pictures of animals on them and I liked them at first and made up games that I could play with zebras and lions and tigers and cats but then I got a bit bored because it's no fun playing those games on my own and my Mummy and Daddy are busy a lot. Baby Joe is too young to play games, Baby Joe just makes noises and drinks milk and makes messes in his nappy. So I think Daddy is bored of us and then I think that I might make him not be bored by making up games to play and by taking him to the Caterpillar ride so that we can laugh and have fun.

My Mummy gave me some gold coins on the day that was before yesterday. My Mummy called it 'happy money' because I was crying because I wanted to see Daddy but Daddy had gone out somewhere and my Mummy didn't know where he had gone. And my arm was sore and it was making a thump thump thump inside its big bandage plaster and Daddy was very very nice to me for days and days after my arm got all broke and that was on February the twenty-third. Baby Joe makes me a bit happy but not a lot and sometimes I feel bad because I don't miss Daddy but sometimes I miss Daddy and I still feel bad. And I know I promised my Mummy that I wouldn't ever run away from home again because it scared her but I think that if I ran away then Daddy would have to come and find me too but I am going to wait until I am old enough to write a letter and I am working really hard at my writing at school and it's good that my left arm got broken which isn't really good, but if it was my right arm I wouldn't be able to practise my writing so that I can tell my Mummy and Daddy why I am so upset and then they might read it and know why I keep crying. I tried to tell my Mummy that I was sad and then I was happy because she gave me some happy money but she didn't make it better like Mummies are meant to. There is a boy in my class and his name is Zac which is the only name that I know that starts with that letter, that letter 'Z', and his Mummy and Daddy adopted him because his real Mummy and Daddy were naughty and went to prison. And Zac is very happy you know and I want to be happy like Zac, so maybe I can be adopted too. But then I would miss my Mummy and Baby Joe and sometimes Daddy so maybe I could just be adopted on the days that they are cross. I have fun when I am at school and I laugh and then I think about going home and my tummy goes all funny and I sit under the table and my teacher has to tell me to get out from under the table and says that it is naughty to hide under there. And I don't want people to know that I am naughty. And I told my teacher that I don't want to go home and my teacher asked me why and I nearly told her that I feel sad when I am at home and that I used to feel a bit sad but now I feel a lot sad, but then I thought that I don't want everyone to think that I am sad because sometimes I am happy. So I just told my teacher that my tummy hurts and she sent me to see the nurse who said I was ok but she said that she would call my Mummy to take me home. And then my Mummy came to get me and the teacher took her into a room and I think they were speaking to each other for a long time and when my Mummy came out of the room she was crying and she seemed a bit cross but most of all she seemed very very sad. And now I know that I have made things go bad again.

Eloise Katherine Bennett

If I could time travel, what would I do? Would I go back in time to before I met Paul and not meet him? I doubt it. I am a glutton for punishment, I am a born victim. My children are suffering because I am not strong enough to stand up to the man that makes us all miserable. It is too late now; the damage is permanent and unchangeable. A broken bone can be fixed, but it will never be the same again. You can glue the handle back on to a broken mug, but you always risk it falling off when you least expect it to, covering you with scalding liquid, damaging you, scarring you, forever. I need to lay my choices out on the table like cards. Take the card that tells me to hold a loaded gun to my head and pull the trigger.

Would I be better off dead? Could I bundle my kids into the car, drive them to their Grandma's, kiss them on their smooth, beautiful foreheads, and then throw myself off a cliff? Or, return home, to take a million tablets washed down with vodka, or whisky, or beer: the very things that have pushed me this far? I am a fan of irony, you know, so it would have to be the latter.

It pushed her marriage until it broke, then it numbed the pain of her death. What a beautiful irony.

Is there a better place than here? A better place than the one that houses my dead marriage and dying soul? I know I can't leave, I have tried so many times, I get dragged back, or I miss him so fucking much that I willingly return. Like a boomerang, flung with vigour, only to return and smack you in the face.

Is death the answer? Could I really do it?

Through the mistiness of my tears and the sound of my sobs, I can see Jessica in front of me, excitedly asking me where we are going.

'We have to leave, darling. We have to go because your teacher is asking questions. Too many questions.'

I had managed to divert a certain amount of suspicion, by saying that Jessica has felt slightly 'left out' since Joseph has been born, and assuring the teacher that I will be sure to pay her more attention.

'*Yes Miss. No Miss.*'

It is only a matter of time before they take my children away from me. Then who will I be?

Childless, soulless, battered, suicidal wife seeks like-minded male for no-strings fun.

'Will it be fun, Mummy? Where's Daddy?'
'Anything can be fun, if you want it to be, Jess.'
I have no idea where Paul is; I dropped him at the job centre this morning, and it is now five o'clock, yet he still has not come home. Should I be concerned? Like fuck, I should.
I wish I could think straight, everything is a fuzzy mess in my cotton-wool head.
Jess is talking, talking, talking.
Joseph is crying.
'Jess, please. Please shhh. Please, baby, please.'
Is this right?
They are unhappy. The teacher said so.

'*Yes Miss. No Miss.*'

Jessica is unhappy. I can't make her happy anymore. I light a cigarette whilst standing in the kitchen. I can smoke where the fuck I like if I'm going to be dead in three hours, can't I?
'Jess. Are you unhappy?'
'Lots of the time I am. Mummy, why are you smoking indoors?'
We make our own fate, maybe this is mine.

I should write a note. What do you write in a note when you are planning to commit suicide?

Suicide. Such a horrible word. Final and gruesome.

I take one last, deep drag on my cigarette and expertly flick it out of the kitchen window. I walk to the computer desk where the pens and paper are, Jessica hot on my heels, as if she cannot wait to embark upon my suicidal adventure, or is still anticipating the answer to her unanswerable question. The computer takes this opportunity to loudly inform me that I have mail. I sigh; distractions are the last thing I need when I have so much to prepare.

I decide not to entertain the computer's whimsical declarations, instead, I walk upstairs to collect Joseph from his cot where he is sleeping. He makes a snuffling noise, and puts his fingers to his mouth. He is hungry.

Does it matter if he is hungry? I'm going to die in two hours and forty-five minutes.

Jessica is still at my heels, and I want to shout at her to leave me alone, but I know that these are our last precious moments together. I squat to my heels, so that I can look her in the eye.

'Jessica.' I say sternly

'Mummy has lots and lots to do, why don't you go and watch the television for a minute?'

'But, Mummy. I want to be with you, you look

sad.'

For a fleeting moment, I see reality. Clear and crisp like an autumnal day, it sends a shiver down my spine, and for a split second, I wonder why I am doing this. Then I see it: unhappiness. Deep inside my baby daughter's eyes lurks a monster that I have made, that we have made. She has seen too much to be able to have a happy life with us. We have broken her. I can feel the hot tears rolling down my face as I gather the only things I will need for my final journey. My car keys and my children.

At this moment, the computer again informs me that I have mail.

'JUST FUCK OFF.'

I haven't written the sodding note. Out of curiosity, I wiggle the mouse to awaken the dormant computer, then click the envelope on the taskbar to see who is so persistently sending me emails.

You have 2 new messages from Sam Merchant on behalf of Newfriends Oldfriends.

My breath catches in my throat. My knees give way underneath me and Jessica holds her good arm out as if to catch me as I fall. I now know that fate is real, fate is true, fate has been sent in an unexpected form to save me from a terrible choice that I was about to make. Fate has been sent to save me from myself. Sam is fate.

Elly. So so good to hear from you. Send me your email address and we'll instant message next

time we are online at the same time. It'll be great to catch up. XXX

PS. Here's mine: sam_merchant_762@vjsystems.co.uk

I reply immediately, then log into my email account, praying that Sam is online.

Elly!

Sam! How are you?

I'm good thank you. What have you been up to all these years?

Married, 2 children. You?

Separated. No children. Oh my god, it's so good to hear from you. I've missed you, Elly. It's been too long.

I think about you sometimes Sam. I think about us. About what could have been.

Just sometimes?

I have too much going on to think about anything more frequently than 'sometimes'.

It's generally good to be too busy to think!

I suppose it is. Sam, I wish we had stayed together.

Elly! You said you are married! Whatever would your hubby say?

It's not really the perfect marriage, by any stretch of the imagination. he'd probably say 'Fuck off then, you slut' and throw an empty can at me.

Oh. You're kidding, right?

Exaggerating, yes. Kidding, no. Unfortunately.

Anyway, enough about me. What's going on with you? Where do you work, what do you do, do you see anyone from school?

Well, I am separated; my fault entirely and if I could change that, I would. I am an electrical engineer, really quite rich (haha) and no, schooldays and school-friends all firmly in the past. But that all pales slightly, since your life sounds far more complex than mine! Are you happy?

No. Are you?

No. Why aren't you happy?

I want everything to be perfect. It will never be. I make excuses, but I honestly think that Paul (my husband) is actually a complete bastard.

Aren't they all?

Not like this, they're not.

What does he do?

Nothing. Everything.

Why don't you leave him?

I've tried.

Why did you go back?

I'm a boomerang.

Seriously, Elly. If you are so unhappy, why did you go back?

Because I love him, Sam. Because the children love him.

The children will be happy as long as you are happy, Elly. They could still see him.

It wouldn't work, Sam. I keep going back.

That's because you have nothing to run away to.

That's true. What are you suggesting?

I am suggesting that if you wanted to leave then you would have done. You have nothing to run away to, Elly. Even if you did, you will always return to where your heart belongs.

Do you have a time machine?

If I did, where would you go?

Back to that day outside the school playground and un-dump you. We'd have been married by now.

Married and divorced, probably. Reality is tough. How do you know that I'm not a bastard?

Because I know you, Sam. I remember you.

People change. I bet you have changed.

A stone or two heavier, perhaps. But I am still the same person inside.

The Elly I used to know would never have put up with a bastard for a husband though. You HAVE changed.

The Elly you knew didn't put up with some-body who couldn't be bothered to love her.

I did love you.

You didn't tell me.

I didn't love you exactly how you needed to be loved. I wish I could have.

We all have regrets. I don't regret marrying Paul. I love him.

If you say that enough Elly, you may convince your-self eventually.

You saved me Sam.

Saved you from what?

Saved me from killing myself.

What the fuck are you talking about? When?

Just then. I wanted to go and kill myself.

But why?

Because I thought they would be better off without me.

You are kidding me?

No.

Elly. I truly don't understand why you are telling me this. What do you want me to do?

I want you to help me.

How?

I don't know. You emailed me just as I was about to go. You saved me. That must mean something?

I didn't save you, Elly. I can't save you.

Stop being so fucking philosophical, Sam.

I don't get what you want me to do, this is all getting a bit heavy.

Heavy? Fuck off then.

I don't want to fuck off. I just want you to realise that I can't save you. I can help you, but I can't save you.

Help me then.

Leave him.

I can't.

Then what do you want me to suggest? You just want me to advise you to stay, don't you? Then you can justify your weakness.

My weakness? I am staying for the children.

Are they happy?

Yes. No.

Yes or no?

No.

Then you are staying for you. You stay and make it better, or you leave and stay away. They are your only choices. Go on holiday or something. Write him a letter.

A letter?!

Tell him how you feel, how he has made you feel.

Such as Dear Paul, when you hit me, it hurts...

He hits you?

Yes.

Why the fuck are you telling me this? What do you want me to do?

I don't know.

Then why? I don't understand.

I need someone on my side, Sam. Someone who won't judge me, someone to talk to.

Meet me.

When?

Tomorrow.

9am outside the school? I have to drop Jessica off, so I'll be there anyway.

Will he find out?

No, he'll be asleep.

Ok. I'll see you then. Chin up Elly, we can sort this out.

Thank you, Sam X
☺ X

Jessica Louise Bennett

Sometimes my Mummy is funny and makes me laugh but sometimes she is strange and sometimes she is not funny. Today my Mummy has been funny and strange and not funny. First of all my Mummy came to get me from school when I was in the nurse's room because my tummy was all funny because I didn't want to go home because my Mummy and Daddy keep arguing. Then when my Mummy got home my Mummy was all weird and crying and packing things like pyjamas. And Daddy wasn't there but Daddy isn't at home much because perhaps he has moved house like when me and my Mummy and Baby Joe in my Mummy's tummy went to live with Grandma and Pops. So then I thought that my Mummy had a surprise for us but then I thought she might not because it was a school night and we don't have staying-out surprises on school nights because we have to get up very early in the morning. And when I tried to ask my Mummy questions my Mummy kept crying and she was crying loads and I thought that she was never going to stop crying. And I wanted my Mummy to stop crying because I love my Mummy so much and I love her with all my heart.

And then I asked my Mummy where we were

going but my Mummy didn't tell me she just said that my teacher knows too much. And then I knew that definitely I should not have hidden under the table and I will try to not do that again and I thought that I don't really want to be adopted because I love my Mummy. And then I hoped that God or Santa isn't trying to punish me for thinking bad things about having a new family. And then my Mummy was still crying so I followed my Mummy to the kitchen and then I followed my Mummy to the hallway and then I followed my Mummy to the computer which made a noise and then my Mummy picked up a pen. And then my Mummy put down the pen and then I followed my Mummy up the stairs to get Baby Joe because Baby Joe was making hungry noises. But then guess what? My Mummy didn't feed my Baby Joe, my Mummy just started crying again, so I followed my Mummy down the stairs again.

Then my Mummy turned round and looked at me and sat on the floor with her legs all bent and pointy and my Mummy told me to stop following her and to watch the television instead and that made me a little bit sad because I thought that my Mummy would like me to follow her to cheer her up because I have a big smile that I can do even when I am feeling really sad. And then I went to go to the sofa to sit down to watch television and my Mummy went to the computer again and so

I followed my Mummy because I really like the computer. And then my Mummy picked up a pen again and then my Mummy wiggled the funny thing on the computer table and then my Mummy nearly fell over and so it was a good job that I was following my Mummy again so that I could catch her with my good arm. And then my Mummy sat down and my Mummy typed lots of things and sometimes she smiled a bit and forgot to make me dinner until late and didn't take me for a sleep-over. That's why I think my Mummy is funny and strange and not funny.

SIXTEEN

Paul Bennett

My life is two roads. The roads head in the general direction of the same destination, a parallel outcome. Occasionally they join together, periodically they branch apart: far, far away from each other. Sometimes, they are the same. Equal in all but name, all but scenery. Each its own journey, each worthy of attention, of laughter, of tears, of pain, of deception. Each beautiful in its own sweet way. Each painful in its darkness. Each with its own choices, its own dangers and its own benefits. Each open to me. Who should I travel alongside?

I often wonder where I would be right now, had I not chosen to split my life into two separate journeys. Between Amelia and Eloise, I should have everything that I could ever possibly want or need. Stability and passion. Love and lust. Who could want for more? Yet, I do. I crave more, like a drug addict. Whatever I am offered, it is never enough. Whatever I am given leaves me slightly cold. I want love from Amelia, and lust from Eloise. I want my children to need me more, I want Joseph to stop crying when I hold him, and I want Jessica to stop flinching when I reach for her. I want another beer. I want a job, I want a bigger house, I want everything I have and more. I want them all to be placed directly into my hands, as I no longer have the energy to feel for them. I am tiring of making excuses, I am tired of lying and I am tired of justifying myself.

Do I really want Amelia?

I want the attention.

Do I really love my family?

I enjoy the status they give me.

Do I have to choose?
Am I allowed to choose?
Or, do I let fate take its course?

Go with it Paul, Eloise will never find out if you are careful. One night a week of that hot, steamy sex, veiled under the excuse of a night away at your recently invented drinking buddy's house. One night a week, she will never suspect. Whilst you are at home, be a devoted husband. Show Jessica and Joseph that you love them. Give them money. Go and get a job, Paul: a job will give you a reason to be out of the house. A reason to be with Amelia. You are a bad man through and through, rotten to the core, like an apple with a bite taken out. It is not your fault, Paul. Not your fault, not at all.

<u>Amelia Marie Francis</u>

Man-eater.

Whisper the words

Home wrecker.

Whisper the words

Mistress.

Whisper the words

Slut.

Whisper the words

Without labels, who am I?
Single

Hush…

Lonely

You misheard

Rejected

Not me

Desolate
Whisper the words.
But, do not judge me.

It is not an easy way to live. Nobody wants me for who I am. I am a hateful person; all I am good for is to be a mistress.

Hush...whisper...

However, I do not care as I enjoy the buzz.
I am a contradiction.

I am a web of yearning.
Do not judge me.

I get the good without the bad, and when I get the bad, I get out. How could life be better than that? I can reel them in, I can make them love me, and then I can spit them out. Occasionally, just occasionally, they come back for more. Perhaps I didn't break them painfully enough the first time?

Untold depths.
Please don't tell them.
Please don't judge me.

Don't get me wrong, I love to love. I have loved in the past, and undoubtedly, I will love again. I don't want to be alone, but I don't want to be tied to one person.

Because nobody wants to be tied to me.
Misinterpret words and lines.

Married men are the way to go.

Listen. Do not judge.

The best of both, the cream of the bargain bin.

Lives entwined.

We have all loved the wrong person, I certainly have.

Hush...

I refuse to do it again.

I refuse to be in pain.

A married man cannot be loved. I will not allow myself to fall into a cycle of love and heartbreak. I make sure I take control from the beginning.

Pretence.
A shallow mask of fun.
A commitment-phobe
A slut
A home-wrecker
Do not judge me.

Power.

A fantasy

Predator.

A passion.

Control.

Darkness.

Every night I go home to myself: my own company, my own life, my own choices. Alone, with nobody to love me, nobody to ask me how my day was.

Words, whispering inside.

I don't care.
Sometimes I feel lonely.

The darkness of a job half done.

But, I don't care.
Don't judge me.

Sometimes I feel that I am throwing my life away on a series of meaningless nothings.

Escape to my arms.

But, I don't care.
Don't judge me.
Sometimes it stings a little when I throw someone away, like an empty sweet wrapper in a litter-bin.

Used and useless.

But, I don't care.

Then I remember who I am. I pick myself up, dust myself down, and revert to being the strong Amelia we have all come to know and tolerate.

The heartless Amelia.
The slut.
But please, do not judge.

I got too close to Paul the first time, so I had to cut my losses and move away to stop myself pursuing him.

Did he feel too little?
Did I push too hard?

I am a contradiction.

Do not judge me.

After ignoring the first text, it became easier. It is a battle of wills, and enjoyable in a masochistic sense. Despite the pain of walking away from someone I had developed feelings for, I was able to revel in the power and control that the situation offered me.

I am a contradiction.
I am being judged.

I was weak when I left town, I had allowed myself to become reliant upon the affection Paul showed me. I have returned stronger, with reinforced barriers that nothing, nobody, can infiltrate. It has returned to how it should have been, it is again the game that I love to play.

Hurt or be hurt.

I don't care.
It is all quite simple. I simply want to be the recipient of unrequited love.

Stifled whispers

I can take the best of them.

A shallow mask of fun.

Then I wonder what that leaves the wives with?

Circles of habit.
Don't judge me.

These are not my morals on trial here, they make the decision whether to love or leave.
Either way, I do not care.
Control.
Power.

Protestation.
Denial.
But, don't you dare judge me.

I intended to text Paul when I returned to town, but then luck intervened.
Love intervened

Fate
It may be meant to be
DO NOT JUDGE ME.
Paul is the only man who is able to give me that intense feeling of love upon which I thrive. Ironically, this intense love would choke and kill me if we were together as a couple.
Protestation

Denial

This is why I love my life.
My world. The best of both.
I am me.
Take me.
Or leave me.

But do not judge me.

It's a game.
I will always win.

Don't judge me.

Stifled whispers
Misheard breaths
A web of yearning
Untold depths

Misinterpret
Words and lines
Misunderstand
Our lives entwined

A fantasy
A passion
A shallow mask of fun
Words from another
Whistling inside
The darkness
Of a job half done

The meaning
Of nothing
Of everything to me
Too near
Too far
Go slow,
and do it quickly
Escape to my arms,
your finger encased,
in a circle of habit
A life not embraced

Do you feel my thoughts?
Do I push too hard?
The silence of night,
the secrets are dark.

Untouched by faults,
a little, but enough

Be false,

yet be true
A belying touch

It's never said;
does it live inside?
Write it, feel it
Speak it
I don't mind

I love you

Game over

Eloise Katherine Bennett

A perspective of perfection.

I walk Jessica to her classroom, and kiss her lightly on her smooth, pale forehead.

'Bye bye, baby girl. I love you with all my heart,' I say softly, letting go of the pram and gently squeezing her hand.

'Bye bye Mummy. I love you and you look happy today.'

'I *am* happy, because I have the best babies in the whole wide world.'

Jessica skips off to put her prized lunchbox in the cupboard, then turns round and flashes me an utterly beautiful smile.

'Bye Mummy. I'm in the big spelling group today and when I come home I will know how to spell 'shopping', then when we go shopping I can spell it too.'

Pride almost overwhelms me, but then I briefly feel the pang that I get every morning; the pang that hits when I know that I have to return home; home to HIM, my life, my hell. Then I remember that today is different. Today I am going to see Sam.

Samuel Elliot Merchant, do you take Eloise Katherine Harrington to be your lawfully wedded wife?
Oh, the dreams of yesteryear.

I slowly make my way out of the school, walking carefully and nervously. I briefly stop to apply some lip-gloss, something that I could not do at home, for fear of Paul awakening and asking questions.

Demanding answers.

I take a deep breath, paste a smile upon my face and confidently push the pram out of the school gates.

Heart, lift high and be proud
Sink low; feel the darkness of reality.

I recognise him immediately: he is leaning against the lamppost outside the gates, nervously picking at his nails.

Is this a date?
You can't go on a date, you are a married woman. A

slut. A whore, wearing lip-gloss.

Samuel Merchant. The love of my life.

Don't pretend you wouldn't. Don't pretend that if he asks, you'd decline. You have clearly forgotten that this is who you are.

'What the fuck are you wearing, Eloise? You look like a fucking whore.'

A whore. The forgotten whore.

The last time I saw Sam, he was leaning against the very same lamppost, only that time I had walked away from him, crying. I hope history does not repeat itself.

I loved him.

That man could have been my husband.

Almost as if he senses me, Sam turns around. He looks straight into my eyes, a smile forming on his face. He is still the same Sam I knew all those years ago. His wiry frame is eclectically clad, his face cheeky, yet gentle. The twinkle is still in his eye.

Yes, this man can save me.
Yes, if he asks, I will.

'Oh, Sam.'

I would.

It lives inside
A wanton monster

Eating reason
Spitting rhymes

'ELLY!' Sam hollers at the top of his voice, before noticing the pram and guiltily holding his finger to his lips.

'It's ok,' I laugh 'He's used to noise.'

'So, where do you want to go?' Sam whispers conspiratorially in my ear, whilst quickly kissing my cheek.

'You stole a kiss! I don't know. Shall we walk in the park?'

It removes the pips
Of reality forgotten
Paranoia and lust
A sign of the times

So, this we do. Like a couple of teenagers, we stroll in unison towards the park, our footsteps falling harmoniously in step. My heart is slowly rising from the chasm of darkness that has become its home, and I feel fifteen again. Joseph is sleeping soundly in his pram, but I know he will awaken at ten o'clock for his milk, and I have brought some with me in anticipation of this. I feel alive. I feel free.

Sam and I sit on a bench, looking intently at each other. I try to read his eyes; feel what he is seeking from me, what he needs from me, who he thinks I am.

A hunt for more
A wife
A lover?
A friend?
A mother
A need for less
A forgotten whore.

This should be it. This should be the moment that he leans in for that kiss, the moment our lips touch and send vibrations of lust and love to our cores. I feel a tear welling in my eye as I contemplate this fantasy and its consequences, because I still have Paul. I need nobody else.

Master
You call me
No tears in this world
A story
created
yet never unfurled.

I know it is Sam I want right now: with me, inside me: it's Sam I need right now - Sam who can save me right now. But, where does it end? When does the grass become greener upon the side you reside? Does it ever, if you're a whore?

You'll be one of many
A lame, hopeless dancer.

I flinch and break the gaze, our knees touching

briefly. I expect to feel a jolt of electricity, but I do not. I look intently at his face as he speaks. He is a good-looking man; the years have aged him well, and as he speaks about his ex-partner, I see that twinkle deepen in his eye. He tells me how he made terrible mistakes in the relationship, yet he never elaborates, nor does he mention her by name. He tells me he felt embarrassed to be with her; perhaps she was overweight, like me? I try to ask, but I can't. That's not why I am here; I am here simply because I need Sam to save me.

I can tell he still loves her and expect to feel disappointment at this realisation, yet I do not. Perhaps Sam is not the man for me, after all. Perhaps I am not looking for a Sam, but looking for a solution. Perhaps fate forced Sam and I apart all those years ago for a good reason. Perhaps fate pushed me together with Paul. Forever.

'Bloody hell, I'm rabbiting on a bit. We came here to save *you*, didn't we?' Sam laughs.

'Yes, but I am probably beyond help.'

Noble.

'It's easy to think that. I thought that. Seeing you and listening to your story has made me realise...'

'Sam, we can't,' I interrupt

'Oh Elly, how egotistical. That's not what I meant.'

'Shit, how embarrassing. I'm stuck. I honestly don't know what to do.'

'Whatever the man has done, he clearly has a hold on your heart for some reason.'

I want you to help me.

'You tell me that he hits you, then you tell me you love him.'

Tell me what to do, Sam.

'You tell me he makes you unhappy, then in the next breath you tell me he makes you happy.'

He does, but it's not all that bad.

'You need to decide what you want, Elly. Do you want to leave him, or do you want to fix him?'

'I want to be happy.'

'Then be happy, Elly. Think about it; you know what to do...'

Sam pauses briefly, as if for dramatic effect, then stands up, his voice breaking as speaks.

'Elly, I'm sorry. I have to go. Stay in touch.'

'Sam?'

He turns around, and I am surprised to see a tear rolling down his cheek. I see something I had not seen in him before, I see a man who has been broken by his own mistakes. I have seen this look before; I have seen it on Paul. They are all cheats, I realise. They are all cheats, they are all liars, they are all normal.

'Sam...thanks. Good luck.'

'You too, Elly.'

Then my saviour, my fate, my man-that-could-have-been-but-shouldn't-have-been, leaves me feeling as if it has all been a dream: a brief, insightful dream. This dream, this dream I did not expect, has climaxed with the realisation that we are all a failure in somebody's eyes. All of us. Yet, we all deserve a shot at redemption.

I walk from the park feeling positive. The soggy grass under my feet feels as if it is swallowing me, absorbing me. The old me would wish it would swallow me. No more decisions to make, no more mistakes to make, I would have wanted to sink slowly into the earth, I would have wanted to BECOME the earth. I would have wanted to cease to exist, in my old form.

Seeing Sam, thinking about Sam, Sam's advice, has brought me to my decision. In front of me had been a man who had been, to me, the epitome of happiness, yet even that had waned. I expected to worship at his moral feet, to listen to his advice - he would tell me to leave - absorb every word he uttered, to hold him, to need him, to allow myself to fall right back inside of him. Instead, I have something more positive: I have learnt that everyone's life is a see-saw of mistakes, the grass is never greener elsewhere; equilibrium teeters and faults wherever you look, whichever life you live. I saw it in his eyes: another man who has made mistakes. Terrible mistakes. Hurtful mistakes. But just mistakes, that is all. Had Sam beaten his wife? Had Sam broken the people who loved him most in the world? Or, have his mistakes been bigger, better, wholly more destructive? Whatever Sam has done, lovely Sam, he deserves another chance: just as   Paul does. Remorse counts for a lot; we are, after all, only human.

Joseph looks up at me from the safety of his pushchair. I wish I could be there; wrapped in blankets and secured to a safety from which I cannot fall. I will fix my marriage, and nestle within the safety of stability. I will change; I will walk away from my past, from my ridiculous expectations. I will write the letter, I will apologise. I have betrayed my husband, just as Sam has betrayed his ex-partner. I will fix this.

Joseph starts to stir, awakening me from my thoughts.

'There there, Baby Joe. Let's go home and see your Daddy, shall we? Let's go back and make the most of our reality. Our fate.'

The beat is inside
A heart with no rhythm
It lies inexistent
Unable
Yet, forgiven.

Happily. Ever. After.

Samuel Merchant

I walk away from Eloise feeling positive. I am going to fix my life, something that I should have done months ago.

Eloise accuses me of not loving her—this is untrue: I adore every bone in her body, I always have done, but to coin a cliché...not like *that*.

1992

I look into the mirror that my mother bought for the new pine dresser in my bedroom. My parents do that, you see: buying stuff, buying things. Things will make me smile.

I study the face staring back at me. It's not an ugly face, it is just a face. An empty face, without a smile. It has a mouth, slightly downturned at the corners: probably because, for once, its owner is not forcing it to smile. It has a nose, a little out of proportion, but apparently the owner will 'grow into it'. The eyes, the windows of the soul. No sparkle, no soul. An angry spot is forcing its way from the otherwise unblemished chin, lurking and throbbing. Volcanic. Ready to erupt.

Detached.

I do not understand this person. I do not understand what is wrong with him. The face looks normal, like that of any other fourteen-year-old boy, but there is something extra, or perhaps it is something missing. Tainted. I touch the face with my left hand, it feels ok, but now my hand is dirty. I squint; it blurs the monstrosity in front of me. It doesn't help. I run to the bathroom to wash my hand.

Water, soap, rinse, dry.

Water, soap, rinse, dry.

Water, soap, rinse, dry.

Water, soap, rinse, dry.

The same ritual in sets of four. My hand is now clean. I must be careful not to do that again.

My best friend, Elly, kissed me today. Straight on the lips, no messing. She held my hand and leaned in, smiling as she heard our school-friends cheering, anticipating something I could not anticipate myself. Nothing. Her lips landed, still nothing. She parted her lips and began to flick her tongue towards my tightly-clenched mouth. Not even a stirring. Poor Elly. Not unattractive, quite the opposite, in fact. Beautiful, curvaceous, vivacious, Elly. My Elly. Just not like that.

I wish I could stand on the very bench on which we sat and kissed, face the boys egging me on and tell them that no, I didn't get a stiffy. I didn't get a stiffy because I don't like Elly like that. I don't like any girl like that. I like boys. But, to say that would make it real. Speak. Reality. Secrets. Reality.

Unhappily. Ever. After.

I spent the best years of my life with an amazing man. Oliver. Slightly shorter than me, he was. Ten years older. Greying hair, slowly receding back towards the crown of his head. 'One day, the front of my hair will meet the back of my head,' he joked on many occasions. He may have hated it, but I loved it. I loved him. I wanted to draw a happy face within the bald spot, without him knowing. Happiness reflecting towards the sun.

He was intelligent; he knew a little something about everything. He taught me politics, he taught me the shape of countries that I will probably never visit, he played songs on his guitar: badly. He sang songs into wine bottles: badly. He kissed me, he loved me: perfectly. Perfect? Well, it would have been, had I not been such a tosser.

I can say it now: I am gay. I couldn't say it then, even to him, even after we had just spent a glorious evening in bed together, even as we were holding hands over the dining table, even when we moved in together.

I still live in the flat, it is a bijou two-bedroom affair, the second bedroom not even worthy of the title 'box-room'. At a push, I could perhaps fit a matchbox in it, slotted neatly between the single bed and the canvas wardrobe. The second bedroom always housed my belongings; my clothes, my toiletries, my books, my life. I shared my life and a bed with my partner, but even to myself I could not admit that we were any more than flatmates. Oliver had enough: quite rightly, some might say. He lived and breathed our life; he accepted that I would tear my hand away from his if we happened upon someone we knew during a meandering walk across the green hills of the

South Downs. He accepted that I would wash my tainted hands, as if cleansing him away, before my mother came to visit. But what he could not accept is that I would never allow myself to be his. My head would not let me. So, he walked. He packed his belongings into a rucksack and he walked.

Sam. I adore you, but, I cannot live with you anymore. I cannot look into your eyes and see the disgust you harbour towards yourself. Please run after me, please reach for me and tell me you can finally be yourself. I will keep my phone number and I will wait until you are ready.
Oliver X

Today, I saw the acceptance in Elly's eyes as she finally realised that nobody is perfect; we are all allowed to make mistakes. Including her. Including me. Excluding Paul. I worried for her, but now I know she will be ok. I saw the light twinkle deep inside, as she realised that she is able to rectify her mistakes: she can be free: she can leave Paul. As for me: I can finally be the person I am. Oliver, here I am.

Happily. Ever. After.

Eloise Katherine Bennett

Running.
I am running. I am running on grass, there are fields around me, over me, within me; looming,

lush, green, soft, beautiful. Jessica? I panic. But she is there. Jessica is holding my hand. I am happy. Clouds. I look to the sky. Clouds are forming, swirling grey and descending; shifting shape, managing me, gripping my mood, holding my hand. Jessica breaks her grip, she has disappeared; instead of her hand, I feel dust. Dust from the cloud, soft grey dust. I am trapped, I am choking, I am stifled.

Paul. Paul is here. In front of me. I stop running. Paul's face has changed, but I know it is Paul. He is holding Jessica, she looks so beautiful. She is smiling. She looks like an angel. Is Jessica dead? Where is Joseph?

I gasp for breath.

I can feel Joseph looking at me. He is locked in a cage to the left of me, but he is smiling. Grey, metal bars. He is holding them, his chubby fingers curled around his prison. Gurgling. Gurgling blood? The fields are now concrete and I am running again. I am running away and my feet are hurting.

Sam is here. He is not smiling, he is pointing into the distance. Mouthing words. The words carry on a breeze of dust. 'Run, Elly. They need you. Run.' Sam floats towards the clouds, a look of tranquillity on his face. Swirling... away...away...away...

Paul, my Paul, Paul is smiling. Joseph is now in his arms. Smiling. Where is the blood? No cage. Freedom. Jessica is smiling. Jessica is moving. Alive.

My face feels stiff, unmovable. I touch it. Cold, cold metal. I run my hands over it, my hands are sticky.

A mask, I am wearing a mask. I look at my hands. They are caked in blood. Congealing under my nails. I turn my hands. I look at my palms. Dripping. The blood is dripping. Yet, bizarrely, no pain. The blood from my family. Am I dead? Am I dying? Can they see me? I try to call them. JESSICA! JOSEPH! PAUL! They can't hear me. They look, then they fade. They are living without me. I cannot let them live without me. I run faster and faster and faster and I see them again. There is a wall. The wall has a window. They are the other side of the wall. I cannot walk around the wall; there are guards with guns. The guards look at me. They are talking about me. They want to shoot me. They want to shoot me because I made my family bleed. They are in my way. The window is just below thigh-height. It is ajar. I push it. It opens. Then it closes. Opens again. Closes again. Open. Close. Open. Close. It finally comes to a stop at ajar. Back to square one.

I lift one knee on to the sill in front of the green, metal window. I feel a sharp pressure, but no pain. There are nails hammered, upside-down, into the wooden sill. I don't care, because my family are the other side. They are living the other side. They think they don't need me. I grit my teeth and bear my body-weight on the knee that is resting on the nails. Still no pain. I feel the pressure of the nails pierce my skin; I feel the pop as each and every one injects me with rust, with fear, with courage. I ease my other knee on to the sill, it still does not hurt. I reach around the frame and feel for a catch. No catch. I feel a padlock; it feels rough, as if it has rusted. How did they get in? I need a key. I need to be with my family. I feel as though I am twenty feet above the ground. I am scared. My heart is pumping blood out of my hand. I tentatively look at the palm of my left hand. There are holes in it, almost through to the other side. I see a key shape beneath the skin under my ring finger. I need my right hand to hold me to the window frame. I bite at my left hand until my teeth hit metal. I still feel no pain. The key. Am I falling? My knees are slipping, the nails ripping the skin. I am naked. Will the guards see me? I lift my left knee, then bang it hard back down on the nails, securing me to the sill. Still no pain. No pain. Both my hands are free. I dig the key from my palm with my right hand, then begin to reach around the window-frame to unlock the padlock. The window swings open before I can insert the key. I feel a hand. Paul is pulling me in. He is crying. The mask falls off, it hits the ground with a metallic clank, then dissolves. Dust. Grey dust. Paul is pulling me in. Pulling me. Pulling, pulling, pulling. It hurts, he has hurt me, but finally, we are together.

Aspects of my being
Clarity, at last
A window, in a wall
of defence.
Open it
gently...

feel free to
peer within
For, behind the glass
lies deconstructed emotion
Evolving
Thriving.
Enter
Unveil me, with care
Love me, or hate me
But, please, keep me unmasked.

Paul Bennett

I am lying in bed, blinking the sleep out of my eyes, wondering why Eloise is slowly opening the bedroom door. She knows better than to wake me.

As Eloise walks quietly into the bedroom, I look at her tired, drawn, tear-stained face and wonder where it all went so wrong. I watch her head towards the bed, a gurgling Joseph over one shoulder, and a piece of paper clutched in her hand. A flash catches my eye, a wedding ring. The wedding ring I lovingly placed on her finger all those years ago, when I promised I would love her forever. I meant it from the bottom of my heart. The heart that is now incapable of feeling anything but anger, hatred and scorn.

Eloise sits on the end of the bed, and clears her throat. An ominous feeling washes over me, and I imagine Eloise standing on a chair, Joseph aloft in her arms, like a trophy of achievement, announcing that she is leaving me.

You're a rapist
You're a loser
You're a bully
An abuser

I shake myself back to reality, and begin to open my mouth.

'Here,' Eloise says, before I can utter a word, handing me a wriggling bundle.

I take Joseph from her arms, and for the first time ever I see him clearly. I look deep into his brown eyes, and as my heart awakens, I remember why I fought so hard to bring him home. This is my son, my heir, yet as it stands right now, all he will inherit are a few empty cans and a head full of traumas. I watch as Joseph's tiny hand grasps firmly around my little finger, as if he is punctuating my realisations.

This is what I am here for,
Fuck the beer
Fuck the arguments.

Eloise silently hands me a piece of paper, then manoeuvres herself so that she is sitting next to me as I read it. It is a holiday booking form.

'Land's End,' she whispers.

'Make or break.'

Then I realise. It is time. It is time for the truth. It is time to save our marriage, for the final time.

It is time to become a family again.

Fuck Amelia
It is just me, Eloise, Jessica and Joseph.

I fucking love my family.

SEVENTEEN

Eloise Bennett
Paul Bennett

Dear Paul,
If we are to start afresh, I think a few things need
to be aired. We can be the family that we have both
always dreamt of, but not whilst we are harbouring
so many secrets, telling so many lies, and ignoring so
much pain.

Dear Eloise
I have always loved you, Eloise, despite what
you may think. We have had our problems, ad-
mittedly most of them caused by me, caused by
alcohol, but I am certain that we can overcome
them if we are truthful with each other. I am
calling an amnesty.

I want you to know the truth about the damage
you have caused this family. I want you to realise
the pain you have inflicted upon us, and the paths of

temptation down which you have led us. All we have ever done is love you, but you turned that into hate.

I want to be able to justify my behaviour to you, Eloise, but I cannot. I am desperate to change; for me, for you and for the children. I have changed before, and I can do it again. I need you to understand how truly sorry I am for everything I have put you through.

Recently, I have become somebody that I have grown to despise more than I despise you. Believe me Paul, this is not an easy feat to accomplish. I have been pushed to the very boundaries of my emotional capabilities, I have had to learn to cope with intense emotions and situations that I would never have even dreamt were possible.

I haven't chosen to be this person; this person has chosen to be me. This person has chosen to change me, chosen to adapt the way I think, feel and behave. This monster has changed me into someone my own family despise. Has this monster always been inside me? Is this why both my parents independently made decisions to move away and forget that I exist? It is not easy, Eloise, it is not easy to ignore something so intrinsically deep and powerful.

I have chosen to be honest with you, Paul. We used to be happy, and I am confident that we can return to the place where we once loved. We were so happy, but was it too good to be true? Are you the person that I see now, that I see today? Are you the person that scares me and hates me? Or, are you the person that you used to be?

I'd like to think that I have never intended to scare you; that all the times I have hurt you or made you cry, have been an accident, a minor incident. But we both know the truth. We both know that when the monster takes over, I revel in the anger that floods me. My senses heighten, and every irk, every fear, every annoyance becomes magnified and converted to rage.

Do you remember me talking to you about Sam, my first love? When I first met you, during that whirlwind romance, I told you everything about me. I stripped myself bare and I told you how much Sam had hurt me, how he had been my best friend, then my boyfriend, but then walked out of my life. I told you how scared I was of losing somebody that I loved again, that I was frightened of pushing you away. You took me in your arms and you promised me that you would never hurt me, you would never leave me, and you reminded me that Sam was my past, and that you were my future.

All the bad things that I have done can be blamed on my alcoholism. See, I said it. My name's Paul, and I'm an alcoholic. Beating, shouting, raping, cheating. Do you remember

the conversation we had about adultery? It was during one of our all-night discussions, when we first met. You had just told me about Sam, your ex-boyfriend, who had broken your heart as a teenager. I did not feel threatened by his existence; I felt smug that I had you and he did not. We discussed what would happen if one day he returned to the scene, would you carry on the love story that you had begun, yet paused? Or, had the story already finished, abruptly and totally? You assured me that I was the only man for you, and always will be. Adultery was wrong, you said, if you do not want to be with someone, do not be with them. Adultery is for cowards.

Sam saved me, Paul. Sam saved me and Sam saved our marriage. That day I saw the light, I had a moment of clarity. I recognised that however hard I try, I will never be able to leave you. I tried twice, yet both times returned, because I love you, and because the force that pulls us together is stronger than the wedge that drives us apart. But I also know that our relationship is self-destructive, dissolving our trust, our love, our sanity. I needed a way to get out; I needed an excuse, a reason. I contacted Sam. I need you to know that without him, I would be dead.

I didn't understand it myself, Eloise. I met you and no longer needed to be wanted by random women, you were everything I ever needed. Then I started drinking again, and all the old insecurities came flooding back. I was convinced that you were going to cheat on me at some point, because something this good could not last forever, right? Something this beautiful could not remain untainted. Then I met Amelia. I had an affair, Eloise. I went back on all those things we agreed on, and writing this, telling you, knowing I am hurting you, it is truly breaking my heart. I justified it somehow; I told myself that you would do it, given the opportunity. I told myself it was ok, because it was not just sex: it was love. But, it wasn't. It was an obsession, and as far as I am concerned the worst thing that I could ever have done to you. The ultimate betrayal. I know that armed with this knowledge, you have every right to leave me, I know that when I had the affair with Emma, it broke your heart, and the last thing I want to do is cause you that pain again. But, we need to wipe the slate clean.

You made me want to kill myself, Paul. You made me want to leave my babies without a mother, because I knew that the only way to escape the violent clutches of our marriage was to die. But, just as I was about to pack the children in the car, and heartlessly abandon them at their Grandma's, Sam emailed me. That email saved me. I admit, yes I considered that perhaps my life would be better if Sam and I were together, but when I met him, I saw it in his eyes. I saw that look that you have, I saw a man who has absorbed his own betrayal, a broken man made from broken promises. It was then I knew that it could happen anywhere, to anyone, at any time. I am not the only victim in the world. I am a survivor. We can survive this.

All I can say to you, Eloise, is that I am sorry. I will never be perfect.

If you consider that a betrayal, then I am sorry, I am not perfect. But then, neither are you.

Every time I hit you, a part of me died.

Every time you hit me, a part of me died.

The times I made Jessica cry are burned into my memory, and will be scarred there forever.

All the times you made Jessica cry will be burned into her memory, she will be scarred forever.

If this were a witch-hunt, I would be burned at the stake.

If this were a witch hunt, you would be burned at the stake.

I am rotten, but not to the core, Eloise. And if you still want me, I will never understand why, but I am here for the taking.

You have been rotten and evil, Paul. But I still want

you, if you are here for the taking?

I will never forgive myself.

I forgive you.

But please forgive me?

Please forgive me?

I love you, Eloise.

I love you, Paul.

Onwards we march, against adversity?

Together we battle, against adversity?

Until death do us part. Paul XXX

Until death do us part. Eloise XXX

Jessica Louise Bennett aged 5 years and 5 months
April 2001

I am five years old. It has been my birthday ages ago and I got most things that I want which makes me happy. I love my Mummy. We live in a house together and also with my brother called Baby Joe and Daddy too.

My Mummy is like a volcano. She doesn't look like a volcano she looks like my Mummy all pretty and soft with a round tummy a bit smaller than my space hopper and a pretty face and lots of hair. My Mummy is sometimes dormant then she gets all cross and her crossness comes out of her mouth like a lava. Then sometimes she doesn't have any crossness and she just has kisses and sweets and cuddles.

My Daddy has a different crossness. He has a smelly crossness that he gets from the pub and sometimes from a big bottle at home and it makes my Mummy scared.

Paul Bennett

I lie
My life is shit
I beat my wife
I scare my children
I'd die without them

Eloise Katherine Bennett

I fell over, that is what I shall say.
I FELL OVER.

Waiting
Anticipating

'It's HIM: it's Paul. It's not the table, it's not the door, it's not the drawer, it's not the cooker, IT'S NOT A FUCKING ACCIDENT. It's the man who loves me.'

My heart breaks as I filter the shouting and accusations to watch Jessica concentrating on her distraction; a tiny face creased into a frown; a frown that shouldn't exist for many, many years.

Demanding, asking, terrifying

I do not love him enough not to be scared.

I am the woman who broke her daughter.

Jessica Louise Bennett

It's a happy day today because even that my Mummy and Daddy are going on holidays without me I had lots and lots of fun with them yesterday and it was more fun than the fun I have when they spend lots of gold coins. And the day before the day that was yesterday, I had a whole afternoon not at school because I had to go to the hospital and I had to sit on a chair for ages and then when it was my turn I went with my Mummy into another room and there was a doctor there and he told me to sit on the bed and he made the curtains go closed which was a bit funny because it was daytime and there was no window. And Baby Joe was there with us too and he was looking at me and his eyes look too big for his head but he'll grow into them. And then the doctor asked me if my arm felt ok and I said yes it felt ok but it keeps getting scratchy and the doctor said that is all normal and then asked my Mummy questions about my arm and my Mummy's eyes went a bit big too and I remembered the secret about not telling all lies but not telling all the truth either and so I didn't say anything else, I let my Mummy talk to the doctor instead. And then the doctor got some really really big scissors which were bigger than the biggest scissors I have ever seen in my life. And the doctor snip snip snipped at the big hard plaster-bandage and then it came off in exactly two pieces and looked funny because it was still the shape of my arm. Then my arm looked a bit thin. Then the doctor squeezed my arm at the top, squeezed my arm at the bottom, squeezed my arm at the side and the other side and then squeezed my arm both sides together. Then the doctor told me to open my arm up and close my arm down and a bit to the side and to open my fingers and then close my fingers like a squeezing punchy fist. And then because that didn't hurt at all the doctor gave me a letter to give to the old thin lady with the dropping face at the table to tell her I can go home and never go back until I have problems. Then my arm felt weird and hangy and I had to keep remembering it could move.

Then the next day it was the weekend and at first I thought that it wouldn't be a fun day because my Mummy was sitting in her and Daddy's room for a long time that felt like hours and when I went in there she was writing a long long long letter that was even longer than the thing I had to write that time at school, when we had to copy the stuff about a poem about a worm and write about the things that it meant that weren't put in the poem. I thought that it was probably just about a worm. When I walked into my Mummy's room, she covered her writing up with her hand and she was sitting on a chair by the window at her cupboard that has bottles on, and the bottles have things in for Baby Joe's bottom when it gets sorely and for that time I had an itch on the inside of my elbow of my arm that didn't get broken and it went all red. And the bottles aren't in a line all neat and tidy like my bottles will be when I have my own house when I am a grown-up, they are fallen over and some of them have some sticky dust on the top. Dust is people's skin. When my Mummy covered up her writing with her hand it was like when I cover up my writing with my hand to stop that Zac boy at school from writing the same pictures that I write when we are describing things. My Mummy says that I have to be extra kind to Zac because he has went through a lot and he is still little and that no little person should have to go through a lot. I am very lucky but I still don't want people to copy my writing and my pictures. I told my Mummy that I wouldn't copy her writings because I really can't read her writings very well anyway. My Mummy laughed and held out her arms and we had a big squeezing cuddle which squashed my arm that used to be bad because I forgot to move it out of the way because I had still forgotten it could move. Bad arm. Then when I thought I should let my Mummy finish writing things and maybe drawing pictures I thought I would find Daddy and that maybe he would lift me up on to his shoulders and make me laugh. I found Daddy and he was sitting in the room with the television in that my Mummy and Daddy call the lounge, but my Grandma calls it the sitting room because we sit in it. It has a table in it too and the table has some scratches on it, but that is ok because my Mummy says that when she is old she will look at the scratches and the scratches will make her think of me and of Baby Joe too because maybe when Baby Joe gets older he will scratch it with pencils too, but that I must try not to scratch it any more. Daddy was sitting at the scratched table and he had a pen and some pieces of paper and he was writing a letter too! My Mummy and Daddy don't always talk nicely so maybe they are writing letters to each other. Baby Joe was playing on his play-mat. He loves his play-mat. He was lying on his back and making a funny noise and he was kicking his legs in the air backwards and forwards and backwards and forwards and he was having so much fun. And Daddy looked at him and smiled and then Daddy looked at me and smiled and so then I went over to Daddy and I put my head on the table which was a bit hard but I didn't want to jog Daddy's hand when he was doing some work and I asked Daddy very nicely if we could have a Fun-day and he said yes! And after a while which was hours my Mummy finished writing and Daddy finished writing and then we had our fun day. First we went to the shop that sells sweeties that I only ever ever go to with my Mummy and my Baby Joe and we bought some sweets and they were all in one bag and we took them out one at a time and we were taking turns and sharing. I got cross with Daddy because he took the last chewy sweet that is in a wrapper that makes your tongue all black and you can stick it out at Baby Joe and Baby Joe laughs. But Daddy promised that next time he would buy extra and we would all eat one at the same time, except Baby Joe because he is too little and then we will say 'Look, Baby Joe!' and we will all stick our tongues out at the same time. But then when we went home down the hill and my Mummy and Daddy said they have something to tell me and they told me that they are going on holiday together on their own together and not with me and not with Baby Joe and that did make me feel a bit sad. So I walked in front of them for about seven minutes and I thought about it and I thought that if I make them promise to have extra

Fun-days when they come back then maybe it will be ok. And they said yes and they said that Grandma and Pops will look after us both very well and yes, Grandma will give me extra biscuits and they will buy some chocolate breakfasts for me to eat on the mornings that I am there. So that bit was ok again. Then when we got home we played a game and we had to spin a spinner thing while Baby Joe was asleep and we had to put our hands and legs on different colours and we got all tangled up and I fell over, but it didn't hurt much even though I landed on my bottom and Daddy and my Mummy laughed, which was ok because I wasn't hurt badly at all. Then it was the evening and it was late and dark and my Mummy said it was ok because it was a special day and a Fun-day and we all went outside, even Baby Joe in his pushchair and we walked down the hill and round the corner and along the road and for-wards and round until we got to the beach bit but not on the pebbles, just on the pavement, and we looked over the railings where the sea flies over when it is really windy and I looked up to the sky and I saw the moon and the moon in the sky was shiny and big and bright and when I looked down at the sea, the shiny bits were showing bits in the sea and if I closed my eyes a bit, it looked like fire-works and I held my Mummy's hand and her other hand held Baby Joe's pushchair handle and on the other side of me was Daddy and I held

Daddy's hand too but very softly because that hand has to be thought about a lot to make it go into a holding shape and this is what should happen every day that I'm not at school. And today I am still so so happy.

Eloise Katherine Bennet

There. Look, right there:
Can you see it?
Take me by the hand.
Show me:
silver moonlight, sifting
its finest reflections
upon our open sea,
perfecting a pathway of sparkling tapestry.
Does it lead us into forever?
Because, my darling, I will stroll
with you. And, they may not be unblemished,
the waves that slide unannounced, into the darkened night.
Yet, they are not unexpected,
nor unwelcome,
as they perform a pattern.
A perspective of perfection.

Eloise Katherine Bennett
May 2001

The light of the lamp on the bedside cabinet casts an eerie glow over the modestly decorated room. A feeling of trepidation builds inside me, I know that now I am forced to talk to Paul, really talk to him. We recently seemed to have settled upon an unspoken truce. We don't speak of mistakes, of choices, of reality. We avoid speaking of Jessica's arm; Paul threw away the plaster she proudly displayed on the table when we returned from the hospital. We sometimes catch each others' eye and exchange a look of mutual fear, but that aside, we have been skimming the surface. Sometimes, we have even found ourselves laughing. Oh, God forbid! Paul has still been drinking, yes, but not to the extent he has in the past. We have had a few blips, a few arguments, a few slaps, but nowhere close to the destruction we were amid before. I am suddenly tempted to drive back home. Back home to suspended reality. Safety. But, it has to be now, doesn't it? It has to be now, or never.

Jessica and Joseph are safe at their Grandma's, their little eyes shielded from whatever this weekend throws at our broken family. I feel inside my raincoat pocket, to check whether the letter is still there. It is. This is the letter that could make or break our family. Will Paul ever forgive me?

Bizarrely, I am comforted by the knowledge that Paul has committed worse evils during the course of our short marriage, yet I am also painfully aware that his tolerance is markedly lower than my own. Nothing was mentioned during the long drive to our weekend of truth, nothing at all, our journey to this beautiful place was conducted in silence.

You do not have to say anything, but anything you do say may be used in evidence. Do you understand?

Paul drove us, occasionally humming along to a song on the radio, his hands gripping the steering wheel to stop the shaking that I have come to accept, ignore, and tolerate. The shaking indicates a change, a change for the better. Soon, we will be ok. We will. I promise.

I look at my watch, wondering how long it will take Paul to find somewhere to buy us fish and chips. I stayed to unpack, as I wanted to give Paul an opportunity to find a pub, to have a drink, to let me throw his weakness at him in the inevitable showdown.

One point to Eloise.

Paul has already been gone for an hour and a half, yet I know that there is a cafe within a ten-minute walk. I am not yet angry, but feel that I should be.

Where are you?

Two points to Eloise.

Sighing, I continue to unpack the suitcase, noting with humour the pointless items I have packed: Joseph's dummy, Jessica's socks...oh, fuck, I remember: the chocolate breakfasts. Jessica is going to hate me for forgetting to buy her chocolate breakfasts. I become distracted as I again look around the room; it is small and cosy, yet bordering slightly on stifling. The walls have paint chips in vertical lines, as if somebody has tried to claw their way out.

Clawing at walls and pillars, trying to escape. Trying to make sense of a room that is claustrophobic, yet comforting. Struggling for breath inside, then struggling for breath alone out in the cold night air. Freedom. Is it? Freedom of choice. A choice, a junction, a signpost. Vers la droite, ou vers le gauche?

I'm outside, look out the window XXX

I tentatively pull back the curtains, almost scared of what I might find. In the gardens of the bed and breakfast, I can see a wooden picnic bench, half covered with a makeshift wooden shelter. There is an old-fashioned lamp-post casting a comforting light on the dark wood of the table, raindrops illuminated as they fall from the grey, early evening, sky.

Droplets of truth.

Paul is sitting on the uncovered side of the bench, his hood up to protect himself from the increasingly torrential rain. On the far side of the table, sheltered by the roof, are two paper packages that look suspiciously like fish and chips. A bottle of wine is next to them, along with two paper cups and a bottle of soft drink. Paul is attempting to light a candle, but the wind is not in his favour, and I laugh as he dramatically throws the lighter on the floor and sucks his burnt thumb.

One point to Paul.

I zip up my coat and grab the keys from the bedside cabinet.

Making my way down the stairs, I feel a draft of cold air enveloping me, protective yet freezing.

Preserving.

I pull on the handle of the heavy front door, which resists my efforts to open it the first three times, as if in protestation at the things that could, that should, be said and done.

Wrap yourself in the blanket of cold. Curl up on the hallway floor, protect yourself, and keep inside what needs to be said. Bury your head back in the sand. Once said, never unsaid. Once said, never forgotten.

I finally manage to open the door, and step with trepidation onto the soft, waterlogged grass. The unseasonable cold air catches at the back of my dry throat, and bites at my nose, making me want to turn back to re-enter the cosy, stifling room that protected me from the elements.

Protected me from myself.

I plunge my hands deep into my pockets to stave away the howling wind and cold rain, tightly clenching my fingers around the piece of paper that is nestled in the corner. I find it appropriate that my secrets have found a home in amongst strands of dried tobacco and lint, in the bottom of a deep pocket, protected from the elements.

The truth, protected from reality. Secrets shrouded in truth. Truth stifled by apprehension.

I feel a desire to rip the piece of paper from its waterproof prison, and throw it to the wind.

Throw caution to the wind.

Let the wind take it, far away, for a stranger to find, to read my secrets, the anonymous confessions of an anonymous woman.

This is my marriage on the rocks, in the wind, and battered by the rain. This is my marriage that needs to be protected, yet needs to opened, needs to be vulnerable, yet needs to be wrapped up warm, until death do us part. This is my marriage that today, will live or die.

Paul Bennett

Make or break.
Bravery: Noun. Brave conduct, courage, valour.

I concentrate on the music blaring from the car radio, meaningless lyrics floating around the car. They make me cringe as somehow, bizarrely, they remind me of all those terrible things that I did. Hit it, baby. Break it down. I grip the steering wheel to stop my hands shaking; the tremors are present to remind me that I desperately need a drink, but I know that this weekend I must stop. Forever. This weekend is the beginning of the new me. The old me. My stomach cramps, and I wince. I look at Eloise, as she opens her mouth to say something, perhaps to check that I am all right, yet no words appear. I turn up the volume on the radio to distract myself from the silence and the pain.

Inside my jacket pocket is the letter that I wrote to Eloise, baring my soul. I need to find the right time to give it to her, but that time certainly isn't now, as I do not wish to be encased in a moving vehicle with a scorned wife. This thought makes me smile wryly, and I briefly let go of the steering wheel to make sure that the letter, the truth, is still there. My fumbling hands grasp it, and as if absorbing strength from the carefully scribed words, with a renewed energy, I stamp my foot on the accelerator. The sooner the better.

The day is threatening twilight as we arrive at the bed and breakfast. The rain is cascading, and the wind blowing furiously through the trees. Eloise walks on ahead of me, and I study her frame. She has lost weight since we first met, and she walks with her head down, sheltering herself from the howling wind.

Like she walks towards you with her head down, Paul. Sheltering herself from the scorn, and the abuse.

I take the bags to our room, which is cosy and secure. I feel safe, comforted by the worn walls, and well used furniture. Old, overused, yet loved. I am aware that I have arrived at my last chance saloon, clichéd but painfully true. I need this symbolic journey to fix us, because I know that I cannot do it at home. Too many reminders, too much pain. If I can plaster over the cracks whilst I am away, I will no longer feel the sting of life when I return.

I decide that I will make this evening extra special, I will make it everything that Eloise wants it to be. I won't drink, I won't shout, I won't accuse. I will buy dinner, buy her some wine, and give her the letter. I will let her shout at me and punish me, when she reads the awful truth, then I will show her that I have changed, and I can be the person she needs me to be.

With this in mind, I leave Eloise to unpack, whilst I go on a hunt for our dinner.

A proper man.
A real man.
Foraging for food.

I can feel the wind picking up around me, as I head towards the local shops to forage our food. The rain is running in my eyes and soaking the bottoms of my jeans. The howling wind and unrelenting rain are perfectly reflecting my churning stomach and the cascade of tears that are threatening to fall.

Crying in the rain.

I decide to walk for a while, in an attempt to walk off the churning in the pit of my stomach. Despite the chill of the night, I am sweating. I know that to stop this, all I need to do is pop into a shop and buy myself a few cans of beer, a bottle of wine, or a bottle of champagne, if I wish to be a more refined alcoholic. Yet, I also know that by doing this, I will become that man again, the one I am trying to avoid. I have ruined so many things, broken so many rules, broken faces, broken bones, broken hearts, broken souls. I will now do everything I possibly can to fix them.

I walk for about an hour, not taking in any sights, not noticing anybody or anything. I am trapped inside my own head, and trapped inside the body that is punishing me for the sins I have committed against it. I walk round in circles, knowing that at some point I need to stop walking, and start doing. I stop at a takeaway shop, and order our tea, then to a convenience store to purchase some paper cups, candles and a bottle opener. Across the road is my nemesis. The off-licence. It is a ridiculous battle, but a battle nonetheless. I feel as though I am inside a computer game, as I take a deep breath and walk in, trying to avoid losing my lives on the various enemies around me. I choose a soft drink for myself and then pick a bottle of wine for Eloise. Any bottle of wine. I need to get out. I am shaking. I am sweating. I am suffering. I hand over the money with shaking hands then leave the shop, praying that I am strong enough to resist the temptation to open the wine, to ease my suffering. The cool rain is welcome upon my sweating face, and I look up to the sky, to my absent God, praying for some help.

The walk back to the bed and breakfast takes only ten minutes, and once there I head to the gardens to set up my romantic evening.

Romance.
Comes before a fall.
A fool.

I walk across the rain-softened grass to lay the wooden table. I text Eloise, requesting she join me, and then pace nervously, awaiting her arrival. As I burn a thumb on my lighter, I realise what a bloody ridiculous idea it was to light candles in such weather. Nonetheless, I soldier on, a bad-man-turned-good, with the truth burning a hole in his pocket.

I finish laying the table, then stand back to admire my handiwork. Not bad, considering the adverse circumstances. As Eloise tentatively walks towards me, I briefly wonder what I am hoping to achieve by telling her the truth. To clear my conscience? To start afresh? Again, I place my hand in my pocket, searching for my strength. The truth will out. The truth is bold. The truth is brave. The truth will win. I know that I am doing the right thing. I stand to greet my beautiful wife, who smiles nervously. Trepidation is encompassing us as we formally hug each other; there is no room for emotion right here, right now.

I can liken this soiree to being on a first date: stilted, nervous conversation, about things that mean nothing, when all you want to do is dig deep and be bold. We discuss the weather, the scenery, the bed linen.

What about our marriage, our life, our problems?

A sudden gust of wind grabs the paper cups from the table and flings them on the grass, at my feet.

'Oh. I didn't really think that one through, did I?'
Then Eloise says it.
'Shall we walk? Shall we talk?'
I nod and pick up the packages of food from the table, passing one to Eloise. I begin to offer the bottle of wine, but she shakes her head at me,

pleading in her eyes.

'We don't need that.'

We don't.

We decide to head up to the cliffs—to walk, to talk, to air our lives, in the driving rain. We make our way to the car and sit inside in absolute silence, the only sound that of paper rustling as we eat our lukewarm chips. The drive along the coast road to the cliffs is carried out in a similar ambience, the windscreen wipers tattooing a regular beat, punctuated by Eloise tapping her fingernails on the dashboard. We see seagulls in the distance, struggling against the wind as they try to reach their destinations.

'Freedom?' asks Eloise

'I don't know. I don't know what that is, I'd like to try it, even if I am flying against north-north-westerly gusts of a hundred and fifty thousand miles an hour.'

Eloise laughs, and then relaxes her head back against the headrest. My heart fills with a fondness for her that I certain I have never felt before. I have felt love, I have felt hate, I have felt lust, I have felt rage, but never this all-encompassing fondness I am feeling now. I want to protect her, protect her from me.

We reach our destination and make our way to the cliffs. It is stormier and windier than I would ever have imagined, the sea air is mixing with the rain, stinging my eyes and saturating my already soggy jeans. I lick the salt from my lips and look to the distance, to the end of the land. Eloise places her arm on mine, but I need to concentrate. I squint at the horizon, realising that if I cannot make this work, I may as well take a running jump right now. I turn to look at Eloise, and smile.

'Let's fix this, Eloise. I've been an idiot, let me make it right again.'

I reach into my pocket, as Eloise reaches into hers.

Reaching for freedom.

'We can be free, Paul. No more lies, eh?'

At the same time, we both pull letters from our pockets.

Apprehension.

Suddenly, I feel scared. My bravado has decreased dramatically, and I wonder whether it would benefit either of us to know the truth.

Coward.

'If we are moving on, Eloise, do we need to know the past?'

'It's make or break, Paul. I want to, why don't you? I want to clear it all up, and start again, or not. Oh, I don't know. You decide.'

'Let's draw a line, make it final, make it real. Throw it to the wind?'

'Yep, I suppose so.'

'On the count of three.'

One…

At that moment, a small dog bounds happily over to us, and I stoop to pet it. Its owner whistles the dog back, he is an elderly gentleman and looks forlorn, as if he is missing a part of himself. His face lights up as his dog loyally returns to him, and he waves and apologises for interrupting us.

Two…

Eloise and I both hold our letters, our truths, above our heads.

Freedom
Sail away, forever. Truth. Deceit. Pain. Gone forever.

We turn to each other, and briefly, I see fear in Eloise's eyes, but as I take her in my arms, I can feel the tension melt away. We both sob with relief, as we consider what we could have lost if the truth was out.

Coward: Noun. Paul: A person who lacks courage in facing danger or confrontation.

Eloise: A timid or easily intimidated person.

Courage: Noun. A quality of spirit that allows an individual to face difficulty without fear.

The elderly gentleman summoned his courage, leaned forward, then plummeted to his death over the edge of the cliff.

<u>Eloise Katherine Bennett</u>

Oh, how pleasant. An al fresco meal, and then a refreshing stroll along the cliff tops towards the end of the world. I tentatively peer over the edge to look at the rocks that have been worn away throughout years, decades, centuries, slowly succumbing to a lifetime of abuse from the raging sea. Yet, they remain. Worn away, yet present, in all their ravaged glory. Cracked, broken, and forever in the way.

Downtrodden.

I am unsure whether I want Paul to read my letter. Part of me wants him to hate me for what I have done, solely to satisfy my guilt complex, yet the other part of me wants to forever hide the truth, because who does the truth hurt if it remains unknown? All it can do is eat away at my conscience, my useless conscience, whose sole purpose is to make me feel guilt for the things I thought I might do. A tenuous link to guilt, and easily broken with a strong dose of tit-for-tat justification.

But, yet again, I let Paul take the reins, because,

although he is not malicious in his persuasion, he is certainly subtly controlling proceedings. I will never know what was written in Paul's letter, yet I suspect it is more sinful than mine, else why would he want to forgo our freedom for yet more secrets?

Imprisoned.

As we are about to let go of our papers, a small dog approaches us. Paul bends down to pet it, and the owner fretfully whistles for it to return. Another example of freedom restrained, I think to myself, as I reluctantly let the truth free into the turbulent wind. Paul pulls me into a hug, which I initially resist then melt into as I feel the warmth from his body, and feel his heart beating against mine. Out of the corner of my eye, I can see the papers whirling by the cliff edge. The old man's dog is chasing after them, but a little too fast for comfort. Paul must also have seen this, as he breaks free, and begins to chase after the dog, who is heading for the cliffs.

Run.
Freedom.
Run.

I attempt to attract the attention of the old man, through the driving rain and descending darkness, but he is looking in the opposite direction, lost in a thought of his own. As realisation dawns, his face drops in absolute horror, and he begins to slowly walk towards his dog, all the while watching Paul in the vain hope that he can somehow catch the errant canine. The dog stops for a brief moment, and I realise that it has been chasing the pieces of paper, chasing freedom, freedom caught helplessly in a tornado whirl. The paper begins to float down to the cliff edge, before it is ripped away again. The dog takes one last leap towards freedom, my freedom.

Absconding.
Escaping.
Freedom.

The dog plummets to its violent grave on the rocks below, whilst Paul runs helplessly towards the edge. I cast my gaze towards the gentleman, who starts to walk towards the cliff edge, and I wonder whether it is advisable for him to view his beloved pet's battered
body.

Imagery of death.
Death induced by freedom.

I begin to make my way towards him, trying to catch his eye with a sympathetic glance, but he is staring straight ahead, leaning heavily on his walking stick. As the old man reaches the edge of the land, he peers inquisitively over, then, clearly having confirmed his worst fears, places his walking stick on the ground, leans forward and calmly freefalls to his death.

Be grateful for boundaries, for this is exactly what happens when they set you free.

Mr Isaac Roberts

One man and his dog.

I walk towards the distant cliff, Rosie pulling frantically at her lead. My worst nightmare would be to see the curious dog plummet to her death over the edge of the cliff, water ravaging her tiny, flailing form. She hates me for this nylon leash, which fetters her freedom, and a part of me hates myself. Rosie is all I have left since Marion passed-on two weeks ago, and I realise that perhaps I am a little overprotective; perhaps Rosie would like some freedom. I will make a decision in ten minutes or so, just let us walk down this path. As I make my way down the stony stretch, two fig-ures catch my eye, illuminated against the dusk sky by beams of light from scattered lampposts. A lady and a gentleman, both dressed for winter despite the month of May, although admittedly the weather is unseasonably windy and rainy. The gentleman looks ill; his face appears pale, and he is shuffling uncomfortably from foot to foot. The wind catches the lady's hood, and it falls away from her head, displaying a mane of beautiful chestnut hair. She is pretty, in a natural understated manner, although even from this distance I can see that her face is worn and tired. The lady is standing still, as if rooted to the spot, her arm reaching for the man, who, despite the imploring look upon his companion's face, appears to be more intent on looking out to the sea. Rosie is again tugging at her lead, and I realise that I should have decided by now whether to allow her to have her way, have her freedom. Freedom generally comes at a price, I realise, and I wonder whether that price is worth paying. Marion paid for her freedom, with death. Freedom from the pain of the cancer that ravaged her, freedom from the endless hospital admissions. I am also free, in a sense. I am free from caring for her, yet I would give that freedom back in a heartbeat, to see my brave, beautiful wife again. I furiously wipe the tear that is threatening to escape from my eye. I am a man, and not allowed to cry. Yet, I cried over her body, cried over her coffin, and every day, I cry over her photographs. I am a weak man, a fool. Fifty-seven years of marriage, and all I have to show for it is a tear and a frustrated dog. I am closer to the couple now, and study them from beneath the peak of my hat. The gentleman is in his thirties, I would say. He is now looking at the lady, they are squared up as if to battle. I can hear snatches of their conversation, carried over with the wind. I catch the general gist, and conclude that they are husband and wife. They are speaking of being honest and free from lies. There it is: that freedom again. They reach into their pockets at the same time, and retrieve identical pieces of paper. They seem almost surprised by this similarity, as if unwittingly their lives are parallel without their permission or realisation. Rosie is looking at me imploringly, so I decide at this moment that she deserves a little freedom too. I kneel to remove her leash, kiss her on the nose, and she scampers towards the couple, as if to smugly advertise her newfound freedom.

The gentleman bends to pet Rosie, still holding his piece of paper in his hand, whilst the lady moves her gaze towards me. I whistle Rosie back to me, and shout an apology to the young couple, who graciously nod in acceptance.

The howling wind is not letting up, but Rosie is still full of energy, so I decide to walk to a little further on, to watch the waves from the cliff edge. The wind is causing the Atlantic to crash against the rocks below them, wearing them away, until eventually it will seem as if they were never there. Clouds are moving quickly above, the early evening sky dark and ominous, lightened only by the pure white seagulls that are screeching overhead, presumably communicating their plans to escape the storm overhead, searching for safety, searching for freedom.

I feel as though I have missed a scene of a film, the couple are now smiling at each other, a look of relief on each of their faces. They hold their pieces of paper aloft, and then simultaneously let them go, watching as the wind catches them and hovers them over the cliff edge. Freedom. For a split second, I see what looks like fear on their faces, before they fall sobbing into each other's arms. I wonder what restraints they have managed to free themselves from, and I feel a sense of resentment that whichever emotion they are feeling is one that I will never experience again. Not without my Marion.

I decide that I have had enough of today, and frankly, need a cup of tea, despite the advancing hour. Rosie is no longer sitting at my heels, so I whistle for her, and wait for her to return. She does not bound back as expected, so shielding my eyes with my hand, I whistle for her again. No Rosie. I can feel worry gnawing at the pit of my stomach, as I look behind me in a desperate attempt to locate her. The young couple are no longer standing together, the lady is shouting something in my direction, and the man is running toward the cliff edge. He looks almost eerie against the dusk sky; his silhouetted arms and legs appear bizarrely elongated. Just in front of him is Rosie, her little legs bounding towards the freedom that I have allowed her. Despite his young age, the man is not fast enough to catch her, and fear has rooted my own legs to the spot, like an old, gnarled tree. I cannot understand why

Rosie is running so fast, until I look ahead of her, to see a piece of white paper blowing back on to the edge of the cliff. A momentary sense of relief washes over me, but the wind picks it up again, taunting Rosie and pulling the paper back over the edge of the cliff. I know what is going to happen, and I cannot stop it. I watch in horror as Rosie takes her final leap to catch the paper, and falls, falls, falls. I don't know what to do, what to think, as my only companion plummets to her death. What I do know, is that tomorrow I will not have to do anything, or think anything, if I go with her.

Freedom.

It always comes at a price.

Jessica Louise Bennett

I actually do not understand why I am staying at my Grandma and Pops house and I know that my Mummy and Daddy have gone on holiday but it's not very nice to go on holiday and not take your children. When my friends go on holiday they go with their Mummy and Daddy and it's not fair that I have to stay at Grandma's house. And I thought it was ok when they promised all the nice things when they told me about it but now I don't think it's ok anymore. Not for me. It's ok for Baby Joe because he only drinks milk but it's not ok for me because Grandma doesn't buy those chocolate breakfast things and I think I should have one to make me happy because I am sad that my Mummy and Daddy have gone on holiday without me and Baby Joe and my Mummy promised, she PROMISED, that she would buy some chocolate breakfasts and give them to Grandma and tell Grandma that I am allowed to eat them because Grandma doesn't believe in them, but she forgot. My Mummy forgot. And forgetting makes me more sad than anything because it makes my head think that my Mummy thinks that being excited about her holiday with Daddy is more important than me having something favourite to eat for breakfast at Grandma's house because I had to have cornflakes which are boring, even when I put sugar on them after I put milk on them and they go all crunchy.

My Grandma and Pops have cakes in a cake tin that are circle size and they have chocolate on them and they have sponge bits like cakes do, and they have orange bits in the middle that are all squidgy and I am allowed to eat three chocolate squidgy things but I took four yesterday and I hid one in my slipper and when I got upstairs to eat it, it was all squashed but it tasted ok anyway. That was fun but not as much fun as chocolate breakfasts. My Grandma said that my Mummy and Daddy have gone on holiday to somewhere that is the end of the land and I wish I had gone because I want to know what happens at the end of the land. I think that the end of the land will be all black and like nothing and then I think that black is something and I can't think what nothing will look like. And my Grandma says that my Mummy and Daddy are coming back tomorrow and that is good because I miss them because I love them and because my Mummy promised me that she would buy me a pencil at the end of the land to put in my collection of pencils that are in the purple pot in my bedroom. And I hope that my Mummy doesn't forget that promise too. And underneath my purple pot that has my pencils in is my special photograph of my Mummy and Daddy and me before Daddy made my Mummy sad that time and before we all got happy again. Maybe we won't ever be sad again? I think sometimes that we were happy before Baby Joe was born then I remember that we were sad sometimes too because when my Mummy ran away it was before Baby Joe was born and my Mummy wasn't happy then. When I am older I want to look after children who aren't happy and I want to get paid to hug them and make them feel better and make them feel special. And one day when I am older I promise that even though I love Daddy I will tell my baby brother Baby Joe how much sadness Daddy made us have on sometimes when we weren't smiling, because then Baby Joe won't love him as much as I do and if you don't love someone then I don't think that they can make you feel sad, not real sad.

Harry at school made me sad one day when he sat on my foot and I don't love Harry, but I think it made me feel sad because it hurt because it made my toes bend the wrong way in my shoe and I told the teacher. I promise that I will tell Baby Joe. I promise that more than I promise anything in the world because I love Baby Joe so much that the love makes my teeth feel soft. And one day before, I heard my Mummy say to Daddy that she feels lonely and that Daddy is never there for her and I thought that was a lie because Daddy is in the house most of the time except when Daddy used to go out in the evening and came back really really late and I heard him come in more than one time and I heard him shout at my Mummy before my Mummy had even said anything. I try to forget about that. I really really want to be able to sleep properly and not think that I might wake up and hear nasty things again, but when I close my eyes and when I go to sleep bad things happen in my head and I have nightmares and I wake up crying and then I think I can hear shouting and I think that maybe bad things don't just happen in my head, they happen everywhere. I am looking out of the window at Grandma's which has a curtain on it that you can see through and I can see a car coming down the road and it looks like my Mummy and Daddy's car, but I know that they are not coming home until tomorrow. But my Mummy and Daddy might have missed me and Baby Joe so so much that they couldn't be on holiday without us for longer. And then I am so happy because I know that I am cross that my Mummy and Daddy went on holidays without me and forgot all about the promise about the chocolate breakfasts and might have forgotten all about the promise about the pencil but now I know that they didn't want to miss me but they have missed me because otherwise they wouldn't come home on a day that is earlier than the day they promised they would come home. Then I feel a little bit upset but only a little bit because I now remembered that yesterday Grandma said that because I had been so good she would buy me that nice chicken from the shop that the shop cook for you that is nicer than Grandma's chicken because Grandma's chicken has vegetables on it. And Pops said that's ok which is good too.

And now I remember something else. I remember that I heard my Grandma talking quietly to Pops when I was sitting in the hallway playing with Buggly Bear because I had been sent to bed but Baby Joe was asleep and I felt lonely and a bit sad, but I knew I would be told off because it was very very dark and it was late and so Grandma and Pops didn't know that I was sitting by the door. And Grandma was talking quietly but not whispering because whispering is rude, and she was talking quietly and also not whispering too because Pops' ears don't work properly and I heard Grandma say that she wants me and my Mummy and my Baby Joe to live with her and that she will do anything to make it happen. And Pops didn't say anything and I think he was probably drinking his tea because then I heard my Grandma tell Pops off for spilling a bit. But I think it's ok to spill a bit because Pops uses a thing called a saucer which is made for catching spilling bits. Grandma uses a swirly pink cup with orange flowers on it. And I look again out of that window and that *is* my Mummy and Daddy's car so I am running down the stairs and I am opening the door and they are outside and they are smiling and I am so happy but my stomach hurts a bit like it does when I get worried. And Daddy gets out of the driving bit and my Mummy gets out of the other bit and they are both smiling. And I know that when they looked this happy and smiling together the last time, that was when we played games the other day when we went to see the moonlight and the time before that, that was when Baby Joe was in my Mummy's tummy. And it's daytime so they haven't been seeing the moon and yes, I love my Baby Joe, but he is very very noisy and I don't think he is big enough yet to look after a baby brother or sister. And I am running to my Mummy because sometimes I run to Daddy but he doesn't always see me or he looks at something else and so I am running to my Mummy but Daddy has his arms open and he is smiling at me and my teeth go soft and I run to Daddy because I love Daddy. My Daddy.

EIGHTEEN

Paul Bennett

Sorry...
It doesn't mean
how I feel
It hangs so daintily,
on a thought;
on the pain
of fragmentation

Square one.
Here I am?
I have sporadically wanted to return to square one for quite some time, but have instead been focussing on drinking my life away, wishing my life away, and praying that I could be transported somewhere, anywhere, but here. I am still drinking. Not today though. I drink for two days, then I stop for two days. Then I drink for three days and I stop for one day. Then I drink, then I stop, then

I smile, then I shout. It is a never-ending cycle, I can't break it. I try. I try so hard, but it sweeps me up and whizzes me round...dizzy...dizzy. Then I open my eyes and I can see it again...clarity...square one.

It all makes sense on square one, you see. On square one, my life is as it was eight years ago, when I was happily employed, happily married and happily teetotal. Fast forward a little, and grab my children for me, will you? Then bring them back to square one, because square one is the place in which we are happiest. I do not strive to achieve anything else in life, other than to return to square one, and therein remain rooted to the spot. If I am pushed, I will stumble, but I will not step forwards. If I am tempted, I will look, but I will not reach. If allowed to return to square one, I promise I will be grateful, I promise I will not taint the square with the grudges and the pain and the memories of the present. I promise I will do my best to live my life in absolute purity, and cast nothing but love upon those around me.

We are projecting
Futile imagery
See nothing,
yet it's there
Abduct your life
the best of you
you gave to me

Unshared

I can't promise the things I tell myself I should promise; the things I want to promise. I can't promise them because no matter how fucking hard I try, I always succumb. I am weak, I am spineless.

I am shaking with withdrawal and I know that under the bed, nestled between bed sheets and towels, is a bottle of brandy. I could take a swig. Just for medicinal purposes, mind. It takes the edge off, doesn't it? I feel like I am dying, I have felt like this since yesterday. The day before yesterday, I had a drink. The day before that, I didn't. Whirling round the wheel of misfortune. The day before that, we returned home from Lands' End, a day early, because to all intents and purposes, we were perfect again. We could not wait to get back to our children and show them how happy we were that we had fixed our marriage. But, three days on and I have barely spoken to my wife, or my children. I either feel ill or angry; there is little scope for balance when you are living life perched upon a precipice. I have broken the vow I made: the vow to be the Perfect Husband. The Perfect Husband let down by his weaknesses, his drink, and the monster that lives inside him, the monster that punishes him when he does not feed it the poison it requires to survive. The Perfect Husband whose wife has taken to sleeping in the children's bedroom, because she cannot sleep next to a man who either shakes, sweats, tosses and turns all night, or who stumbles into the bedroom late at night, waking his wife with the squeaking door, the creaking floor, the noisy, interrupted sleep of a man with a lot to hide.

The Perfect Husband who refuses to see a doctor, because the doctor will tut disapprovingly at the failure to stay off the booze, despite all the stark warnings given last time.

The Perfect Husband, who despite knowing what will happen next, is reaching between the towels and the bed sheets with every intention of finishing the secret bottle of brandy; he simply cannot take the pain anymore.

Reflecting...
Dusty mirrors,
Oh, the pain
will disappear,
you will know
I feel and say
What right now,
you cannot hear.

Sorry.

Eloise Katherine Bennett
June 2001

Do you remember the song I had going round and round in my head a while ago? It was comforting at the time, something to listen to when I became scared of the sound of my own thoughts. Now it is a broken record, symbolising the return of my marriage to square one. Paul sometimes mumbles about square one, as if it is a positive place to be. I need to move on, move forwards, evolve us into the couple I have always strived for us to be.

Forced evolution.
Forced happiness.
Modified marital bliss.

Each time I take a step forward, towards our future, Paul drags me back to where he prefers me to be. He is drinking again, sometimes just in the evenings, but I am sure that
some days the approved time has arrived a little earlier: teatime, lunchtime, breakfast-time. Just as before. Like a broken record.

Drink
Drink
Drink.

The violence? Of course. It goes hand in hand in hand with Paul, doesn't it? Sometimes, he waits until after nine o'clock, like an unspoken watershed. I can see the anger building, but now Paul is trying so hard, he holds it all in through his gritted teeth, until the children are in bed. However, I know Jessica hears everything, because I hear her crying, but I have no energy left to do any-thing other than hug her tiny, scared body and whisper promises that I can never keep. Promises that we will be safe. Promises that I will make it all better. And I try, oh, how I try. I remember the day we returned from Land's End, I remember how Jessica ran so lovingly into Paul's open arms, after faltering for a split second. And my eyes filled with tears, because that was it: The Moment. With my mother standing at the door with Joseph in her arms, that was The Moment. That moment was my family. My stomach flips with excitement when I occasionally remember that one day it might be ok, if I just keep trying, keep marching, keep ignoring, keep loving. It will all be ok, it will. I just need some support, some help. Somebody, anybody, please, please, help me.

Paul Bennett

Shouting is ok, isn't it? I mean, if I have to do *something*, then shouting is better than hitting. There is a fine line though, just as they say that cannabis leads to heroin, and killing flies leads to murder. Shouting leads to hitting. Hitting leads to crying. Crying leads to shouting. A vicious circle, I think they call it. If I am walking, sprinting, run-ning around in circles, how am I ever meant to reach square one? I am not a bad man—I am ill, I need help. I am misunderstood.

Yes, I have been drinking. Not always all day though; I'm nowhere near as bad as I was. I am on the 'hard stuff' now, it's easier to manage, none of this lager shit for me anymore, no. Breakfast for breakfast, lunch for lunch, dinner for dinner, vodka for supper. Interchangeable. Vodka for breakfast, lunch for lunch, vodka for dinner, supper for supper. Vodka for breakfast, vodka for lunch, vodka for dinner, forget fucking supper.

It could be worse.
It could be better.

Where do I go from here? I cannot return to the shaking, sweating and cramping. I cannot go to the doctors; he cannot help me. I tried. He did a sympathetic head-tilt and presented me with a prescription for medication. The tablets ran out months ago, and they do not touch the craving inside; the desperate longing for that warm, peaceful feeling induced by a glass of my finest.

I do not know what to do.
My name is Paul, and I am an alcoholic.

I do not know what to do.

My name is Paul, I can be the man who changed.

I do not know what to do.

Somebody, anybody, please, please, help me.

Jessica Louise Bennett

Everything was happy after my Mummy and Daddy came back from the end of the land. Everything was happy but I didn't see Daddy much because Daddy spent a lot of time in bed and my Mummy said he felt poorly and it was best not to go to the bedroom and the time I did, Daddy shouted at me quite loudly which made me jump because I thought that he would be pleased to see me and I had drawn him a picture with the pencil that my Mummy and Daddy bought me from the shop round the corner because they had forgotten the promise they made about the pencil from the end of the land. The picture I drew was the picture of the day that me, my Mummy, Baby Joe and Daddy all went for a walk and saw the sea and saw the moon and saw the pebbles and stood on the pavement. And it's quite difficult to draw the sparkles that the moon made on the sea but I was going to tell Daddy what the spots on the sea that I drew meant. And in the picture we were all holding hands except for Baby Joe because Baby Joe was in his pushchair, remember? And then so I went into Daddy and my Mummy's room and it smelt a little bit stinky and it was all dark because the curtains were drawn but I could see a bit and I could see that Daddy was asleep with his mouth open a bit and that funny snoring noise coming out of it. My Mummy told me that I snore too but that's because my tonsils are really big and maybe that's why Daddy snores. And I tiptoed quietly quietly to the bed and I was going to put the picture on the bed but I thought no because I wanted to see Daddy and I wanted Daddy to give me a cuddle and so I said 'Daddy?' quite quietly because it's nice to wake up to quiet voices and then Daddy made an even louder noise and opened his eyes a bit and he looked at me and he looked like he didn't know who I was and my stomach went funny and he did a frowning thing and then in the BIGGEST BOOMIEST VOICE EVER, Daddy shouted 'WHAT ARE YOU DOING IN HERE? GET OUT GET OUT GET OUT GET OUT,' and then my Mummy ran up the stairs and said sorry to Daddy even though it was my fault and my idea and my Mummy picked me up and brushed a bit of hair out of my eyes and said to me 'What were you doing, you silly girl?' and kissed me which I think made me feel a bit better about the boomiest voice thing which I did not like one bit, not at all.

When I hear things and see things that I don't like I have decided to not look at them or not hear them and then it is ok. I have learnt a new song that I sing that has happy words and I sing it a lot and I sing it loudly so that my Mummy and Daddy shouting and screaming and crying and being mean doesn't get into my brain. Clap your hands clap your hands clap your hands. And I sing it to Baby Joe too because Baby Joe is too little to sing and I don't want the bad sounds to get into his little brain too but I don't clap my hands because it makes a loud smack noise that might scare Baby Joe. I am his sister, I am his expert sister, and I will not scare him and I will look after him and I will stop him being sad and so I sit on my bed and I put my fingers in my ears and I sing as loudly as I can and I can't hear anything except the song in my head that I am singing and making a funny noise inside my ears and I close my eyes and I can't see anything and I need someone to help me because I don't have a big sister or a big brother to sing to me. And my Mummy is meant to help me because that is what Mummies do. Mummies are on the television sometimes and Mummies give money to their children and Mummies stop their children falling and Mummies stop bad men taking and hurting their children. But Daddy is a bad man and they don't tell you that on the news. They tell you that a bad man is in the park and on the road and outside the school and he will give you sweets and take you to his car. They don't say that the bad man is your Daddy and that you will love him and he will make promises and say that he will take you places and then just shout at you instead. And my Mummy promises me that she will help me and she will keep us safe and everything will be ok, but it isn't, it isn't, and she isn't helping and I need somebody, anybody, please please help me.

NINETEEN

Eloise Bennett
22nd July 2001
0100 hours

I am sitting on my threadbare sofa, looking out of the window. The window needs a clean, I notice—there are water marks on the inside, from the time the shower leaked through the ceiling. I look up at the ceiling, it got away pretty lightly, but there is a small damp patch and the lining paper is hanging down. I expect Paul will get round to fixing it, sometime, perhaps. It is raining heavily, and the trees outside are clearly lit by the eerie lights of the lampposts, the rain turning the lights into showerheads. Oh, how I would love to be standing underneath, feeling the refreshing liquid washing away the stifling hate around me. I can hear the droplets hitting the roof tiles, and the distant sound of clattering thunder. One ear is tuned into the rhythmic pattering above me, and the other is tuned to pick up snippets of Paul's rant. Today, I think it is something to do with me not paying the gas bill. I am unsure how Paul expects me to pay the bills, when he takes money out of my purse for alcohol every day, but I dare not ask. Quite frankly, I cannot be bothered. I do like to pick my battles, you see. Call me a drama queen, but I am certain I have bigger things to worry about. I sigh, and then retune the ear that was listening to Paul to make sure the children are asleep. I cannot hear any sobbing or screaming, so I assume they are sleeping soundly. I am long past asking Paul to be quiet for the sake of the children, because I am not allowed to accuse him of being a bad father. Yesterday morning was a different story; yesterday morning Paul was sober, so we had sex, had a cup of coffee, and then watched a film together. I accept that Paul is actually chronically ill, he has good days and bad days. Peaks and troughs. Recoveries and relapses. I would not leave a man to fend for himself with a physical illness, so I am not giving up on Paul just yet, although I am dangerously close to doing so.

I yawn, as it is at least four hours past my usual bedtime.

'I'm sorry. Am I boring you?'

I retune my ear yet again, cursing myself for my idiocy at taking my mind off the ball.

'No darling, I'm just really tired.'

This is actually one of our more pleasant arguments; Paul is not in the least bit threatening, yet. The children have not woken up. I will be a little tired in the morning, but that is better than waking up with a black eye, or split lip. I laugh at the strangeness of the situation, then immediately wish I hadn't. Paul is heading towards me, face like thunder, one arm raised...

Paul Bennett

...I lower my arm, because it is not right. It is not right to hit your wife, is it? Despite the things I have done in the past, I know it is not right.

The past? Yesterday? Last week? When does the past become the past? The second it has gone?

What I actually really want to do is tell her to stop being such a fucking whinging, whining, moaning nag.

Amelia isn't a nag.
I will text Amelia, she will want me.

Why did I choose Eloise, the selfish bitch?
I want control. I want Eloise to stay up all night begging me to love her, not sit there fucking yawning and laughing at me. In exasperation, I throw my can of beer at her. In slow motion, it flies through the air, amber fluid fizzing out in front of the flying can, like a rocket in reverse.

Eloise looks at the can flying towards her, then ducks at the last second. It whizzes over her head and hits the window, showering the curtains in beer. Eloise mutters something under her breath, then heads as if to go past me

'Where you going?'

'To get something to clean up that mess, Paul. You go to bed. Please.'

She is not scared of me. I can feel it. She is not scared of me anymore.

I grab hold of Eloise's wrist to stop her leaving the room. She expertly twists it around, forcing me to let go. I feel a sudden pang of shame.

'When did I become this person, Eloise?'

'What?'

'This person who bores you. This person who makes your life a misery? Make him go away.'

Eloise stands still for a second, and then rises on tiptoes to kiss me on the lips.

'Let him go, Paul. Let that person go. We can be happy, remember?'

I pull Eloise down on to the sofa with me, and kiss her hard on the lips.

Lightning strikes, illuminating the room, Eloise's face briefly lit by the eerie flash of light.

Eloise pulls away from me, stands and walks towards the door.

'Not now, Paul. I need to clean up that mess.'

She is rejecting you, Paul. What are you going to do?

I let Eloise walk away from me, trying to ignore the anger rising from the pit of my stomach.

What are you going to do?

Thunder

Do not let her reject you.

Lightning

What are you going to do?

Thunder
Lightning
Thunder lightning thunder lightning.
'BE QUIET.' I roar.
I hear Eloise clattering around in the kitchen, and then tiny, soft footsteps on the stairs. I rub my face in exasperation, trying to become the person I should be, for the sake of my daughter.
'Daddy?'
Jessica is standing in the doorway, her sleepy eyes half closed, and one hand clutching her favourite toy...

Jessica Louise Bennett

...Buggly Bear. Buggly Bear looks after me so when I heard Daddy shout and I heard the storm and I heard the thunder and I saw the lightning then I thought that I should take Buggly Bear with me in case I need to be protected to be safe. Daddy looked a big bit angry when I went into the room to speak to him and to ask him to stop shouting but he looked a different angry to the angry he looked the other day. Daddy looked tired angry and there was a smell of funny drinks and I just really wanted to hug Daddy and so I walked towards Daddy and I put my arms out to him to get a hug and Daddy picked me up and I thought he was going to hug me but he held me too tightly which hurt my tummy a bit and he walked with me up the stairs which was quite fun, up the stairs past the stair I broke my arm on and up to the bathroom and past the bathroom and to my bedroom and smacked my bottom and dropped me on my bed which scared me and then he put his finger up to his lips like it was a secret and now I don't know if I like Daddy anymore because my tummy AND my bottom hurt and also when Daddy dropped me I put my bad arm out and now my bad arm hurts...

Eloise Katherine Bennett

...It hurts like mad where he had grabbed me around the wrist. The bastard. I don't really care that the curtain has beer on it, I just wanted to get out of the room, because the look in his eyes reminded me of that night. *That night.* But, before that, he softened, I saw the other Paul again, the one I have been waiting for all this time. The Paul who loves me, the Paul who would never hurt me, the Paul who is trapped inside the horrible monster I see every evening. Now I know he is definitely there, struggling to break through the barriers of hate, now I know that for sure, now I know I can fix him. I run up the stairs and along the hallway to Jessica's room to comfort her. I can hear her sobbing, but I know that Paul will get angry when he realises...

Paul Bennett
0200

...She is comforting Jessica. I can hear Jessica whining, and Eloise's soft voice comforting her. She has been in there for half an hour, whilst I am out here, alone, unable to unravel this mess Eloise has tangled us in. I feel pushed out and unwanted; my children have suddenly become more important than the man who made them. Without me, they wouldn't even exist. I stagger into the kitchen and slam the door; I cannot stand to hear another second of that shit. Where's my fucking beer? My mobile bleeps inside my trouser pocket, and I wonder who the fuck is texting me at this stupid time in the morning.

Amelia

Beautiful, wonderful Amelia.

Amelia who I have cruelly ignored since my weekend in Land's End.

When I have sorted out the mess Eloise has got us into, I may well leave to live the life I deserve with Amelia.

Where are you? I haven't heard from you for ages.

That's another thing Eloise has cocked up; she made me choose her, when I could have had the best of both worlds. Then, she starts this stupid argument by not paying the gas bill and getting us cut off. I'm only angry because I CARE.

Sorry baby. Things happened at home. I think this is it. I think I can leave soon XXX

I think it is time Eloise knew how lucky she is to have me. I put my mobile on the worktop, leaving it unlocked, because then she might look through it, saving me the bother of telling her. The amazing thing is that I believe I can escape without leaving too much mess behind. Jessica clearly hates me, and Joseph is too young to ever remember me. She can find them a new Daddy, another mug. I bet Jessica is telling Eloise lies right now. I bet Jessica hates me. I'm better off without them, they are better off without me. I bet that's what Jessica is thinking. I'll bet Jessica is saying that...

Eloise Katherine Bennett

...Paul hurt her. Why would she lie? I can't understand. He loves her, Paul loves her. This moves the goalposts completely; if it is true, we will have to leave. Maybe it isn't true. Children exaggerate, children lie, it's what they do. I hold Jessica close, whispering softly into her ear, praying that she is lying. I feel like I am in the middle of a horror movie, I feel like at some point things are going to go terribly, terribly wrong, and I will forever pay the price.

Leave then, why don't I leave?

Leaving. Loving. Living. Dying.

I can't leave.

Why am I staying?

I'm staying because I can fix him. Dammit, I can fix him. I have glued him together so many times that he is no longer the person he was. I have created a monster.

I love that monster.

That monster will kill me.

I will not let him. I will change him; I will change everything. I will make us the family I desire, the family I need, the family I crave.

Jessica is finally dropping off to sleep, so I gently place her back on her bed, and tuck her in. I drop a kiss onto her forehead, and tell her I love her. I can hear Paul banging around downstairs, probably looking for the beer I have emptied down the sink. I am beginning to regret that rash decision already, as I try to anticipate the outcome. What is the worst that he can do? I want to go to sleep, but I am so tired that I just know I can't…

Sandra Alice Harrington

...Sleep. I need sleep. I have a funny feeling tonight, you know when you can feel in your bones that something is not quite right? I quietly get out of bed, trying not to wake George, and then creep silently into the hallway, turning the light on as I walk, blinking against its sudden, almost blinding, brightness. Looking out of the window in the hallway, all appears to be in order. Yet, I can't quite shake the feeling that it's not. I walk down the stairs, which look bizarrely alien, as if I am viewing them for the first time. A nice cup of tea, that's what I need.

Whilst I wait for the kettle to boil, I try to think outside my own head, as if a different perspective will enlighten me. I pour my tea and take it outside to the garden, so that I can have a cigarette. The rain is pelting intensely, like a monsoon, and lightning is highlighting the navy sky. I lean backwards against the wall, sheltering my freshly blow-dried hair under the overhang of the back door.

'Should have given you up years ago,' I say to my only vice.

I take a deep drag, listening to the cigarette crackle against the background of darkness. I pause as the smoke hits the back of my throat, suddenly realising the only thing that could possibly be wrong on this eerie night.

Eloise.

I have a sudden, intense feeling that Eloise needs me, but I can't quite focus. I clamp my cigarette between my lips, and run back into the kitchen, where my mobile phone is laying on the table.

Nothing.

No messages.

I consider this for a moment, and then send her a text.

Eloise. Please, please call me. I need to know that you're ok. Mum.

I love that girl.

If only I could tell her.

Eloise Katherine Bennett
0300

VOLCANO noun, *plural* –noes, -nos.
A gap in the earth's crust, through which lava, anger, steam, emotion, are expelled, either constantly, or sporadically.

I am standing in the street outside our home, feeling the refreshing rain cascade over my tense body. I have always loved summer rain, nothing can beat the smell of it soaking into fresh grass cuttings, and the nights are still and warm. Tonight, however, it feels different. Warm: too warm, oppressive, stifling, unfinished. There is something else out there waiting to force itself upon me, waiting to make the night one that I will never forget. Perhaps there is a psychopath lurking around the corner, waiting to pounce on the woman crazy enough to be outside, alone, in the pouring rain at three am. Or, perhaps I am being overdramatic, and it is a night like any other, a night where a husband and wife have a stupid argument. A night where a daughter tells a lie and a baby son sleeps through a storm. A boring night in a warped suburbia. The air is still thick with thunderstorm, so I stand still waiting for the inevitable lightning. Even better would be if I managed to get a picture of it to show Jessica in the morning. I reach into my trouser pocket for my phone, to take a snapshot of this beautifully ugly night. A message is on the screen from my mother, asking me to call her. It strikes me as a little odd, as it was sent at two o'clock, far too late for her to be awake. I consider replying, but assume she is now safely tucked up in bed. I hold my phone to the sky, waiting for the lightning. When it comes, it is magnificent. It forks through the still night sky, lighting up the trees and houses and cutting through the rain. As quickly as it arrived, it disappears, melting back into the navy night sky, as if it had never existed. I step into the road, and lift my head up towards the fresh raindrops, feeling them mingle with my salty tears. Innocence tinged with hate.

As the thunder claps, I hear another noise. A scream. I look up to the window of the children's bedroom, and see that the light is on. Part of me does not want to go inside to see what is happening. That part of me, that selfish part of me, wants to stay outside, being soaked by anonymous, innocent rain. The rain that has no secrets, no fears, no hate, unlike the tears of my children...

<u>Paul Bennett</u>

...Jessica and Joseph are getting on my nerves now. *She* will not stay in bed, *he* has woken up crying, and Eloise is nowhere to be fucking seen. I need another drink, but *she* has poured away my beer.

Pour me a drink

I am tired now, but I can't stop this bloody baby crying. I am holding him, rocking him, and doing all those things that *she* does, but *he* won't go to sleep.

'FOR FUCK'S SAKE, JOSEPH.'
Versez-moi une boisson

Now Jessica is crying.

Pour me a drink

Viértame una bebida

I am at the end of my tether

Pour me a drink

Giet me een drank

I feel anger rising in me.

I am going to snap.
I do not want to do this anymore.

I am snapping.

My head is going to explode.

I snap.

I put Joseph back in his cot.
I pick up Jessica, and drag her screaming downstairs.
'GET IN THE CUPBOARD.'
'NO DADDY. PLEASE DADDY. NO DADDY PLEASE NO NO NO MUMMY DADDY NO PLEASE.'
'Get IN. Come out when you can behave.'

Pour me a drink

Close the door.

Pour me a drink

Versez-moi une boisson
Turn the light down low.

Pour me a drink

Viértame una bebida

Hear the crying quieten.

Pour me a drink

Giet me een drank
Breathe. Relax.

The international demand of the damned…

Natural diamonds are formed inside some dying volcanoes. The beauty thrives, long after the volcano's death.

<u>Jessica Louise Bennett</u>

I am so scared I am so so scared. I tried to be quiet but there was a storm and some thunder and some lightning and it went on for ages and ages and then the thing happened when Daddy picked me and threw me and the lightning carried on and my Mummy, she made me feel better and so I pretended to be asleep. Then the lightning happened again and Baby Joe woke up and I went over to him really really quietly to tell Baby Joe that it will be ok and to tell him to be quieter because if he wasn't quieter then Daddy might get cross because I know that today Daddy doesn't like any noise at all because I think that's why he hurt me the first time.

And now I am in the cupboard and I have been in here once before but only because I was hiding from my Mummy and I could hear her laughing and I was hiding for fun because it was my turn to hide because my Mummy hid behind the door which was a silly place to hide because I couldn't open the door properly so I knew she was there. But I have been in the cupboard for a long long time and I have counted more than twenty buttons and it is quite small in here even though it is a big cupboard but there are shelves and the shelves have tins of food on them and there are also bottles of things that my Mummy uses to clean stuff and I am not allowed to touch them but they make the cupboard smell funny and I am just waiting. I am waiting for my Mummy to come and get me but I am so scared and I don't know if my Mummy will know I am here. And I don't want to shout because Daddy made me go in the cupboard for being noisy and so if I am noisy again I might have to be in here for longer. And I am so scared right now and Daddy turned the light off in the kitchen I think but I am not sure because the cupboard has a big door and so I might not see any light anyway even if the light was on and not even a little bit of light is in this cupboard and there are probably spiders and I am so scared. I am trying to push the door but it won't move and I know it has a lifty lock on the other side of the door because I like to lift it up and down and up and down because it makes a squeaky noise and I have only just got big enough to reach it since I grew up a bit taller. And when I went to whisper to Baby Joe to be quiet, that was when Daddy came into the bedroom and he switched the light on and I know that won't make Baby Joe be quiet, that will make Baby Joe be noisy because Baby Joe doesn't like bright lights when he is meant to be sleeping, but I didn't tell Daddy because I knew I had to be quiet but Daddy looked so angry and I was so frightened that I had an accident and I don't like having accidents because only babies wear nappies and so I cried a little bit, but only quietly I promise. And then Daddy was rocking Baby Joe really hard which won't make him sleep either because you have to rock Baby Joe softly and sing a song to him and I couldn't tell Daddy that either. Then Daddy looked at me really crossly and told me to stop crying and I tried, I promise I tried, and then Daddy put Baby Joe in his cot not very nicely, and then Daddy shouted at me and then Daddy made me go in here and I am scared, I am so so scared…

Eloise Katherine Bennett

…I am scared of what he has done. The noise inside the house is a direct contrast to the tranquillity I discovered in the street. This has been waiting for me; this is where the oppression was borne. I step outside the front door again, to absorb one last breath of warm, quiet air, then, with the calm of the night flowing through my veins, I step back inside the house; back inside the nightmare. I can hear Joseph crying, but I cannot hear Paul, and I cannot hear Jessica. I resist the urge to call out to them, as, after all, it is just another ordinary night. I feel my phone vibrate in my pocket.

Eloise. Please, please call me. I need to know that you're ok. Mum.

I wonder whether this feeling I have, this ominous feeling, is being felt by everyone, far and wide. Carried in the thunderstorm, transported in the heavy, dark clouds.

It is just another ordinary night.

I walk carefully through the dark hallway.

The beast may be sleeping.

I can hear three separate sounds, melting together in a rhythmic arrangement.

Joseph screaming.

A scratching noise.

A sobbing.

I realise each noise needs to be investigated separately, in order of priority, like casualties at a critical incident of mass destruction.

Screaming

Sobbing

Scratching

I head towards the kitchen, then change my mind and walk back towards the stairs. I must go upstairs to remove the screaming from the arrangement. It suddenly stops, and lessens to a whimper. He must have screamed himself to sleep.

Sobbing

Scratching

Whimpering

I head back towards the kitchen, walking past the larder cupboard in the corner, to see Paul crouched down opposite it. His head is in his hands, his face crumpled like a two-year-old who has lost their favourite toy.

Sobbing

'No no no no no no. Stop it stop it stop it.'

It is just another ordinary night.

I kneel next to Paul, as he is next on my list of priorities.

What is the scratching?

'I know it can get too much, Paul. He just wants a cuddle, that's all. Just a hug.'

Paul is rocking. Backwards and forwards, backwards and forwards.

'Paul. It's ok. It'll all be ok.'

The scratching has stopped.

I realise that perhaps Paul is upset that Jessica lied.

It is just another ordinary night.

Just another lying child.

'I know she was fibbing, Paul. I know that you would never hurt her. I know that you love her, that you love Joe, that you love me. It is just another ordinary night, Paul. Let's just go to sleep.'

Scratching

'What is that scratching, Paul? Where is it coming from?'

Scratch. Scratch. Scratch.

Paul tries to speak, but no words come out. I hear the scratching again. The cupboard. It is coming from the cupboard. A rat? A mouse?

'Paul. It's coming from the cupboard. What is it?'
Instantly I plunge back into the horror movie, the calmness I felt only moments ago replaced by intense fear. I rise to my feet, but Paul grabs at my ankle.
'No!'

It is just another ordinary night.
'Oh, don't be silly, Paul. It's probably just a trapped bird or something.'

Bird. Cupboard. How would a bird get in a cupboard? How? What is it?
Just. Another. Ordinary. Night.

'No!'
'Let go.'
'No!'
I wrestle my ankle free.
I lift the latch.
The scratching stops.
A rat?
A mouse?
A bird?
Not a rat.
Not a mouse.
Not a bird.
A child.
My child.
My sobbing, broken, tear-stained, frightened, shaking, abused, Jessica.
That is what it is.
This is not just another ordinary night.
This is not ordinary…

Jessica Louise Bennett

…This is horrible horrible horrible. It is still horrible horrible horrible even though I'm not in the cupboard anymore and it still makes me scared even when I just think about it. I thought about lots of things while I was sitting in the cupboard. I thought about pretending to pretend it was a game and I thought that if I pretend that I was hiding then it would be easier and I wouldn't be scared and then I would stop crying. And then that worked for a little while and then I thought that I would play a closing my eyes game and I would pretend to go to sleep and then maybe the pretending would stop and I would really go to sleep, and so I tried that and that didn't work because even though I pretended not to be scared I was still scared a bit. Tears came out of my eyes lots and I could still hear Baby Joe crying and I really wanted to go and see Baby Joe and I really wanted to hug Baby Joe because I am an expert big sister and I can make Baby Joe feel lots better and he would make me feel better too because I love him and he snuggles and makes my heart go thumpy in a good way.

And I thought that because it had been a scary horrible night that it would be ok to put Baby Joe in my bed and cuddle him so that we could fall asleep together. And I thought that I could have Buggly Bear one side and Baby Joe the other side and I would have a person that I love a lot on one side and a bear that I love a lot on the other side and then I would really stop crying lots. And then I got sad because when Daddy held my arm to put me in the cupboard Daddy didn't pick Buggly Bear up to put Buggly Bear in the cupboard with me even though Daddy knows that Buggly Bear goes everywhere with me except school because he's not allowed because he might get taken.

When I go to school every day except at the

KARINA EVANS

weekend I put Buggly Bear on the windowsill in the room with the sofa and the television, which is called the lounge and the sitting room and Buggly Bear looks out of the window and makes sure no strangers come near my house and he looks for me all day and waits for me all day to come back from school. And I don't have to put Buggly Bear on the windowsill tomorrow because it is Sunday and I don't go to school on Sunday because everyone needs a rest because it is the weekend. My Mummy said that some people in another country go to school on a Saturday and I wouldn't like that very much because sometimes I like to go out with my Mummy and Daddy on a Saturday and if we go to the Caterpillar ride we go on a Saturday and I wouldn't want my Mummy and Daddy and Baby Joe to go without me and that is for two reasons. The first reason is that it would make me very sad that I had to do reading and writing at school when my Mummy and Daddy and Baby Joe were outside having fun and the second reason is that my Mummy and Daddy and Baby Joe would be sad if I wasn't there to have fun with them. And I know that they will be sad if I wasn't there because I know that that time I went from Grandma's house when I wasn't allowed, when my Mummy found me my Mummy told me that it wasn't any fun when I wasn't there and that I must never not be there again. And then in the cupboard I thought that maybe

Daddy doesn't want to have fun with me anymore because maybe Daddy has stopped liking me and that made me frown because it made me think and then I wasn't sure if it was true or lies in my head.

And then I cried quietly because I know that Daddy loves me when he hasn't had funny drinks and I don't understand why adults have to drink those funny drinks because they make them act all differently. My Mummy had some of those funny drinks once and it was a day that Daddy didn't have funny drinks too and Daddy was laughing at my Mummy because I heard them and then I went to sit on my favourite stair which is where I can see up and down, I saw my Mummy walk out of the lounge all funny like she had been turning around and around in circles and looking at the ceiling and had got all dizzy, and then my Mummy tripped and Daddy was behind her and Daddy caught her which is good because then my Mummy didn't hurt herself, and my Mummy and Daddy were not angry that I wasn't sleeping in my bed and that I was on my favourite stair because my Mummy said hello to me in a funny voice and laughed and Daddy said that he would have to carry us both back to bed because we were both tired.

And I tried to think of other things that I could do in the cupboard to make it fun and I thought that it might be fun to make raindrop noises because it was raining outside and then it would be like it was raining inside too and it wouldn't be noisy because the raindrops outside were making a noise anyway and so Daddy wouldn't get cross again. So I tap tap tapped my little fingers on the wall and then I remembered that it rained a lot tonight in straight lines so I made straight lines down the back of the door with my nails which needed cutting but my Mummy forgot to cut them and I think she will cut them tomorrow. And I made lines over and over again and thought it was a very good game and then I stopped to listen because I heard my Mummy's voice and then I started again and then I stopped again because my Mummy asked Daddy what the noise was and then I thought it must be noisy because my Mummy had heard it. And then I thought that I would carry on making a noise because I had been in the cupboard for a long time and if Daddy gets angry and hurts me it is ok because it is better than being in a cupboard. And then the door opened and I saw my Mummy's face and my Mummy looked so upset to see me and my Mummy held her arms out and I held my arms out and even my bad arm worked again and my Mummy stopped the horrible game that Daddy made me play.

Eloise Bennett
0400

Help me please Mum. I don't know what to do.

I hit send, and, holding Jessica tightly against me, I wait for a reply, something to tell me we will be ok, we will be saved. Jessica is shivering with fear. My daughter, who does not lie, scared half to death by her sadistic father. I want to run, but I have done that before; I know it does not work. I want to protect us, I want to lock us all in a cupboard, as the bastard did to his daughter; a cupboard where he cannot reach us, he cannot hurt us. I close the children's bedroom door, and flip my phone on to silent, because I cannot let Paul know that I have broken out of the bubble he has trapped us in; broken free and begged to be rescued. Joseph is finally asleep, his little chest quivering with each inhalation. I bend down to kiss his tiny face, and I can taste his salty tears upon my lips. My children, my angels. They could have been so happy if I hadn't been so weak.

I'm coming over

I don't know what I want my Mum to do. All I know is that she is a mother, she is *my* mother, and she is meant to make everything ok again. I am stuck, I am broken, and she is the only person who can free and fix me.

I am frustrated; I cannot live with Paul anymore, not after what he did to Jessica, yet I cannot go back to live with my mother. I will not let her take me home; I will not let anyone control me, ever, ever again.

Should I stay?

Look at Jessica, I cannot stay. I owe my children a life free from pain, free from fear.
Should I go?

Look at Jessica, I cannot leave. I owe my children a life with a father, a life with a Daddy.

I know what will happen; my mother will turn up, calling the shots, calling Paul all the names she has learnt watching late night television when she cannot sleep. She will not consider my feelings or the children's feelings, she will tell me to leave with her, she will not understand, she will force me to go; she will not give me a choice. I refuse to leave, I refuse to be controlled, I refuse to live with my mother, I refuse to stay here, I refuse to go to a refuge. I refuse all help, I refuse all advice, I refuse to be a fool.

I do not know where Paul is, for all I know he could still be perched on his heels in the kitchen, weeping in self-pity because he allowed his actions to be controlled by the monster inside him. Sometimes I want to kill him, but I refrain; I am a human and I possess self-control. It would be so easy for me to finish him, to grab that knife and stab him in his cold, evil heart. I wonder how much force has to be used to pierce the skin, the muscle, the beating heart. If I kill him today, I can stay here with my sobbing daughter and my sleeping son. I can stay in the house I have lived in and nurtured, I can keep my family together. I can claim diminished responsibility; I have seen it on the news.

He pushed me to it, your Honour. He raped me, he beat me, he scared me, he broke me.

Then, when they are old enough to understand, I will show them the newspaper cutting of my story. It will show them that I had no choice. And, they *will* understand, because Jessica will remember the fear she felt when he locked her away. She will thank me for taking away the bastard who hurt her and made her cry.

Or she will hate me for killing her Daddy, for the pain she felt when she saw her Daddy die in front of her sleepy eyes. Watching as her beloved father's blood dripped from the knife that her Mummy used to slaughter him.

I suspect there is another way. A more difficult way. Another avenue open to me, which will take inner strength to walk. I could stop being so weak and I could walk away from this situation forever.

I could build a new life somewhere else, without the intervention from my mother. Jessica and Joseph could still see their Daddy, could still love their Daddy, because Paul would make darned sure that when he had access he would be sober.

He is a good father.
He is a good man.
He deserves another chance.

I remember the fear I saw etched upon my daughter's face, as I opened the cupboard that her Daddy locked her inside. Shaking, crying, scared to talk.

'I'm sorry Daddy I'm sorry Daddy I tried to be quiet I tried I'm sorry.'

I am no better than Paul.

I saw you
need me with unending hope.
A new belonging, bonding souls.
Then I felt you
grasp a finger, wholly within a
tiny hand.
Your dreams inside my palm.

I have a monster too. The monster inside me is weakness, contrasting beautifully with Paul's anger. I cannot control it, so why should I expect or demand that he controls his anger? Maybe this is how we are meant to live—heads buried in the sands of our mistakes and ignorance, until something external drags them out of the comfort of their hiding place. Drags them out of the place we have come to know and accept, until we are forced to open our dry eyes, look around ourselves; a new perspective of the reality we are suffering. We spit the dry, gritty sand of acceptance and lies from our parched mouths, then we can move onwards, for it is only then that we see what everyone else can see. It is only then we see that the sand is uncomfortable and painful, we realise that the others we have forced to live this life with us are suffering too.

I told you
to cry, when others gifted a mask.
You listened, then wiped away
my tears.
I hurt you
with imperfection, standing higher than
you could reach.
Travel, with hope that my mistakes have
taught you all you need to learn.
Be strong, be fair, be you.
Now your dreams are yours.

We will walk from the desert, and quench the craving for fluid with water from the beautiful oasis we discover en route. Only then, as a family, forced from our hiding place, only then can we learn how to survive today, only then can we begin our journey...

<u>Sandra Alice Harrington</u>
0430

...Towards tomorrow. The only way to survive today is to concentrate on tomorrow. I wonder how this night will end, as I drive through the quiet, lonely streets towards Eloise's house. She needed me; I could feel it all night, like an irritating itch that will not go away however enthusiastically it is scratched.

Since I awoke, I could feel the night heavy with impending disaster, the menacing hold of destruction gripping around my heart. I am acting the role of a knight in shining armour; it invigorates me, it excites me, and for this, I feel guilt. I should not be excited by my daughter's pain, even though the excitement is attached to the crown of saviour I will achieve. I should be saving her because she is my daughter, because I love her, because I am a mother, and because altruism exists. If we push somebody out of the path of an oncoming vehicle, thus saving their life, then we feel good about that act, does that not make us selfish? Altruism can only exist if one achieves no satisfaction from an act that benefits another. If I feel no glory from my mission of mercy, then I will be truly altruistic. I cannot help but feel a little self-righteous, because although I think the world of her, I did tell her...

Paul Bennett
0440

...I told her that there was no need to involve her mother. There is never any need to involve her mother, but look who is driving up the road now. Hands clutching the steering wheel, in exactly the right position, as if she has only just passed her driving test.

Ten to two, Sandra. Ten to two.

Work the wheel, Sandra. Work the wheel.

I feel like clapping, as she manages to execute an almost flawless turn in the road. I swig from my bottle of brandy, whilst watching Sandra slowly pull up outside the house. Reverse, forward, slightly closer to the kerb, reverse, forward, too close to the kerb, reverse, forward, and stop. I am feeling slightly mischievous, despite having locked my daughter in a cupboard and made her cry, for reasons beyond me. Sandra is now fiddling about in her handbag, maybe calling for back-up. The thought tickles me, as I imagine Sandra's bingo-playing cronies all pulling up outside in a similarly composed manner.

Group.
Regroup.
Disband.

I do not know why I suddenly feel so unbelievably joyous, perhaps I have finally let the monster take over, finally let the monster *be* me, achieving freedom from the panic of having to suppress something that is so almighty.

Oh, almighty monster
Who controls my actions
Controls my mouth
Controls my feelings
Oh, almighty monster
You win
Take me
Eat me
Kill me
Control me
But save my soul.

I swig another mouthful of brandy, whilst watching Sandra carefully ensure all her car doors have locked, despite probably having only unlocked one of them. Then she checks them again. Thank God it's not a fucking emergency, eh? I forget to be angry that Eloise has called Sandra, but I suppose I will have to put up a bit of a fight for my family. It was just a game. Jessica didn't mind really. It was a punishment. The punishment fits the crime. Children need discipline. It was just a game. Don't take them away from me; it has all been a terrible misunderstanding. It was just a game. Just an argument. Nobody got hurt.

I briefly wonder what is wrong with me, as I touch my face to feel the tackiness of drying tears. Why was I crying? It all seems so far away, so yesterday. I feel detached from myself, every-thing that has happened before this moment, be-fore now, happened to somebody else. They're all laughing at me. I love them all. I love them all so much. Don't leave me.

The doorbell makes me jump.

I love you.
'Eloise.'
Who is at the door?

I recall that I know who is there, but nothing is real. I look out of the window, see Sandra's car, and then I remember again.

'Where is she?'

How should I know?

'She's coming with me.'
'Nope. She isn't.'

Sandra opens her bag and starts to pack random things inside it. A used bottle, a dummy, a teddy-bear.

Playing along, I reach across and take the items out, then throw them on the floor. This is fun.

Sandra gives up, and heads out to the hallway.

'Sandra, take your shoes off, you will ruin my stair carpet.'

Ignorance.

'ELOISE.'

'Grandma!'

Here we fucking go.

'Jess, go to bed.'
'Mum…'
'Come with me, Eloise. You can't stay here, have you seen the state of him?'

Ha. Go with her? That stupid old hag?
'Jess, darling, go to bed.'
'Come with me, Eloise.'

I love her. Don't forget.

'Eloise. Don't go. I love you. Yep, I love you.'
'Jessica. Go to bed. Go to sleep.'
'Eloise, come with me. I am your mother. Do as you are told.'

I don't understand.

'Stop trying to control me.'
'I know what is best for you, come with me. You asked me for help. What on earth has been going on, Eloise?'

What's happening? Why is she trying to make her leave me?

'Don't listen to her, Eloise. Listen to me. I love you.'
'You torture me.'

I love my family. Why would they want to leave me?

'Stay with me, Eloise. I love you, I love you all. I want to make it better.'
'How?'
'Eloise, don't be a silly girl. Come with me.'

I can be the man who changed.

'I can change.'
'I hate you. You BEAT me. You RAPED me. Joseph is here because you raped me, you bastard.'
'No, I didn't. It wasn't like that. Stay, stay with us, please.'
'I. HATE. YOU.'

Anger.
Rage.
The monster.

'YOU BITCH.'
'PAUL. NO, PAUL NO.'

Shit. What have I done?

'Jessica, go back to bed. I'm ok, I promise,'
'You're bleeding Mummy you're bleeding,'
'Come with me Eloise.'

Shut up.

'It's ok Mummy hugs are good and I'll make you better,'

'Go to bed, Jess. Please. Go to bed.'

For fuck's sake. Go to bed.

'Ok Mummy and I love you.'
'ELOISE. COME WITH ME IMMEDIATELY. THINK OF YOUR CHILDREN.'

My children.

'Mum, let go of me. LET. GO. OF. ME!'
'COME WITH ME.'
'YOU'RE HURTING ME.'
'Hurting you? Does this hurt? Huh? Does it hurt more when I hit you, or when he hits you?'

The monster is inside Sandra.
We all have a monster.
I love her.

'Jess, sweetie, thank you. Please darling, please go to bed. Everything will be ok. I promise.'
'Promise?'
'Eloise, don't go, please don't go. I love you.'
'Why do you want to stay with him? Why? He is a disgusting bully.'
'I love him. I can help him change, can't I Paul?'

She loves me.

'You can't stay *here*. In this disgusting house, with that disgusting man. LOOK AT HIM, ELOISE. JUST LOOK AT THE STATE OF HIM...he is disgusting.'

Her husband.

'I'd rather be beaten every day, for the rest of my fucking life, than bring my children up in a house with a cold-hearted bitch like you.'

Pull her. Pull her to you, Paul. Pull her closer. She will stay.

'YOU HORRIBLE, HORRIBLE, UNGRATEFUL WOMAN.'

Scream.

Bang.

Scream.

Bang.

Scream.
Bang.
Scream.
Bang.
'I love you, Paul. I love you…'

Eloise Bennett
0452

I feel a hand on my left wrist and a hand on my right shoulder. The hand on my shoulder suddenly jerks forwards as my mother's face looms towards me. I see venom in her eyes. My feet slip from the top stair. I try to regain my balance, but I cannot. I cannot reach around to steady myself.

I can see her. I can see Jessica. My baby, watching me fall. Falling, falling. It hurts. I feel my back snap against the wooden stair. I can see her eyes, Jessica's eyes, full of pain and fear. I can feel my head bounce off the banister. The banister that broke Jessica's arm. I can hear screaming. Crying. It hurts. I cannot breathe. No air. Pain.

'I love you, Paul. I love you…'

0456

Darkness.

0505

'Eloise, wake up. Eloise. Stay with us, Eloise.'
'Eloise I love you.'
'Does she have any medical issues?'
Jessica's voice.
'Mummy mummy mummy mummy.'
Paul's voice, strained and gritty.
'Shhh Jess. It'll be ok sweetie. Go to bed for me. Go to bed for Daddy.'
'Eloise. Come on. Eloise…'
Darkness…
Breathe.
Voices in the distance.
Paul's voice.

'What have I done? I didn't mean to hurt her, I really didn't mean to hurt her.'

Lifting...

Breathe

My Mum's voice.

'Look what you have done, Paul. Look what you have done. She's bleeding, she's really hurt. What have you done?'

Falling...

Breathe.

A stranger's voice.

'C'mon Eloise, you can do it. Stay with us.'

Lifting...

Breathe.

Noise...

Breathe.

Everyone's voices.

Jessica crying.

'Mummy mummy mummy.'

Paul's voice.

'It's ok baby, it's ok. I'm sorry. What have I done?'

A stranger's voice. A stranger helping me.

'We're doing everything we can…'

Too much noise…

Breathe.

Pain…
Breathe.

'We need to operate. She's bleeding from her brain.'

Too much pain…

Lights…

'Defib.'

Shock…

Breathe.

I can't do it. It hurts…

Voices…

Too many voices…

'I've got it.'
Breathe.

Lights…

'Shit. Faster.'

I'm tired.

Breathe.

Bright lights...

Sleep...

0655

Breathe.

Live

Jessica. Joseph. Paul. Mum.

Love

I'm here...

Life

So tired...

Leave

Darkness.

Peace.

Death...

<u>Sandra Alice Harrington</u>
0705

The doctor looks miserable as he walks towards the family room. I stare at him, hoping that with the power of my mind I can change what he was going to say. I suppose that it is difficult to find an appropriate facial expression to break the news of demise. I also suppose it is difficult to find the appropriate words. 'I'm afraid...' is a bizarre turn of phrase, I think. 'I'm afraid,' implies that he is scared. Or, that there's another option. 'I'm afraid that the wolf may eat me alive.'

Then again, the wolf might sniff at my feet, then

decide there's something tastier around the corner.

The fear would be wasted.

I know that within the next ten seconds my life could change forever. I look around and absorb some information from the life I know right now. I know that I can call a number if I wish to cut old people's toenails. This, of course, will be slotted between bereavement counselling and playing for the local over 50's band. Just as I am about to contemplate which instrument I would like to put my hand, or mouth, to, the door opens and the doctor, full of fear, steps gently inside.

He is a huge man; his feet are at least a size 14, and his big, hairy hands do not look nimble enough to carry out delicate procedures. He is afraid.

'Mrs Harrington...?' he begins, almost tentatively. The fear shows on his face. He is going to use that phrase, I think. He is going to be afraid.

'I'm afraid that your daughter sustained a very serious head injury. We did everything we could, but unfortunately, Eloise didn't make it...'

I wonder when it will hit me. This is the news I have been expecting ever since I felt something was wrong, ever since I saw my beautiful baby lying at the bottom of the stairs. Maybe it had hit me before it happened; when I felt the thunderbolt and awoke in a panic about nothing. This is it; the escape has become the end; the demise. Eloise's chestnut hair matted with blood. When did it start bleeding? I wonder. The top stair? I can hear screaming, but I am unsure whether I am screaming now, or hearing the scream from earlier, or hearing somebody else's screams. Whoever it was, whenever it was, it breaks my fragile heart some more. There is nothing like realising you are upset, to upset you some more.

Emotional bulimia.

'Mrs Harrington...'

The doctor lifts me from the floor where I have fallen, my lukewarm cup of hot chocolate staining the linen slacks I have seen fit to wear the day my only child is murdered.

'I'm...I'm...I'm...'

'It's OK, Mrs Harrington, I have you here. Is there anyone we can call?'

I consider this in my fuzzy brain. I cannot call George; he has already had one panicked call from me tonight, and one certainly cannot break news of death over the phone. Death has to be broken in person. You have to say that you are afraid.

I feel stupid sitting in the big room, I should go home. Another mother or father or daughter or son will need this room now, while somebody they love has their head cut open, their heart shocked, and their dignity removed. I am wasting a room, wasting this doctor's time. I need to sort this out. I need to speak to the police.

'I'm OK, doctor.' I reply

'I really just need to talk to the police.'

My daughter is dead, and I need the police.
I need to be afraid.

'I need to tell George...'

Many deaths caused by volcanic eruption are from unpredictable surges of hot rock, as it is difficult to ascertain when and where these will come from.

0800
Statement of Sandra Alice HARRINGTON.

This statement consisting of two pages each signed by me is true to the best of my knowledge and belief and I make it knowing that, if it is tendered in evidence, I shall be liable to prosecution if I have wilfully stated in it anything which I know to be false or do not believe to be true.

It was approximately 0430 hours on the 22nd July 2001. I had driven to the house shared by my daughter, Eloise BENNETT, her husband, Paul BENNETT, and their two children, Jessica BENNETT and Joseph BENNETT. I had visited the house because I had received a text from Eloise stating that she needed help. I know from past incidents that Paul has been physically violent towards Eloise, which, on one occasion culminated in rape and the birth of their second child. I felt fearful for the safety of Eloise and her two children, so I went to the house with the sole intention of bringing them home to live with my husband, George HARRINGTON and myself. When I arrived at the address, Paul was clearly intoxicated. He was swigging from a bottle of brandy and stumbling as he walked. Paul was aggressive in demeanour. Paul refused to tell me where Eloise was, so I went upstairs to find her. Upon reaching Eloise's bedroom, I noticed that Jessica was awake and Eloise was visibly upset, asking that Jessica go to bed. Jessica was also crying. Paul followed me up the stairs and began to shout at Eloise, I recall Paul shouting, 'I will change. I love you.' I took this to mean that Paul intended to stop being violent towards Eloise. Paul took hold of Eloise's left arm, and pulled her towards him. I took hold of Eloise's right shoulder to try to steady her. Paul released Eloise's arm, thus I released her shoulder. Eloise appeared to have her balance at this point, but she was positioned within two inches of the top stair; Paul was standing behind her and she could not move back-wards. Eloise shouted at Paul, telling him she hated him, and then Eloise slapped Paul's face. Paul hit Eloise, I believe with a closed fist, causing Eloise to hit her head on the wall. I grabbed Eloise's shoulder and reached across to attempt to push Paul away from Eloise, this is when I inadvertently caught Eloise's face with my hand, causing reddening. When Eloise regained her balance, Paul grabbed hold of her arm and then flung her forwards. Eloise lost her balance. This is when Eloise fell down the stairs. Eloise fell to the bottom of the stairs. I could see straight away that she was badly hurt, as she was struggling to stay awake. I called an ambulance from my mobile phone. Paul BENNETT was clearly distressed, and he was trying to calm their daughter, Jessica, who had come out from her bedroom. Paul then said to me 'it was an accident. Don't tell them anything.' I took this to mean that he wanted me to lie to the paramedics. The paramedics then arrived, and began to treat Eloise. As the paramedics were leaving with Eloise, Paul turned to me and said, 'I did not mean to hurt her,' or words to that effect. I took this to mean that Paul had deliberately pushed Eloise down the stairs. At this point, I got into the ambulance and travelled to the hospital with Eloise and the paramedics.

Signed

SANDRA ALICE HARRINGTON 22/07/2001

This statement was taken on 22/07/2001 by PC Dillon.

Statement of Daniel Saunders

This statement consisting of two pages each signed by me is true to the best of my knowledge and belief and I make it knowing that, if it is tendered in evidence, I shall be liable to prosecution if I have wilfully stated in it anything which I know to be false or do not believe to be true.

I am a paramedic, employed by the East Sussex division of the NHS Ambulance Service Trust. I was on duty on the twenty-first of July from 2300 hours and finished my duty at 0700 on the twenty-second of July. At approximately 0455 hours on the twenty-second of July, we received an emergency call to a residential area in town. The call was pertaining to an Eloise BENNETT who had fallen down the stairs. Upon arrival at the scene, we identified the caller as a Sandra HARRINGTON, mother of the patient. Also at the property were the patient's husband, Paul BENNETT, and I believe there were two small children in the house, although I observed only one. Mrs BENNETT was lying at the bottom of the stairs. She was bleeding from her left ear, and from a deep would to her right temple. Her left arm was bent underneath her, and I could see that her right ankle was broken. Mrs BENNETT was still breathing at this point, but her breathing was shallow and her pulse was critically low. My colleague Joy NICKOLLS, and myself, administered first aid at the scene, before preparing to take Mrs BENNETT to the local accident and emergency department. As my colleague and I were transferring Mrs BENNETT into the emergency vehicle, I heard an altercation between Mr BENNETT and Sandra HARRINGTON. Mr BENNETT was clearly intoxicated, he was swaying as he stood, and his speech was slurred. Mr BENNETT was shouting that he did not mean to hurt her. At the time I took this to be in reference to Sandra HARRINGTON, as I had observed a small scratch to her face. At this point, I turned around and saw Sandra HARRINGTON grab hold of Mr BENNETT's jumper and say, 'look what you have done, look what you have done.' I could not clearly hear the rest of the conversation. At this point, the police arrived, and we transported Mrs BENNETT to hospital, accompanied by Sandra HARRINGTON.

Signed
DANIEL SAUNDERS 22/07/2001
This statement was taken on 22/07/2001 by PC Dillon.

JULY 22ND 2001

Hastings Police Station

'Time of arrest?'

'Zero nine thirty hours.'

'Offence?'

'Murder.'

'Place of offence?'

'154 Wallgrave Street, Hastings.'

'Circumstances of arrest?'

'A female died at the location in the early hours of this morning. Detained person named as possible offender. Detained person located at home address and arrested for the purposes of securing and preserving evidence and to obtain evidence by questioning. Detained person was distressed and volatile, therefore handcuffed at time of arrest.'

Detained person presents tearful and struggling with officers.

'Paul, do you understand why you are here?'

'I killed her. I fucking killed her.'

'I suggest you don't talk about the offence right now, you will have your chance to talk about it during interview. Just calm down, Paul. I need to ask you some questions and book you into custody. Calm down.'

'FUCK OFF. I KILLED HER.'

'Paul, are you willing to sign this entry in my notebook to that effect?'

'What? Fuck off.'

'At zero nine fifty hours, in Hastings custody, you stated

'Fuck off. I killed her.' Are you happy to sign to that effect?'

'FUCK OFF.'

'Paul, I'll give you one last chance to do this the easy way. Stop struggling, calm down...'

'FUCK OFF. I KILLED HER. YOU WANKER.'

'Take him to the cell. Seize his clothes. Dry cell. Hand swabs.'

DS MANSFIELD

I am investigating an offence of murder.

This interview is being tape recorded and it may be given in evidence if your case is brought to trial.

It is eighteen hundred hours on the twenty-second of July two thousand and one.

We are in the interview room at Hastings police station.

I am Detective Sergeant Mansfield.

The other officer present is Detective Constable Pollard.

What is your full name?

Paul Bennett

What is your date of birth?

The fifteenth of August, nineteen-seventy-eight

Also present is:

Sophie Green, solicitor

Do you agree there is no one else present in the room?

Yes

At the end of the interview I will give you a notice that will explain the procedure for dealing with the tape and how you can have access to it.

You do not have to say anything. But it may harm your defence if you do not mention when questioned something which you later rely on in court. Anything you do say may be given in evidence.

Paul Bennett, do you agree that you were present at 154 Wallgrave Street, Hastings, East Sussex at approximately 0430 hours today, the twenty-second of July?

Yes. I was present

Paul, do you agree that you and your wife, Eloise Bennett, entered into a heated verbal exchange at the location?

Yes.

Tell us about that.

She...I...we...were arguing. Her mother wanted her to leave me, to take away everything I loved, my family, my Jess, my Joe...I couldn't let her do that. I had to stop her.

Who are Jess and Joe?

My...our children.

How did you propose to stop her leaving you?

I told her to stay. I told her I was sorry.

Sorry?

Sorry for everything. Sorry for being a failure. Sorry for hating her, hurting her.

Hurting her?

I...yes...on a few occasions. I...I...hurt her.

Can we take a moment please?

Interview suspended for further legal advice.

Eighteen thirteen hours. I have treated the prisoner in accordance with The Police and Criminal Evidence Act.

Interview recommenced. Eighteen fifteen hours.

No solicitor present.

I will tell you everything. I don't need a solicitor here. I will tell you everything.

Are you changing your mind regarding legal advice?

Yes.

It is your right to have independent legal advice free of charge. This is an ongoing right and you may change your mind at any time.

Ok.

Ok. So, Paul. You said you hurt Eloise. Can you tell us about that?

I have a problem with alcohol, it changes me. Eloise doesn't...didn't understand, nobody could understand. The cravings, the shakes, the need. She was no angel. She taunted me, she told me nobody would want me, she abused me.

How did Eloise abuse you, Paul?

Verbally. She told me I was a waster. Right in my face, she accused me of raping her, she accused me of being all those things I detest. An alcoholic, a wife-beater, a rapist. How could I just sit there, stand there and let her say those things?

When did she say these things?

Over and over again. Every week, every day,

every time I disappointed her.

And how did this make you feel?

Like a loser.

How did you react to this?

Once or twice I hit her. Look, I know I'm going to prison. Why all the questions? I am telling you the truth, stop trying to trip me up.

We are not here to trip you up, Paul. We are here to establish the truth.

I slapped her.

When?

I don't know. A few weeks ago. How would you feel if someone you love, someone who says they love you, they stand there and accuse you? Accusing you of rape? How would you feel?

Paul, tell us what happened last night.

I snapped. She did it again. I snapped.

Did what again?

For fuck's sake. Why the fuck do I have to keep repeating myself? I need a fucking drink. I killed her, alright? I killed her.

Paul, you say you killed Eloise. What happened? What happened exactly?

I told you. She told me I am a crap father. A rapist, crap father. She fucked with my head. I loved her.

Tell me the events that culminated in the death of your wife, Paul.

Sandra was trying to drag her home...

Sandra?

Eloise's mother.

Ok, carry on.

Sandra was trying to drag Eloise home. Well, to Sandra's home. I wanted to stop her. Despite everything she has done, I loved her.

Yes...?

So, I grabbed her arm to stop her going. Eloise shouted at me, shouted at me that I beat her and I raped her. She said this stuff all the time, mostly to get sympathy from her mother. I killed her. It was an accident, her arm slipped from my hand and she fell.

Her arm? You were holding her arm?

For fuck's sake, I can't remember exactly, hand, arm, shoulder, whatever.

It makes a world of difference, Paul.

Ok, her arm, I was holding her arm and I tried to pull her towards me, but she slipped and I was angry and she slipped from my grasp...then she fell. I'm not saying anymore, you have what you need. No rape, no murder, just a manslaughter, diminished responsibility.

Diminished responsibility?

She drove me to it. She drove me fucking mad. We argued, she died. I didn't mean to. She drove me to it. I loved her. You have the evidence, you have my fucking prints, no further fucking comment.

Paul...

I said, no further comment.

P...

No comment. No comment. No comment. NO FUCKING COMMENT.

Interview terminated. Eighteen fifty seven hours.

THE HASTINGS ECHO

16 August 2002
by Luke Williams

A man standing trial for murdering his wife by pushing her down the stairs at their marital home has been convicted of manslaughter and sentenced to twelve years in prison. Paul Bennett, of Hastings, East Sussex, killed Eloise Bennett on the twenty-second of July, 2001 during an argument at their home. Giving evidence during his trial, Paul claimed diminished responsibility following years of verbal abuse from his wife. The judge, Lord Justice Ralph, described Paul as a 'vindictive, manipulative bully, who deserves to bear the weight of his abhorrent crime and subsequent trauma caused to his two young children.' Eloise's mother, Sandra Harrington, said outside of the court 'twelve years is not enough. He has extinguished the life of my beautiful daughter after years of sustained mental and physical abuse. His children have been left technically orphaned and all he can bring himself to do is sully the name of an innocent woman, whose only failing was to love him.'

TWENTY

Jessica Louise Bennett.
Aged fourteen.

Paul,

I don't know how to start this letter, there are so many things that need to be said so I'll just come out and say them. You may wonder why I am writing to you after so long and the answer is so that I can finally be free from you. I've always loved you, like any child loves their Daddy, but when I needed you, you weren't a father, you were a monster.

Last week was the anniversary of Mum's death. Each year I hope it'll be easier, but if anything it gets harder, because I look back and realise all the stuff she has missed out on, like sports days, shopping, laughing, and even arguing with me over clothes and make-up and my choice of friends.

Grandma asked me to get an old photograph

out of the drawer for her the other day. I went to the drawer and underneath the photographs, I saw a screwed up letter. I know it was wrong, and I know it was nosey, but I suppose I can blame some of my character flaws on my childhood. The letter was a letter to you, and while I read it, everything came flooding back to me. That day, that night, everything. It was like a dam being opened, and suddenly I was a scared little girl again. The letter was an admission, Paul, an admission of Grandma's part in Mum's death. It was an accident, but it was Grandma who killed Mum, not you.

Suddenly, I remembered.

Daddy said that remembering is dangerous.

There was a struggle at the top of the stairs. You were trying to make Mum stay, you were begging her not to listen to Grandma and to give you another chance, because you love us all and you wanted to make it all better and you were sorry. Were you? Were you sorry? Or could you just not imagine life without someone who loved you as deeply as my Mum did?

Daddy was shouting at my Mummy again today and Mummy looked tired. They said cross stuff to each other. Then Daddy looked at my Mummy with crossness and then he hit her face which is naughty and then my Mummy looked scared and so I went to my Mummy and I gave her a hug and Daddy was behind me and my Mummy was shaking and I said it would be okay because hugs are good. And then I went to the kitchen and got some kitchen roll and climbed onto the shelf and got a plaster because I know that kitchen roll wipes away tears and plasters make poorlies better. Then I gave my Mummy the plaster and the kitchen roll and everyone kept telling me to go back to bed so I went back to my room and got into my bed. Everything would be OK now.

Grandma was trying to make Mum leave with her and take Joseph and me with her. There was a scuffle and Grandma hit Mum really hard, on the nose I think. I remember that there was some blood.

Then I heard the noise I heard my Grandma shouting and I saw my Grandma and I saw my Mummy and I saw Daddy. I was being naughty because I was meant to be asleep but the door was open a little bit and the hall light was bright and I looked at it and it started hurting my eyes and making little dots when I closed them. Then I opened my eyes and I looked through the light and I saw them and my Mummy was crying and my Grandma was still shouting and Daddy was holding on to my Mummy's arm and crying 'don't go don't go don't go I love you'. Daddy loves my Mummy.

The argument went on for ages. I was so scared. I remember thinking I should go back to bed, but I couldn't. I remember thinking I should stop everyone, but I couldn't move. My mouth was dry and my little legs were stuck to the spot.

My Grandma shouted and asked my Mummy why she wants to live in a disgusting poky house with a disgusting horrible man. I think she meant Daddy. Mummy shouted 'why would I want to live with you? I'd rather be beaten every day for the rest of my life than bring my children up in a house with a cold-hearted bitch like you.' Bitch is a bad word and I was confused because tonight my Mummy said she was going to leave Daddy and then when Grandma came my Mummy said that she's not going to leave Daddy and I think I don't know if I want to go or not because last time we stayed with Grandma it was fun but I was sad because I missed Daddy but tonight Daddy hurt my bad arm and I don't like being hurt.

Then Grandma shouted in Mum's face, and then Mum fell down the stairs.

My Mummy shouted at Grandma and then Grandma hit my Mummy hard but not as hard as Daddy hit my Mummy and I think I saw a bit of blood on my Mummy's head from where it hit the wall and I know that hitting is bad because if we do it at school we get a sad face on our charts. My Grandma had her hand on my Mummy's shoulder and my Grandma moved her face to shout in my Mummy's face a bit and I know that because I saw that and she tripped a bit and my Mummy fell a bit and then my Mummy looked into Daddy's eyes and then I saw her fall and then I didn't see her anymore I just heard the bang bang bang bang bang bang bang and heard everybody screaming so I covered my ears. Then I didn't see my Mummy again because I knew I shouldn't have looked and that now I had to pretend that I didn't remember. I got back into bed and hugged Buggly Bear and I hoped that it would be like in the films and that everything would be OK in the end.

You are in prison for a crime that you didn't technically commit. Yet, that aside, I think you should be there for all the disgusting things you did to Mum over the years. I know you beat her and I know you raped her. I know Joseph was born because you raped her. I know that Grandma and Pops love Joseph more than they love me because they feel he needs protecting from the truth and surrounded in a bubble of 'things'. But what about me? Does nobody ever think of the little girl who lay awake at night, hearing her Mummy beg her Daddy to hit her quietly so she wasn't woken up? The little girl who thought that if she just went to sleep with her eyes tightly shut, that Buggly Bear would take it all away and make it end like a happy film? Life isn't like a film. Life is what you make it, you made it the dress rehearsal for hell.

I'm not telling you this because I think you deserve to know, I'm telling you this because I KNOW that I am a better person than all of you put together. You have all lied to me, deceived me and made my life a misery. Even Mum didn't care enough to protect us, why didn't she leave you? She had so many chances to break away from you, but always returned. I can break this cycle of secrets and lies that you started. I don't want you to reply to this letter, I don't want to visit you, I don't want to see you, I don't want you to love me. I want to get on with my life knowing that I have done the right thing. You didn't physically kill my Mummy but you set it up and you led her to her death. I can never forgive that and I can never forget that.

And then a taxi came and it had Pops in it and then I saw Daddy laying on the floor asleep and then I wondered how he could sleep when my Mummy was hurt and then Pops got a bag and put some things in it like bottles and nappies and a few toys and then Pops and me and Baby Joe got into the taxi because it waited for us and we went to Grandma and Pop's house but Grandma wasn't there. And then Pops put me to bed after he had given me a hot chocolate and he also gave Baby Joe another bottle of milk which means Baby Joe will sleep too late in the morning and his day will be all confused a bit. Later on when I was in bed but I don't think I had been to sleeps, Pops came tiptoeing into my bedroom which is always my bedroom when I sleep at Grandma and Pops' house and it was late and it was dark and I if I had been to sleep, I had only been to sleep for a tiny time and maybe not at all because when I closed my eyes I could hear screaming inside my head. My Pops sat down on my bed and he was sitting quite close to my head and so I had to move my head a bit. And Pops was looking at the wall that wasn't near my face, it was the wall behind my head and he didn't look at me at all. Pops put his hand on my hand and then he put his nose on my head and he had his eyes closed and he still wasn't looking at me and he said the words that he loves me and the words that said my Mummy has gone to heaven and that she will watch me and Baby Joe and the words that she will look at us and look after us forever. And Pops' voice was a bit crackly and I know that earlier before I closed my eyes was the last time I will ever ever saw my Mummy and I am so so sad and I have never been this sad before. I miss you, my Mummy. I miss you so much.

You don't deserve me, you don't deserve Joseph, you don't deserve anything, Paul, and certainly not our love. From Jess.

<u>Joseph Bennett</u>
Aged 9

Dad,

All, I want is a Dad and all I want is you to be my Dad. I don't rememmber you becuse you are in prison becuse Jessica said, that you did some thing really, really bad. Jessica shuldn't have told me that because it's a bit of a secret but Jessica, dosn't like secrets, but I don't know why because some times they can be fun like birthday pressents and going on a coach to a zoo. The other day Jessica said that may be you diden't do what every one thoght you had done. I think I know that, every one thinks that you killed my Mummy, becuse that's what the childran at school say, but nobody else really talks about it. I have herd some horibel, things said about you, some really narsty things and may be they are true but one day I would like to find out for my self. Jessica says that it's no good trying to be freinds with you or trying to make you be my Dad becuse you won't like, me much becuse I am just like my Mummy and you diden't like her much eether. Jessica can be really horible some times but   I think that is becuse she is upset becuse she rememmbers my Mummy but I am upset too because I don't. My teacher at school tells me when I write things down I shuld, put some commas in becuse it makes it really hard to understand if I don't, so I am trying my best. What I really want to say is, that I know that peeple can visit each other in prisons becuse that's what happens on that programm on the telly. Jessica told, me you are in prison. Grandma and Pops tell me that, you are on holiday. Is it nice like a holiday? You know my adress so can you send me an invitashion please? Jessica said that I can put this letter in the onvalope with her letter and then, you will be able to read them to gether. Joseph XXX

TWENTY-ONE

<u>Paul Bennett</u>

I love my family

Paul Bennett closed his eyes and grunted. He was waiting for the inevitable. The dappled sunlight forcing its way through the cell window was sharp and painful. His head jerked back as the ligature took hold and stole his final breath. As his life ebbed away from him, he knew that soon they would be reunited.

I am the man who I despise
I am the man with hate in my eyes
I am that man
That man who couldn't change

Thank you for purchasing Volcano; your support is hugely appreciated. To demonstrate my gratitude at your awesomeness, I'd like to offer you a free story.

Yep, free.

Just visit my website to get your very own copy of *Building*, an award-winning short story observing the lives of the dysfunctional residents living in a block of flats. *Building* is part of short story collection, *Echoes*.

Get *Building* here:
www.authorkarinaevans.com/building

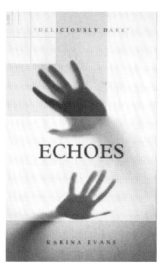

Please do your bit to support independent authors by following them/

liking their stuff/sharing links to their words on social media. You can find me all over the place, but mostly at:

www.authorkarinaevans.com

FACEBOOK: AUTHORKARIN-AEVANS

INSTAGRAM: @authorkarinaevans

You can also hunt me down on Goodreads, if the above doesn't fill quite enough time.

Thank you so much for your support; for reading (and hopefully reviewing). Reading and reviewing is where it's at, for sure.

Printed in Great Britain
by Amazon